THAT
SUMMER
IN PUGLIA

First published in 2018
by Eyewear Publishing Ltd
Suite 333, 19-21 Crawford Street
London, WIH IPJ
United Kingdom

Graphic design by Edwin Smet
Author photograph by Julia Warszewski © 2017
Cover image photograph by Salvo d'Avila © 2017 all rights reserved.
Reproduced by permission of the artist.
Printed in England by TJ International Ltd, Padstow, Cornwall

The English translation of Lucretius's *De Rerum Natura* is by the Rev. John Selby Watson,
in *Lucretius on the Nature of Things – A Philosophical Poem in Six Books*, Henry G. Bohn
(London), 1851.

Set in Bembo 12 / 15 pt
ISBN 978-1-912477-99-9

WWW.EYEWEARPUBLISHING.COM

THAT SUMMER IN PUGLIA

VALERIA VESCINA

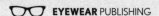 EYEWEAR PUBLISHING

For my parents,
who taught me about strong sails
and good anchors,
with love.

PROLOGUE

If I pass the shop windows more slowly, I should get a good look at his reflection. He's still walking behind me, and it *is* him – every day that shabby leather jacket.

How can the same person keep running into me for a week? There must be an innocent explanation. Could he just have moved into the neighbourhood? Probably an Imperial College wiz. Isn't that what Zoe said yesterday when I pointed him out, sitting opposite us at Starbucks in South Kensington? In which case, no surprise I keep seeing him in Queensway: this area is always teeming with students. I'm hardly the only man who lives on this side of the park but works mostly on the other. In his mid-twenties, so he could well be a postgraduate – his autumn term will have just started.

When I told her how fixedly he looked at his laptop screen, Zoe seemed bemused by my curiosity. I pretended it was casual – I couldn't let her suspect my alarm. I ought to trust her judgment: he was ignoring us, to all appearances a middle-aged couple long at ease with each other. No match for the delights of particle physics or of computer games, I suppose.

And yet the other day, in the chemist, didn't I have the impression he was watching me? I know that a moment later I told myself he was just scrutinising razors and I happened to be in his line of vision. But surely, bumping into the same stranger for several days in a row justifies some anxiety. What's confusing is that he looks so unthreatening – not what I had anticipated, but I suppose murderers and thieves don't come with a warning tattooed on their foreheads, either. He was wandering about the aisles with shoulders so hunched and a step so gangly that I wished I could tell him to straighten up and stop looking like an underfed titan carrying the heavens. 'What's wrong with you?' I was tempted to say. 'A more confident bearing, and you'd be amazed how much easier life gets.'

And what was he doing inside the bin shed of the Hallfield Estate some days earlier? When I stepped inside that murky, reeking shack to dispose of my rubbish bag, the eyes staring out at me made me jump. Then I made out the rest of his body. I can still hear his 'Sorry' in a bass voice strained to a higher pitch by fright, followed by his more composed 'Didn't mean to scare you,' as he walked straight past me into the grey morning. Could he be innocuously renting in one of the blocks next to mine? That'd explain things.

But what if he *is* tailing me? What if his laptop yesterday was a secret video camera? No, no, that's ridiculous. Maybe it's only the taxman – though why bother now with my absence from the register? The sum it would cost to find me would outstrip my pathetic assets.

Let me slow down. That's it, to a snail's pace. Why isn't he overtaking me? I'll have to stop somewhere and see if he carries on. That cash point will do – with such a queue, I won't even have to pretend I'm tapping into my non-existent bank account. There – he has walked on. Calm down, heart. Calm down. Best to rest against this wall until my legs aren't quite so wobbly.

Panic over for now. But it goes to show: I still need to be prepared for the prospect of being found. How long has it been since I last rehearsed what I might do if that happened? A decade? I'd have been forty-two then, and had an escape plan. Now I'm too tired to start afresh in yet another place. Today there'd be only one strategy left. Honesty.

CHAPTER 1

Sorry to disappoint you, Mr...? Mr. Barker. A true inhabitant of the British Isles, then – not like me. Sorry, but I can't think of a single reason to be glad to have been tracked down. Sure, I've been expecting you – noticed you circling around, over the past week. But when you called out to me, back there on the Broad Walk, I still thought I had misheard. Tommaso Spagnulo. The name sounds so unfamiliar, after all these years.

Come, let's sit on that bench. You won't mind the ducks and the Canada geese wandering over from the Round Pond, will you? Excellent. I don't know why some people think the geese vicious – the poor creatures have every reason to fear us, not vice versa. The view from that bench is priceless: whatever you may think of the Albert Memorial, the sight of the spire through the foliage casts a spell, especially against this morning's sky – grim, isn't it? And I need to sit down.

Me, in shock? I suppose I am – more than I imagined I'd be. No, no, not because of her: she was already dead to me. She's been dead a long time. My astonishment is at having been found.

Where did I go wrong? Was it complacency? The web, and 'new investigative methods', as you say. Still, fresh-faced, but you must be God's gift to your profession or else we wouldn't be sitting here.

A funny pair we make, don't you think? You, so pale and tall, and I, olive-skinned and a full head shorter; your shock of red hair, and my greying mop. Oh, it's good of you to say it but if I look younger than my age it's hardly down to personal merit. I inherited a leanness that gives that impression. Sometimes I feel centuries old.

My English puzzles you? Something too perfect about it. That's a kind way of putting it. I love books, and much of your language I learnt from your classics: Shakespeare, Austen, Forster, Orwell... Colloquial talk still catches me out – gives away the foreigner in me, even after more than thirty years.

How pleased you are – it's obvious from the glint in your eye and the excitement in your voice. I take it there's a reward in all this for you – and recognition. Even so, I must ask you to pretend you never found me. Don't look at me like that – I'm not mad, but I don't want the inheritance. Four million euros, waiting for me in an Italian bank? Perfect: there'll be plenty of vultures squabbling over that kind of money – let them have it. As to the recompense – tell me what it'd amount to, and I'll pay you. It's the least I can do. I'm an honourable man.

You went out on a limb to find me, because you thought you'd make me happy? Sorry – I didn't mean to offend you by laughing. I'm moved that anyone should be driven to act by such unselfish motives. Just my luck. But happiness is a tall order, and I'm living proof of the adage that money doesn't buy happiness. Yes, I can appreciate that as a P.I. you don't often get the chance to give your clients good news – but I didn't hire you. I don't want people back home to know I'm alive. A valid reason? Simple: she was a murderer. My mother killed my love.

I can see that I'm asking a lot of you. Bouncy as a puppy, barely five minutes ago, and there you are, sagging into this bench as if I had winded you. But chin up – if you've managed to find me, you'll manage the same feat with plenty of others. And keeping quiet about this triumph will cost you far less than announcing it would cost me: I couldn't guarantee that I'd stay alive if you were to reveal my existence. It's conceivable that the threat against my life uttered long ago in anger might never have been acted upon and never will, but I can't be certain. I see from your alarm that this – more than my dread of being shackled to the nightmare I left behind – might persuade you to hear me out. You sounded sincere, when you said you had hoped to make someone happy, for once. I believe you. This is your chance – even if not in the way you presumed.

Yes, I guess the price is fair: without the full explanation you demand, I can't expect you to understand, and even less, to comply. I give you my word that my account of events will be faithful, though I confess to some apprehension. I've never confided the story to a soul. From time to time, I've been tempted to tell Zoe, my best friend, but I've always stopped short. Why? Good question. It's not that I don't trust her. I even feel I owe her an explanation, after all her years of putting up with the mystery surrounding my past. I wonder whether the prospect of putting it all into words is what has petrified me – words take on a materiality that random threads of thought lack. I suspect it has been compounded by fear – that once Zoe knew, the past I had escaped would become present and too real every time I saw her. Zoe belongs to my life in this country, the life to which I have earned the right. But with you, it's different: you will know, and hopefully, because you'll know, you'll let me go free and never seek me again.

★★★

I can pinpoint the beginning without hesitation: March 1982, the evening of my nineteenth birthday.

From the window of my bedroom on the first floor of our villa, I watched my guests streaming in. They arrived in twos or in small groups through the wrought iron gate left wide open for the occasion. They pushed their mopeds and motorbikes under the tiled canopy of our parking shelter by the entrance. The few who already drove cars must have left them along the edge of the hill leading from the centre of town up to our home on its green outskirts. They made their way towards the building, along the paved trail across the lawn. Their chatter and laughter invaded my bedroom even through the closed windows. I couldn't put names to half or more of those faces. I had done as told: invite your class and tell everyone they can bring a guest, because you are a *signore*, hence cannot be so vulgar as to restrict numbers. Which was just as well: given the effect my dislike for gossip and cliques seemed to have on making friends, thank God for a ready-made class of other teens and their mates, all of them over-joyed to step inside Villa Emma.

To them, my birthday was an opportunity to enter a gild-ed realm. Unlike their modest flats or houses in central Ostuni, Villa Emma evoked a sense of unconfined space. Whatever the season, its white form stood out – the mainsail of a ship demanding to be unmoored – against the sky, the lawn, the fruit trees and the rose bushes. The row of French windows along the ground floor reflected garden and sky, so that they appeared to extend inside the house. That first impression was confirmed when one stood indoors looking out, especially from the interminable sitting room, which was flanked by the kitchen at one end, and the library at the other. With its stark contours, the building could have appeared imposing, had the first floor – which contained the bedrooms – spanned its entire length. Instead, it was limited to the central section of the building, the one above the plain stone arch framing our entrance door. Did my guests perceive the fusion of lightness and solidity in the overall design, or were they too dazzled by the wealth behind a home like this, to take notice?

I finally caught sight of Giorgio. He strode into the garden with an arm around Lidia's waist, and with a girl I vaguely recognised from another class at our school, the Liceo Classico. I opened my door and, at the sound of the disco music and of the voices rising up from the sitting room, took a deep breath. I marched down the steps to the relentless beat of bass guitars. 'Happy Birthday, Tommaso' greeted me in all its variations as I walked past groups of schoolmates until I reached Giorgio and Lidia.

'You spoilt son of a bitch.' Giorgio slapped me on the back. 'I thought your eighteenth was impressive, but your mum's managed one better, eh? Isn't that the DJ from Radio –?'

'Yep, he is,' I interrupted.

'Wow.' He removed his blazer, took his girlfriend's black sequinned cardigan from her, and placed them on the nearby sofa. 'Warm in here.'

'Happy birthday.' Lidia pushed her black mane away from her face and kissed me on the cheek. I caught a whiff of her perfume, its deep, seductive notes out of tune with her usual straightforward looks and manner, but not with tonight's tight blouse and plunging neckline, worn to highlight surprising curves. Things were obviously evolving between her and Giorgio.

'Thanks. I'd much rather have celebrated by having dinner with you two,' I said. 'Can't wait for this to be over and it hasn't even got going yet.'

'Come on, we can have dinner any evening. Just enjoy this. If you can't consider it fun, maybe consider it funny, to see your boring old sitting room transformed into a disco.' Giorgio gestured with an arm to encompass the coloured spotlights, the mirror ball, the DJ and his sound equipment and the manned bar corner at the far end of the room. With the oriental rugs removed for the occasion, and the sofas and coffee tables shifted to the sides, the disco lights bounced off the floor and French windows, glistening on my guests.

'By the way, you look cool.' Giorgio smirked and pointed to my shirt and trousers. 'Try wearing that combination a bit more often, and when you score, come thank me...?'

I smiled. 'Incorrigible.'

'Me or you?' He turned to Lidia. 'Do you know anyone else who has to be dragged to Diego's to buy himself some clothes? Most guys do a happy dance for the smallest thing from that shop. But not young Mr. Spagnulo. His best friend has to kick him all the way there, and work bloody hard to emerge with an outfit, even one as classic as this one. Honest, Tommi!'

'You see, Lidia, the poor boy is convinced he's my elder brother –'

'Anyone saying I'm not?' Giorgio made a shocked face. 'I've been your elder twin brother for as long as I can remember.'

'– Though we all know he's born a month after me. But he's been like this for years. How're we going to break the truth to him?'

'Well...' Lidia laughed. 'Tonight you could pass as twins – if it's possible for one to be dark-haired and the other blond.'

'Ah, but here's your mother,' Giorgio said. 'Signora Emma, what a party.'

My mother, in one of her signature knee-length black dresses, was heading towards us. With her short fawn hair re-layered and blow-dried into the perfect bob that afternoon and with the subtle make-up enhancing her light brown eyes, you'd have thought the birthday was hers. She extended her arms towards my best friend and squeezed his hands. She acknowledged Lidia with a nod, the half-smiling, half-icy gesture reserved for those on whom she was still to pass judgment.

'Giorgio, *carissimo*, can I count on you to ensure Tommaso enjoys the party? You know he always does, in the end.'

Giorgio always managed to exude *grinta* – grit, a quality my mother prized – despite the cherubic curls and green eyes. This was one of those moments in which I could have sworn she must think that all I had inherited from my father were his looks – the jet black hair, the blue eyes, the wiry frame of respectable height – but that in a son she'd eagerly have swapped those for other attributes.

'I'm here and I'm not invisible, Mum. I just don't see how at my age I should still have parties foisted on me – but no point boring my friends with this discussion. Sorry, guys.'

'Indeed. But I'll repeat my piece: it's probably the last year you'll be here in March. Next year you'll be away, and your birthday parties at home will be a memory.'

Thank God for that, I thought, but simply smiled. My mother left us, to check on the preparation of the food, but not before saying goodbye to Giorgio with the warmth that he alone drew out of her.

'I thought you guys had brought someone with you,' I said.

'Yes, Anna. She got cornered by one of her classmates the moment we came in. Somewhere over there.' Lidia pointed towards another area of the room. 'She's a good friend of mine. Same year as us, but in B. Tommi, do you realise you've ended up with almost the whole of B, here? And it looks like people didn't stick to inviting only one guest.'

'Who cares?' I said. 'If they enjoy this kind of thing, let them. There'll probably be food and drink for an army, anyway.' I pointed to the dining table, in the area closest to the kitchen. 'The treats will pile up in a minute.'

Giorgio nodded. My best friend since primary school, he had seen enough parties – and more – here to know that my mother didn't do anything in half measures. Lidia, on the other hand, was a relative stranger to the villa. She had been our classmate for the full five years of secondary school, but Giorgio's girlfriend only for the last two months. Bets were open on how long she'd last. He went through girls the way jewellers go through pearls: one after another, leaving them seemingly unscathed, though threaded together. Surely, by now, any girl who went out with him must know it. That must account for the miraculous lack of heartbreaks – presumably both sides accepted from the start that things shouldn't get deep. It takes so long for an oyster to produce a pearl, but so little to crack those nacreous layers.

'Well, I guess I'd better 'mingle'. See you guys in a bit,' I said.

I did the rounds of the huddles of people standing and dancing in the room. I behaved with competent sociability, containing my irritation at the rising volume of the disco music. We had to shout over the voices of Madonna, Michael Jackson, Duran Duran and their ilk. The famous DJ must have long lost his hearing. I was relieved when eventually I found myself in front of the wide glass door separating the room from the terrace at the back. I slunk out, sliding the panes shut behind me.

The chill and humidity of the evening made me shudder. The air was thick with microscopic water droplets. It felt liberating, as if they could soak through my shirt and rinse away all remnants of the confusion I had left behind. I took a deep breath and exhaled in a satisfying rush. I breathed in again, and this time made out the familiar smell of the rosemary bushes growing, against all odds, on the cliff beneath. I walked towards the far end of the terrace, and propped my elbows against the iron railings.

The olive groves beneath me stretched towards the shore like a dark blanket dotted with the glimmers of farmhouses and villas. Further ahead, the lights of Villanova marked the boundary between earth and sea. From this distance the centre of Ostuni to my right could have fooled me into believing it a kasbah in which time stood still since the fabled times of *The Thousand and One Nights*: our Cittá Bianca, the 'White Town', sat perched on the hill, its coils of ancient walls illuminated by orange-tinged streetlamps. Our terrace offered one of the best views of the town and of the valley at our feet. The vista was the reason my father had built our home on this spot.

How could he not be here, in the Eden he had designed for our little family? How had any of us deserved this? On dates which we had used to celebrate with joy – birthdays, Christmas, New Year... My anger rose up. Every little ritual – blowing out the candles on the cake, slicing the *panettone*, clinking the glasses – summoned memories of when he too had been there. No party crowd could fill that void. I still remembered details my father had pointed out to me as we stood on this terrace during my childhood: how to distinguish the hue of centuries-old olive groves from that of newly planted ones; at what time various kinds of fishing boats set off from Villanova harbour, and which species of fish they caught in the high seas; where exactly, in Ostuni's hillsides, archaeologists had discovered prehistoric pottery... He'd hear out my questions – his eyes fixed on me, any distraction on hold – and answer them with patience. Sometimes he'd say, 'You've got me. I'll have to think about that one,' and rub his nose while considering an explanation. Now and then, when I walked into the entrance hall, I was still ambushed by the memory of his cheerful 'Hello, darlings!' upon his daily return from the office.

'Too loud, eh?'

I jumped – a girl's voice – and turned around.

'Too loud, inside.' A slight figure was silhouetted against the bright sitting room like an apparition. She walked towards me, to the far edge of the terrace. The outlines of her skirt swung softly from side to side. 'Sorry. Did I scare you, or something?'

'Well, yeah. Didn't know there was anyone else out here.' And, I thought, I was aeons away, so you've given me a bigger jolt than you can presume.

'I was sitting there.' In the darkness, I made out her arm indicating the wooden deckchairs by the oleander hedge, and her hand gripping the railing. 'What a view. Imagine it by day. Imagine waking up to this every day.'

I avoided picking up on that observation. 'It *is* much too

loud in there. Awful music, too.'

'I don't like it either.' She laughed. 'I thought everyone else did, though. That must make everyone in Ostuni, minus two. Good to know.'

She had a gentle voice, brimming with energy and humour. Replying to her didn't feel like an effort – and by now I had recovered my breath.

'When there are singer-songwriters like De André...' I said.

'Ah, yes. But you can't dance to those.'

'Fair enough.'

'Can you imagine a party of this many people, all sitting quietly listening to De André? At a concert, they just might – but more likely, they'd profane it with chatter.'

'I went to the last concert he gave in Lecce.' Giorgio, his girlfriend of the day, and I had been driven there by his elder sister. The heat that summer afternoon became bearable only by early evening, as we sat on the stadium seats. To my friends, De André was one of the few hip names who deigned to appear in Puglia, so far south, and therefore counted as one of the year's hot tickets. To me, those ninety minutes spent taking in the sight of the man behind songs I loved was a revelation: he perched on a stool, face scrunched up with emotion as he sang, eyes closed. On the journey back to Ostuni, I struggled to engage the others in a conversation about the concert, until I gave up. Loneliness rarely feels as acute as it can in the company of one's friends.

'Lucky you. I'd have liked that,' the girl said. 'Which of his songs is your favourite?'

'If I really have to choose one, 'The Fisherman', probably.'

'Why?'

'It's about how we should live and let live, isn't it, and that's how I'd like things to be, I guess. What's your favourite?'

'"Marinella's Song", definitely.'

'Ugh. That's a sad one. Girl seduced by cad, and one way or another – can't do without the obligatory ambiguity – girl dies.'

She laughed. 'If you put it like that, then half the world's most famous novels and poems are 'sad ones' you'd dismiss without a second thought. It's how the story is told that matters. De André is a poet.'

'And a musician.'

'Sure, poet and musician. He makes 'Marinella' sound like a fairy tale or a dream.'

'A dream turned nightmare,' I said.

'I suppose. But he does it poetically. I guess that's why we love him.'

There was an awkward pause in our conversation. A whiff of oven-fresh *focaccia* and of Concetta's fried *ricotta* parcels escaped through the kitchen vent. My old *tata* must have the gastronomic feast in hand, as ever. No need for supervision.

'I'm Anna, by the way.'

'Tommaso.'

'Ah, like the birthday boy. Not that I know the guy. I came with a friend in his class.'

'You mean Lidia?' She must be the girl who had walked through the gate with her and Giorgio. I tried to piece together that fleeting image of her and the indistinct one I could conjure up from school. She wasn't the kind that stood out: straight mousy hair, shoulder-length, if memory served me right, medium height, and skinny.

'Yes. How did you guess?'

'I didn't. Lidia told me. I'm the 'birthday boy'.'

'You shouldn't have led me on like that. It's cruel.' She spat out the words.

'What?'

'The music's too loud, eh, and awful? You jerk.' Her tone called to mind a child furious at being cheated in the middle of a game. 'You chose it.'

'No, I didn't. My mother organised the whole thing.'

She didn't reply.

'I swear it's true,' I said.

'Oh?' She paused. 'Well, I guess it's sweet of your mum.'

'Not when she knows I can't stand parties. I'd rather celebrate with a few good friends than with a whole lot of strangers I couldn't care less about.' I cleared my throat. 'Sorry.'

She was quiet for a while. 'Why not look at it as a present for your mother? She's probably mourning already the day you 'fly the nest', as they say. You should hear Lidia's parents going on and on about it – it's lovely, in some ways.'

'Are you some kind of wannabe shrink? Going to read psychology or something like that, in October?'

'No. And you really do have a knack for being offensive. I should never have come to this party: either I get my eardrums burst in there, or I freeze out here in the company of a smug twit. I'm stuck till Giorgio and Lidia can give me a lift back into town, otherwise I'd be out of here.'

'Please don't go,' I said. 'Can the smug twit get you something to keep you warm? He's in desperate need of a jumper, too.'

***

21

Extraordinary, how the course of lives can depend on trivia. What if Giorgio hadn't brought Anna along? What if the music hadn't been so loud and the room so crowded? What if it had been too cold on the terrace? And yet on the concatenation of such nothings did the entrance of the most important person in my life depend. How ironic that my first encounter with Anna was so unpromising and yet we became so close, while with Zoe it was the reverse: auspicious beginnings, and today no more than friendship to show for it – though ok, a deep friendship, for which I'm grateful. Perhaps intensity – yes, even in the shape of Anna's and my frustration with each other, that evening – is the only hint of the forces at play beneath.

But you've seen Zoe – the woman enjoying a sumptuous Starbucks lunch with me a few days ago. She was on a break from the RCM library – she's carrying out some research for an article on a Mozart concerto. I had just dropped off a translation at the agency for which I do some work.

Zoe is only a friend – though the word 'only' doesn't do the friendship justice. She's so beautiful: tall, slim... and her smile is disarming. She's a clever and hard-working woman. Not easy, the life of a musician: the quartet and orchestra tours, the private tutoring, the freelance writing for the press... Constantly on the lookout for the next source of income. Not that my life is any easier: tutoring schoolchildren in Latin and Ancient Greek, and carrying out Italian translations whenever the agency calls. Everything is strictly cash – the only way to stay hidden from the authorities. But I don't hurt a soul, unlike seemingly law-abiding citizens such as my mother.

I owe to Zoe the introductions to the families of my first pupils, nearly twenty years ago – she taught them violin.

From then on, it was all word of mouth. The tutoring keeps me afloat. I don't ask for more. And yet, despite my passion for the Classics, if on my nineteenth birthday you had fore-told that I'd end up helping secondary school pupils in West London wage their private battles against the Greeks and the Romans, I'd have called you a lousy fortune teller.

CHAPTER 2

On the day after the party, we were in class translating Menander's *Dyskolos*. You'd have thought it was a multi-volume oeuvre, judging by how long it was taking. True to form, old Mr. Santoro wouldn't settle for sloppy vocabulary. It didn't help that some of my mates were regretting having chosen the Liceo Classico. There couldn't be a more tailor-made school for those who happened to love Latin and Ancient Greek and be good at them. For those with no such luck, however, that type of secondary school turned into a five-year sentence with a sadomasochistic twist: it condemned them to incessant frustration, and inflicted boredom on the remaining pupils. The masochistic element was not easily measurable, courtesy of the prevalent obedience towards parents who knew better, and whose ambitions for their offspring were presumed to be for the best.

'No, no,' Mr. Santoro was saying. 'Think, Carlo, think: how could Sostratos possibly be saying that?'

Very quietly, I tore a piece of lined paper out of my ring binder. 'Please tell me what she said,' I scribbled, and folded the note. I passed it to Lidia behind me. A minute later, the tip of her pen was poking one of my shoulder blades. I stretched my arm backwards and grabbed her reply.

I unfolded it. 'Spoilt, cowardly and cocky. Congrats, T. Great first impression.'

'What?' I swung round to face her.

'What's going on, over there?' Mr. Santoro said. 'Would you care to let the rest of the class know, Tommaso?'

'Sorry, sir.'

'Let me see.' He strode towards me and picked up the piece of paper from my desk. He held it between his bony, sun-spotted fingers. Heat surged up to my face. He scanned the note before looking me in the eye. 'The discovery of a brilliant student engaging in puerile pursuits is always disheartening. But how much more disappointing it is, when that student is Alvaro's son.' He placed the piece of paper in my hand and returned to the front of the classroom.

'She's got me all wrong,' I said.

Lidia took a bite of her *panino*, and nibbled at the strands of mortadella dangling from the bread. The hubbub of the ten o'clock break surrounded us. Voices bounced against the walls of the corridor in which we were standing. From the open windows, the high-pitched cries of swallows flew into the building and mingled with the babble of hundreds of teens.

'She seems to have got you down as a selfish posh git out to charm a nice girl.'

'That's not true. Well, ok – maybe I *was* out to charm her. I liked her. I liked what she said. At first I couldn't even see her properly, for Christ's sake. It was dark. Anyway, admit it: she looks kind of ordinary. I had barely noticed her all these years you say she's been here.'

That made it sound as if Anna was unattractive, which wasn't what I meant. When we had left the terrace and returned inside the house – noisy, but still a refuge from the chill – I had got a proper look at her. Her hazelnut eyes seemed to laugh whenever her mouth did – though never at my jokes. She wore no lipstick, and her smooth, light-olive complexion was devoid of make-up. She exuded an air of neatness, of attention to detail, like the blue of the ballet pumps which matched that of the gingham full skirt. That outfit might not have been out of place in the *Roman Holiday* wardrobes of thirty years before, and yet it suited her.

'Ordinary. See? You *are* being a real git.'

'Please, Lidia. She's not *un*attractive. I just mean I didn't like her because of some sensational beauty or anything like that. Come on, I'd have thought that's what every girl wants.'

'And not every boy?'

'Don't know about every boy. But me, yes, for sure. Look, there's nothing complicated about what I'm saying, so just try and help. Please?'

'I told her you were sweet, actually. Also, that I could guarantee you've never even had a girlfriend.'

'Who says?' Her look told me we both knew who the source was. I'd give Giorgio a piece of my mind, when he returned from his caffeine fix at the vending machine.

'That puzzled her, by the way. She asked if by any chance you were, you know... if you had other preferences, because you were seriously handsome, so she didn't get it. Handsome, Tommi, heard that?' She twirled her hair to underline her meaning.

'Giorgio's efforts to get me dressed up must have paid off,' I joked.

'I know you're being facetious, but know what? You have the looks, the brain, the money... And beneath that... diffidence of yours, you're so nice, that –'

I leaned forward. 'What's the 'charm offensive' for?'

'To say that you could have it all, if only – '

'– I listened to Giorgio a bit more.'

'Hmm.' She nodded.

'Not you, too. I already have one mother, and that's plenty. I've no intention of aping Giorgio.'

'No one's asking you to.' She lifted her gaze upwards, as if praying for patience. 'Where had I got to – about Anna?'

'You said she had asked –'

'That's right. I said no, that you can just be a bit awkward. So, maybe the door isn't totally shut.'

'Awkward? I just don't want to break any hearts: not mine or anyone else's. I'm not going to go out with a girl unless there's some chance she might be the one.'

'Spare me: 'the one', no less.' She groaned. 'What are you afraid of? You win some, you lose some. That's life.'

I knew enough about losing someone you love. The thought crowded out the possibility of any other. I stared at her.

She laid a hand on my wrist and kissed me on the cheek. 'Just tell her what you said now. About 'the one'. Easy.'

When the bell rang at one o'clock, I joined the throng making for the exit through the corridors and down the grand staircase. At the doorway I waited for Anna. Since the mid-morning break, I had considered how I might address her, but my heart pounded as I reviewed the various permutations. 'Hi, could I have a word?' Too formal. 'Excuse me...' Uncool, dithering. 'You got me all wrong, you know.' Risky: might even confirm her first impression. Hopeless. I shrugged, tugged at my rucksack straps and slunk through the crowd and around the corner, where my motorbike awaited. I stroked its silver top, got into the seat, gripped the handlebars and revved the engine.

As I roared out of the street onto Via Pola, the town's

commercial thoroughfare, I caught sight of her. She was standing at a bus stop, with other Classico students, chatting with two girls. She looked my way. 'For goodness' sake work up some courage,' I told myself. I took a deep breath, turned the bike around and rode to the bus stop.

My mouth felt dry but it didn't stop my voice from rising above the engine's growl. 'Jump on. I'll give you a lift.'

'No, thanks. I'm off to the Old Town, and your home is in the opposite direction.'

'That's for me to worry about.'

The two girls with whom she had been talking were sizing up Anna, the Suzuki, and me.

'I don't need a lift. See?' She pointed to an oncoming bus. 'But thank you.'

'All right. See you around.'

'Jump on, I'll give you a lift': what an idiotic thing to say to a girl who thought me arrogant – and after wasting the morning thinking up a clever line. Comical, really. I rode home, a wounded centaur. I wished it had been possible to follow her bus, to halt at each stop until she descended from it and we could talk. There'd be plenty of walking to do from there, as no bus could enter the Old Town's narrow lanes. Some imaginings: in novels or in films, following a girl on a bus, on a hunch, might be romantic, but in real life it'd be downright creepy. I wondered where she lived, though. I knew nothing about her. And yet, on the night of my party, out on the terrace, I had felt something I couldn't pinpoint or put into words.

'Smells good in here,' I said, stepping into the kitchen. No one could beat my old *tata*'s Neapolitan *ragú*: a waft of it, and my taste buds longed for the flavour of the beef softened for hours in herbs and tomato sauce.

Concetta, by the stove, was stirring some of the *ragú* sauce into the *orecchiette*. 'Sit down, sit down. It's ready,' she said without lifting her eyes from the task.

I took a chair at the table. Her arms, so robust that her dress sleeves were too tight, hauled up ladles of pasta into two bowls. One of these she placed in front of me, before sitting on my right with her portion. I shifted my chair sideways to make space for her bulk, while she removed the headscarf which covered her crop of grey hair when she cooked.

'Where's Mum?'

'Brindisi. Seems things are happening on the project.'

I laughed. 'That'd be the day. Nothing can ever be happening on that front.'

'Don't be so sure, *signorino*. She's having lunch with the mayor. The *ingegnere* arranged it.' She gulped down a mouthful of pasta.

'Ah. The wonderful *Ingegner* Forgalli.'

'Scoff as much as you please. That man's a godsend. Goes to show what they say about silver linings: if the company he used to work for hadn't folded, they, and not your mother, would still be employing him.'

'Ooh. Since when do you know about business?'

Concetta shook her head. 'Honest, son, sometimes I don't know what world you live in. I don't need knowledge. I just notice things.'

'Like what?' I aimed for a particularly large *orecchietta* among the round pasta shells – no doubt shaped that morning by Concetta's roughened fingers – speared it with my fork and brought it to my mouth. She watched me and waited.

'Oh, all right,' I said. 'I guess she's spending more time at home, properly talking with us. And I haven't heard her snapping at you for a while about a badly ironed collar, or badgering Elena over the phone. What are the chances of the Pope proclaiming Elena patron saint of secretaries, now?'

'It's done your mother good to let the *ingegnere* take stuff off her plate. She's managed on her own for too long. And a construction firm's no job for a woman, especially around here.'

'It's certainly easier for a man, in this country, to lobby for building permissions. But as for everything else, Mum is a steamroller. I doubt Dad would have done half as well.'

'Steamroller. You make her sound like some hag, your poor mother.'

'Poor who? She's tough as old boots.'

'Not really. And she'd lay down her life for you.'

I shrugged. 'I'm not questioning her love – or her version of it, anyway. It's just how she is. Fact.'

'You shouldn't say such things.'

We chewed in silence.

'I've been wondering,' Concetta said after a while, 'whether the *ingegnere* might not be a good companion for her.'

The thought of that dull man skulking about our home nearly made me choke on the swig of water in my mouth. 'I can't imagine that.'

'Why not? He's divorced – available, that is.'

'And past it. They're both too old for such things.'

'You're a charmer. Your mother isn't even fifty. And the *ingegnere* must be about that, too.'

'I thought things were officially declared antique when they hit fifty.'

'Things, maybe. Life hasn't even begun.' She grinned.

Of course – *her* fiftieth was only months away. 'Concetta, dear: I'm afraid that can't be true of everyone, even if it is of you, who are *semper iuvenis*.'

'Speak Italian with me, young man.'

'Forever young, Concetta. A compliment.'

'I better treasure that one, then. God only knows when I'll hear another.'

'That's unfair. You know you're my sweet *tata*.' I put an arm around her shoulder and gave her a squeeze. 'Anyway, I thought you didn't approve of divorce. And Mum is one of those who voted against it, in '74.'

'That was '74. Now she's more' – she paused – 'mature. And alone.'

The discussion was starting to make me queasy. I cleared my throat. 'Let's leave aside any wild conjectures about my mother's intentions, eh? You should have done some match-making for yourself: a lovely lady, and no man in your life.'

'You're into compliments, today. Feeling all right?' She grabbed the jug of water and watched the liquid pour into her glass. She re-filled mine, too. 'I had a man in my life once, if you must know. Didn't work out. I was young. I thought Mr. Right had to be Mr. Perfect. I let the chance slip. And after that, another Mr. Right-enough failed to come along.'

'You're a romantic, Concetta.'

My response struck me as unfeeling. I struggled to think how to fix it.

'No, a realist: better to spend life single than miserably paired up. But you can hardly talk, *signorino*: nineteen, and not a girlfriend in sight. There must be some girl you can like, somewhere. Finished?' Without waiting for a reply, she grabbed my empty plate.

'You stay, I'll do it.' I took our bowls to the sink, picked up from the stove the pot of *ragú* meat, and placed it on the old ceramic trivet at the centre of the table.

'Well, actually, there's this girl I like,' I said while sitting back down.

'I knew you must be running a fever.' She dished me out a chunk of beef.

'Her name's Anna.' I told Concetta about the evening on the terrace, about the exchanges with Lidia, and concluded with my failed approach.

'I like her already.' She rubbed her hands. 'Come on. Tuck in.'

One stupid mistake after another: impossible to solve algebraic problems when my mind kept flitting elsewhere. I shut the maths textbook with a thud which filled the silence of the room. I reached once more for the telephone on the desk but withdrew my hand before touching the receiver. Terrible though it might be to let chances slip, the prospect of torpedoing them by ineptitude was even more frightening.

I spun round in the office chair and got up. From the glass door behind the desk, I caught glimpses of the first oleander buds on the terrace, tips like white and pink crinkle paper bursting out of green wrappings. I wandered down to the opposite end of the room, to the window which framed the view of the almond trees in blossom in the front garden. Within months, all those white flowers would be transformed into hard fruit, and later, into the almond nectar and traditional sweets that we consumed year-round. I had never asked whether the trees were here already when our home was built – I was only a toddler, then – or whether my father had them planted there. Either way, I was sure he would have relished the sight today.

With his quickness to connect the infinitesimal to the infinite, what would he have said of those almond blossoms, now? His approach to warning me about oleanders, when I was five, was typical of him. Other parents forbade their children from touching the plant – that was that. My father encouraged me to examine it with him: he, not I, would handle it, as children's reactions to it could be especially unpredictable; but I must promise never to go near it on my own. So I learnt how thick and leathery its leaves were, how soft its petals. But also, that wise men and women across the ancient world had discovered how to turn the oleander's poison into medicine. And that the plant had been capable of a kind of miracle: it was the first to have blossomed again in a far-away city destroyed by a terrible bomb, though experts had predicted nothing would grow there for seventy years. Its flowers had given hope to the survivors.

This room had been a sanctuary of sorts for my dad. It was so narrow that arguably it might have made more sense for it not to have been created at all: its ceiling-high library could easily have formed the far end of our sitting room, instead of being separated from it by a wall. And yet it had been vital for him.

It was also my favourite space in the house. The views from the windows were the least important reason, though the front garden's almonds, figs and carobs, or the vista of valley and sea from the terrace behind the desk were sights of which I could never tire. In the winter, when the centuries-old fig trees shed their lush canopy and turned into dark, naked grotesques, I looked to their branches for early signs of spring's return: for the first new leaf and for the first whiff of the syrupy fragrance that heralded the fruit of the next summer.

The arched walnut bookcases lining the library on both sides gave it the air of a cathedral or a temple, but it wasn't only the room's architecture that produced its hold over me. Over the years, the books had become increasingly compelling. Their mix of literature, history and philosophy, from Ancient Greece and Rome to modern times, vied for my attention almost as if the authors were all each other's and our contemporaries, engaged in discourses whose contexts changed but whose substance endured. Most of those books were once my father's, though I had added present-day ones – the latest a satire by Dario Fo whose sharpness would have made Aristophanes proud, notwithstanding their political differences.

For all the fineness of his library, the spell it cast over me came from childhood memories of moments spent there with my father. As an architect, his foray into property development on his own account was almost accidental. It started out as an occasional small-scale adjunct to designing and project-managing seaside villas for clients. But in the sixties and seventies, more and more Italians were demanding holiday homes, and to that boom we owed our wealth. To his own surprise, by 1972 my father had done well enough to be ready for his first large-scale development. It was with that project that the objects dearest to me, which I kept tucked away in a desk drawer in the library, arrived in our house.

You must think I'm rambling – after all, I set out to tell you about the telephone call I kept being tempted to make, that afternoon. Lidia was the one I intended to speak to. But once I had paced up and down long enough to clear my mind, I opted for ringing Giorgio. It wasn't in response to Lidia's words of that morning – I had long been in awe of Giorgio's common sense. But I decided which of his advice to take and which to disregard. Today, for once, I needed to consult him about how to approach a girl. He wasn't just more experienced than me when it came to girls. Most important of all, we shared the kind of childhood friendship rarely replicable with people you meet later in life. We were relaxed with each other and accepted one another as we were – which was just as well, as by that age we differed so greatly in certain respects, that I sometimes wondered whether we would have chosen to become friends, had we met then rather than as six-year-olds. On this occasion, however, I recognised the value of our discrepancies – someone too similar to me wouldn't have known what to do.

'I'll be at your place around five, ok?' he replied from the other end of the phone line, after listening to my garbled justification for being impatient to talk to Anna.

True to his word, he arrived just after five. At the door he gave Concetta the time-honoured monster hug, then dumped his jacket on one of the sofas and made himself at home on the other one, occupying it length-wise, shoes discarded in a jiffy. I made some space for myself by shifting his jacket to one side and sat down opposite him.

'All done,' he said.

'What's all done?'

'It's fixed. You're picking up Anna from aerobics at seven and walking her home. Here's your chance. This is the gym's address.' He handed me a piece of paper, scribbled in Lidia's handwriting.

'No, no. My friends fixing me up? She'll think me pathetic.'

'She won't. Relax. Tomorrow just thank Lidia, ok?'

I sighed.

'Look, this kind of thing goes on all the time. What are friends for? It works like this,' he said. 'Anna is a friend of Lidia's, right? But Anna doesn't know you well. Lidia does. So Lidia says one or two things about you to Anna, who trusts it's true, and... You follow me.'

'Duh. I wasn't born yesterday. But what did Lidia tell her?'

'Not sure, but I've faith in her and it works. Good luck.' He rolled his eyes. 'Honest, a bit more enthusiasm won't kill you, I promise.'

'I wasn't expecting it, that's all.' I ran my hands through my hair. 'What do I say to her?'

'*Cristo*, Tommi!'

'Ok, ok...' After all, it wasn't as if boys and girls hadn't gone out with each other since the beginning of time. 'I'll have to skip guitar class.'

'Are you getting cold feet?'

'No, no. Just saying.'

Giorgio shook his head. 'Lovely chick, Anna is. If you're re-considering, tell me, because if things don't work out between me and Lidia, then I might, you know, give that girl a go.' He laughed.

'Very funny.' I failed to contain a smile.
'But it worked,' he said, and grinned.

CHAPTER 3

I don't like the look of those clouds, Mr. Barker. Let's head indoors, to my home. It's so near, and surely you won't deny me that comfort while I make the effort to dig up the past. I'm hardly the type who might harm you and escape, the way suspects do in films. Let's go then, down the Broad Walk. Maybe on the way you can tell me how you found me.

Well, well... Psychological profiling based on questions you sent my mother's notary. The instructions she gave him in her will – all those announcements to be placed in newspapers across Europe – give you some inkling of her single-mindedness. It's just like her, not to let go, not even when everyone else must have presumed me dead for decades.

I'm aware that many find the Hallfield Estate a little grotty, but I wouldn't live anywhere else. Mine is a sub-let: the only way not to be discovered – or so I thought. I love the modernist lines: the geometric patterns; the contrasting heights of the different blocks; the arrangement of all the buildings like notes across a stave; the alternating blue and red brick panels; the quirky angles of the balconies. I love hearing the children's voices when they flock in and out of Hallfield Primary School. I love the post-war idealism behind the whole project: decent accommodation for all, and facilities and areas to bring people together.

So what if the clash with reality has bruised that idealistic vision? The wonder is how much of it has survived, despite the windows and doors that don't match the originals, the bungled repairs to brickwork and tiles, the dangling wires and the satellite dishes. I love the open lawn and the London planes, the magnolias, sycamores and maples. This garden lacks the opulence of Villa Emma's but it's no less wonderful, so lush in spring and summer, and so mellow in autumn. Winter, I endure. We're almost there: up that external staircase, then second door along the balcony. But your smile reminds me I needn't tell you.

Here we are. As you can see, it's very basic: the minimum furniture required, and most of it from DIY stores. No clutter, and plenty of natural light. But yes, lots of books for such a tiny place – though stacked sufficiently neatly on the shelves, I hope, for them to disappear into the background like wallpaper. They're my only indulgence – if something vital for inner tranquillity can be called an indulgence. Can you understand that this is where I belong, now? Not sure? Well, then – you take that armchair, and I, this one.

I guess you must be wondering what came of the opportunity Giorgio and Lidia set up for me. I went to pick up Anna, of course, as they had arranged.

'You don't want to get close to me. I stink,' she said, stepping out of the gym onto the cobbled street. A memorable opening line. While I struggled for a reply, she zipped up her navy blue track top and swung a kit bag across her shoulder. Her hair stuck to flushed cheeks.

'I hadn't got you down as the aerobics type,' was all I could think of saying. 'I thought you didn't like disco music.'

'It's useful for aerobics. And I don't mind it if I'm in the mood to dance.' She shrugged. 'Lidia said you wanted to talk.'

'Erm... Yes. Just wanted to say I was sorry that, you know, the other night, I wasn't completely straight with you.'

'I detest dishonesty.'

'Me too. But I wasn't playing with you. It isn't as you think.'

She twisted her lips. 'Do you often do things you detest?'

'All the time, but not out of choice.'

She laughed and raised her hands. 'I wasn't being exactly 'nice' either, I guess. Sorry. I felt awkward.'

'That makes two of us.' We exchanged grins. 'Can I walk you home?'

'Sure. My parents are sticklers when it comes to supper time. And I need to shower, first.'

I had a fleeting vision of Anna under the shower, water streaming over her face and her shoulders, small breasts and slim limbs. I swallowed hard and focused on the uneven brickwork of a patch of wall opposite us, where the plaster had peeled off, and on the rumbling and clanking of an old Cinquecento which came up the narrow street, spewing fumes.

'So, what do you like, aside from listening to De André?' she asked as we made our way towards Piazza della Libertá.

'I also like singing his stuff, and other singer-songwriters: De Gregori, Dalla... I play guitar – not brilliantly, but well enough to strum the chords.'

'Really?' She tilted her head and looked at me as if from a new angle. We were crossing the Piazza, now. Groups of people were huddled in front of the town hall: teenagers chatting, and field labourers negotiating the next day's work and wages. Difficult to believe that many of the former, in puffer jackets and tracksuits, would be related to those stubbly men in faded shirts, weathered blazers and flat caps. Later, at the supper table, the Italianised dialect of the young would clash with their elders' archaic version, a hotchpotch of Mediterranean tongues. In the space of a single generation, the joint power of schooling and television had dissolved countless traces of our history: of ancient Greek, Latin, Longobard, French, Arabic and Spanish. But I was one to talk...! As was typical of the wealthy, I hadn't grown up speaking dialect. I barely understood it. And yet, whenever I caught sight of those two groups in Piazza della Libertá, I mourned the annihilation of an endangered species.

'And you?' I said to Anna. 'What do you like, aside from prancing around in a leotard to the beat of synthesisers?'

She smiled. 'Sexy, eh? But not if you saw us sweating through silly exercises. Handy for putting on some muscle, though, if you're a bag of bones like me.'

We traversed the main street which ran along the square, and dived into Via Cattedrale, which led to the heart of the Old Town.

'You're beautiful,' I wanted to say. 'You're not a bag of bones. But you haven't answered my question,' was what came out.

'What do I like best? Reading, I think: novels, plays, history, philosophy... If you lived in a home like mine, you'd understand.'

'Big library, you mean?'

'Not quite.' She chuckled. 'In my family no one but me cares for books. I borrow them from school. My parents say they don't know how they've ended up with a daughter who'd read toilet paper if something were printed on it – which is unfair, as I am selective.'

I raised my hands in mock surrender. 'I believe you.'

She smiled. 'Thing is, I never give up hope, so it is my

fault if I keep getting disappointed. I should know better.' Only the previous day, she had come across some lines in Lucretius, 'Of the kind that really gets you thinking,' she said. She clenched her fists as if the intensity of her thoughts could be held beneath her curled fingers and be revealed by loosening the grip.

'I know exactly what you mean,' I said. How often had I come across sentences that I longed to share? The dilemmas faced by Antigone on an ancient Greek stage could have beset the sister of a terrorist today. And Blaise Pascal's simultaneous sensations of insignificance and of belonging to the universe whenever he observed the stars, could have been mine. But no one around me was interested. Not my mother, too occupied with work or with a set of people whose company gratified her. Nor Concetta, for whose warmth and common sense I was grateful, but whose basic schooling meant our references were miles apart. Nor Giorgio, who lost patience with topics that weren't of immediate utility, regarding them as obligatory evils during school hours, as did most of my school mates. And yet, lessons at the *Liceo* provided only the tedious structure for more interesting discoveries we could make on our own.

'What were the lines from Lucretius about?'

'Oh, about fear of death being not only irrational, but harmful.'

'So, you're into happy stuff.'

'I am, actually. He's liberating.'

'He is. I was teasing. Not that I understand his diatribe against love, though.'

'Me neither. Unhappy marriage?' We both laughed. 'Anyway,' she added, 'I translated the verses there and then for

Barbara – my sister, two years older than me – and do you know what she answered? 'Can I practise a new haircut on you?' She's training to be a hairdresser, mind you, but have you any idea how I felt? I can't wait to start at university.'

Her hair was still plastered to her forehead and cheeks. I was tempted to ask if Barbara had got anywhere close to it but Anna might not realise I was in jest. 'Which course are you going for?'

'*Lettere Classiche*. Literature, Ancient Greece and Rome... I love them.'

'I hadn't guessed.'

'Yes, well... I'll enrol at Bari, and get there for some lectures and for exams. Plenty of people prepare at home. I'll manage. Mum and Dad picture me already as a secondary school teacher in Ostuni. But I might enjoy teaching at university instead, or becoming a journalist and living in a city. Who knows? No use discussing it with them now. How about you?'

I told her that after the *maturitá* – Italy's equivalent of A Levels – I would study business at Bocconi University, in Milan.

'With a family company to run, it's expected of me. Ours is a property development firm. The alternatives would be architecture or engineering, but I'd have to be an artist or a maths wiz for those, and I'm neither.'

'What would you choose if you could?'

'Don't know. No point considering other options, when that obviously wouldn't be sensible. I'm grateful I've a business waiting for me.'

'Are you?'

'Of course. Who wouldn't be?' Failing to recognise my

good fortune would have been feckless. So, better not to indulge in unrealistic dreams. If, as Plato warned, they could become uncontrollable and bring unhappiness all-round, why choose them over contentment? My father had earned his daily bread with a level-headed job, and pursued other interests. 'I'll be able to carry on reading the classics and to play music in my spare time,' I said.

'Ok.' She sounded unconvinced. 'But I bet that up north you'll miss our bakeries – and more. You should see how the Milanese raid this place,' she said, pointing to the *panificio* on our left as we climbed up the street winding its way towards the hilltop cathedral, 'when their holidays have come to an end. They stuff their cars with all they can carry back home.' The aroma of freshly baked bread, *tarallini*, biscuits and focacce wafted through Via Cattedrale; I wouldn't have been surprised if it had saturated the whitewashed walls of the houses flanking the street over the decades in which the bakery had been churning out its goods.

'Yes, I'm sure I'll miss the food of home,' I said.

We turned into the narrower stretch of the street. Over the centuries, carts had carved smooth grooves into the white flagstones. The further we climbed, the more closely huddled together the houses became. Arched alleyways opened up alongside us and snaked their way towards partially-seen buildings and hidden corners. Only a few people walked by – not like in the summer, when Ostuni was teeming with tourists. We reached the cathedral square and crossed its length until we came to a small area where several passageways began. In some of these, the houses had been built at disparate levels in order to cling to the hill's contours, hence the lanes were stepped, either wholly or in part. The orange-tinted street lights bounced off the whiteness of walls and flagstones, adding to the labyrinth's air of mystery and magic.

'My father called this the medina,' I told Anna. 'He said there was more beauty and wisdom in this than in most 'designer' architecture – though he was an architect.'

My childhood walks with my parents through the Old Town were still vivid in my mind. I remembered my father, enraptured, turning to my mother and me as we entered a little square, a pomegranate tree in its centre.

'Isn't it wonderful,' he said, 'how this space is so cared for? No one is paid to look after this tree – the land between these buildings is unclaimed – and yet someone does. No one is paid to keep the ground so immaculate – but these flagstones were evidently hosed today. No one is paid to keep those geraniums or those bougainvillea creepers so neat...' Arms wide, he pointed to the green doors of the dwellings. 'No one, and therefore everyone, who lives here owns this space. Apparently it's the same in medinas elsewhere: in Greece, Spain, Morocco, Tunisia... How wonderful.'

My mother gave him a big, indulgent smile whilst rolling her eyes, as was her habit whenever he shared intuitions like that one.

'Wisdom?' Anna's question and her puzzled look brought me back to the present.

'Sure,' I said as we entered an alley flanked by houses with puny square windows. 'The defensive purpose, obviously; but also the narrow streets that keep houses in the shade during the summer; and all the unplanned meeting areas...'

'I never thought about it. I like that.' She smiled. 'Well, I'm home. In the medina.'

The alley ended on a paved open space with an unrestricted view of the valley below; in the dusk, Villanova stood out by the shore. We were almost at the edge of the town's defensive walls, which plunged towards the bottom of the hill, and whose white rendering concealed – when viewed from a distance – their mix of live rock and boulders, quarried limestone and bricks. An ancient cast iron watering fountain, one of the many in the Old Town, kept guard, stout and austere, in the square, which narrowed gradually. Some thirty meters further on, it became an alley, tall houses either side buttressed by successive arches. Anna pointed to a small three-storey house by the fountain, with the main entrance on the first floor, at our level: whitewashed, like all the others, with slatted green windows and door. The ground floor was built against the rock's steep gradient. On the first floor was also a small terrace overlooking the olive groves which carpeted the earth all the way to the sea.

'It's just like ours,' I said.

'Hardly. A fraction of the size. Old. Only humble geraniums. And the view is nothing like that from the top of your hill. Here, you can only look ahead. From yours, you can do that and take in the whole of the Old Town.' She stared at her feet. 'Listen – I like you. Really. But I can never be your type, can I?' She indicated her house and looked up at me. 'Plus, you're off to Milan in a few months, and I'm not the kind who... It's better not to get attached now, don't you think? If we ended up liking each other, erm, a lot, then we'd just get hurt. I'm not the kind who just –' Again she left the sentence unfinished and opened the house door.

'Nor am I. But we can still get to know each other better. Anyway, as it happens, once I'm at university I'll be home every few weeks.'

She shook her head and stepped inside. 'See you at school. I'm glad we're friends now.' She smiled and clicked the door shut.

Maybe she was right, I thought while searching through the books of the Latin authors in our home library. We hardly knew each other. My feelings must be pure infatuation. Why set my heart on this girl, all the more when we were bound to go our separate ways within six months at most? I asked myself: would Plato have called this, too, an 'unnecessary dream' best cut short by reason? Or was it something else?

I soon found Lucretius's *De Rerum Natura* and remained standing by the bookshelves to sift through it. I lingered on the section about there being no suffering after death, as mind and soul die with the body: 'When I proceed to speak of the soul, teaching that it is mortal, suppose that I also speak of the mind, inasmuch as they are one... Death therefore is nothing, nor at all concerns us...' I paused over the stanzas in which Nature reproaches us: 'What mighty cause have you, O mortal, thus excessively to indulge in bitter grief?' As to the verses dealing with how illogical and harmful fear of death might be, they were scattered throughout Book Three: 'Avarice, and the blind desire for honours, which drive men to transgress the bounds of right... these passions, which are the wounds and plagues of life, are nourished for the most part by the dread of death.'

Lucretius had done such justice to the teachings of his master Epicurus that his questions still struck with force, masked by the beauty of the perfect word, sound and rhythm in the original Latin. But which were the phrases that had affected Anna? Where were they hiding? My lack of a definitive answer seemed proof that I knew her too little to justify even mere infatuation.

At the dinner table, I asked my mother if she had ever read Lucretius, although, like Anna with her sister, I should have known better.

'No. We didn't read him at the Liceo Scientifico when I was your age, and you know I've never had a soft spot for that kind of stuff. Classics were your dad's thing. We were different – I, down to earth, and he, the dreamer.'

'He built a company – not bad for a dreamer.'

She studied me before replying. 'Yes, he learnt to be practical. It went against the grain, but he learnt. The artistic and the practical, in one person, are a powerful combination. Your father could *be* that combination. I never could tell how long it'd last – before I knew it, he had done something fanciful. But then, somehow, he'd make it all good again.'

'And the moral is?' I sneered, sensing the hint that I should follow my father's example – it should have been obvious to her that I already did.

She threw her hands up, as if in despair, and shook her head.

'There's no moral, Tommaso.' She was good at feigning total innocence.

CHAPTER 4

Maybe, I thought, mine was a frenzy stirred by the discovery of my capacity to fall in love. If so, it was self-absorption, which would end up hurting Anna. But over subsequent days, whenever I saw her at school I was unable to remain indifferent. During breaks I'd catch glimpses of her in the corridor and notice endearing details: the way she stood on one leg and twisted the other foot slightly inwards while chatting with friends; the grace with which she tucked a tuft of hair behind her ear; the arc of her spine when she held her hands behind her back. I could make out her laughter among the hubbub; it provoked my smile and a yearning to be party to the joke, to know what had amused her.

Almost every day I'd walk past her group and stop to talk to her, but only briefly: it was awkward to stand with people from parallel classes whom I hardly knew, though she was friendly – warm, even – and included me in her conversations. I listened out for any allusions she might intend for me, but I never could tell whether I stirred in her the turmoil she did in me.

Her words seemed invested with special significance. She might talk of an absurd shop window on Via Pola – with a mannequin dressed so vulgarly and ridiculously that, irrespective of the expensive labels, she couldn't imagine any woman buying such clothes – and then I'd have a philosophy lesson and make the connection between what she had just said and Plato's distinction between ideal beauty and its real-life distortions. For Plato, we should strive to imitate the perfect forms of the invisible world beyond our knowledge. As its essence were beauty and goodness, that's what we should seek. So when people placed a high value on an outfit as crass as the one Anna had pointed out, what did it say about the world around us? I longed to discuss that and other questions with her, if only to hear her voice.

Places, people and objects outside school took on new meaning whenever – and it was often – they confirmed something she had said and which had never occurred to me. My prior knowledge of concepts I had studied, or of feelings met in literature, seemed vacuous and abstract when compared with my new awareness of their truth – with palpitations to prove it. It felt as if until then I had lived on reality's surface, ignorant of the layers beneath.

Everyday actions triggered musings as to what Anna might say or do: whether she took the same pleasure as me in the blossoming almond trees at this time of year; what she made of the cringe-worthy picture, in the windows of the photographer near school, of a bride baring her lucky red garter; whether she ate her *focaccia alla cipolla* – oozing from every side with its succulent filling of sautéed onions, capers, tiny black olives and fresh tomato chunks – with fork and knife like my mother, or with bare hands like most of us. In those moments, I wondered where she was and what she was doing. Actions I normally performed with attentiveness now seemed unimportant and I became fretful, feeling that I was only treading water.

It wasn't long before I was certain that I wanted her to give me a chance. I had never wanted or cared for anything so intensely. Was it Eros – Venus' mischievous son – running wild? Hadn't Plato called desire 'want' – the first rung on the ladder to higher forms of love? Unknown to ourselves, he said, desire stemmed from our yearning for all that is *really* good and beautiful. I had heard that in Spanish '*te quiero*' means 'I love you' but also 'I want you.' Maybe now I knew why. And yet, there seemed to be more to it. The first flicker of mutual recognition had flashed in nearly total darkness out on the terrace of Villa Emma. It had flared up again during our conversation on the way to her home and during our brief chats in the school corridor. There was an immediate understanding beneath our initial awkwardness and differences. Those differences captivated me: I reflected on her throwaway comments; and I wondered if any of mine had earned a little place in her mind. But what if my suppositions were born of one-sided hope? What if I turned out to be in the grip of a ludicrous fantasy, like one of those film characters who, unbeknown to themselves, elicited our squirms and laughter?

I needed to find a way of telling Anna how I felt, but I also wanted to avoid an embarrassing rejection. Humour might be the answer. Maybe, I thought as I rode home from school, I could write for her some tongue-in-cheek lyrics to the melody of 'Marinella's Song'. I got to work on it the minute Concetta and I finished lunch. I rushed to my bedroom, sat by the window facing the front garden and waited for inspiration, but dismissed every potential verse as daft. It seemed not even the muse of love could make the task easy. I tore the hopeless pages off the paper pad, scrunched them up and tossed them into the wastepaper basket. Then I got up and drifted over to the window overlooking the terrace.

This is the story of lovely Anna
Whose voice on a dark terrace frightened Tommaso

She's lucky he survived the heart attack
As there's no other girl he'd call so wonderful.

Those are the first and only lines I can recall of my attempt. It was laughable. The remainder told, in flippant tones, a love story that, unlike 'Marinella's Song', ended well. I gave them to Anna on a sheet of plain writing paper, in an envelope which she insisted on opening there and then in my presence at the exit from school. She stayed behind while her friends rushed to the bus stop. My face hot and sweaty, I watched her scanning the words across the page, and restraining a giggle. When she finished reading, she gave me a big smile.

'This is so sweet. Thank you. I love the funny bits.' She paused. 'I don't know what to say.'

I cleared my throat. 'How about I take you home?'

Within minutes I was riding through the streets of Ostuni with the girl I loved leaning against me. I could sense the tension of her body. She was trying to keep it as detached from mine as the motorbike permitted, her hands gripping the rack behind her seat. I wanted to jump, to shout, to tell Giorgio... We dismounted in front of her house and looked at each other.

'Come to dinner with me?' I said, encouraged by her smile.

'I have to ask my parents for permission.' She put a hand on my shoulder and kissed me on the cheek. 'I'll get back to you tomorrow – promise.' She entered the house and waved to me before closing the door.

'Tommaso, why so silent?' My mother jolted me out of my reverie. 'And Concetta has made you a *tajedda*. It won't kill you to thank her.'

'Sorry. It's tremendous, as ever. Thanks for taking the trouble, Concetta.' I felt their eyes on me while I chewed. I had almost finished my portion of that divine dish, and yet only now was I noticing and savouring the amalgam of fresh mussels, potatoes, *perini* tomatoes, rice and olive oil, all baked together to perfection.

'What's the matter?' my *tata* asked.

I looked at them. I was so happy that I'd have hugged and kissed them both. The midday sunshine bathing us through the windows gave the kitchen a bright air.

'I'm taking someone out this evening. A girl I like.'

'*The* girl? Anna?' Concetta asked, and I nodded. 'Ah!' she said, lifting her arms up in the air as if the Almighty had answered her prayers.

My mother shot us glances. 'What's her surname? What do her parents do?'

'Saponaro. No idea about the parents – I didn't ask.'

My mother rolled her eyes and sighed.

No self-respecting Southern Italian goes out to dinner before eight-thirty. Nonetheless, I agreed to collect Anna at seven-thirty, as her parents insisted on her returning home by eleven. Nowadays, especially in a metropolis like London, where girls as young as fourteen are clubbing until late – and I know it, from the rows between parents and teens to which I've been a reluctant witness, as a Classics tutor – it must be difficult to imagine that a nineteen-year-old girl could have such an early curfew. But times were different, Ostuni a small town, and Anna's parents less liberal than those from the educated bourgeoisie with whom I was more familiar.

It might amuse you to hear me talk of class, when the

British have a reputation for being more class-conscious than other nations. It's nonsense: in every nation, class distinctions are simply made and perpetuated in different ways. The lines are drawn either by money or by culture – sometimes, by both. The newly wealthy are almost always the keener on the demarcations; they need to renege on any traces of a humbler past, while the learned already hold the seeds of their eventual loss of privilege. I'm not being pessimistic – quite the contrary. Distilled to its purest essence, culture places the highest value on things which aren't 'things': on what money can't buy.

Look at my friend Zoe. An intelligent woman – with her expensive education, she could have chosen to earn no less than her wealthy father and grandfather did. But you only have to watch her playing violin, eyes closed, her head and shoulders an extension of the instrument, swaying with the music, body and mind flowing into the fingertips' pressure on the strings, and you can have no doubt that all this is worth more to her than an exclusive address or jewels, clothes and status.

But I've digressed. My comment about Anna's parents was simply one of fact – I was in love with her, and her family's 'class' was irrelevant, but for the curfew. When I rang the bell, she emerged well prepared for the motorbike ride down to the shore, in a fuchsia jacket which would otherwise have been too heavy for the early-April evening, and a pair of trousers. Her mother appeared behind her in the doorway.

Under the cover of polite smiles, Mrs. Saponaro and I sized each other up. Though barely forty, she was wearing a shapeless flowery dress such as my *tata* favoured. Still, I could see where Anna had got her slight build, the medium height and the light brown hair. She had not inherited her mother's green eyes, though. Green eyes like hers, or blue ones like mine, were among the enduring gifts left to Apulians by a long series of North European conquerors. Centuries of their presence weren't evident only in the castles and cathedrals studding the region, but in the looks of thousands of the living, blending in with those of other – Mediterranean – conquerors. Anna's mother was one of those Apulians whose features seemed to astonish foreigners, who didn't expect to encounter them in such numbers in the South.

I shook her hand. 'Tommaso.'

'Assunta Saponaro.' Her gaze shifted from me to my Suzuki and back again. 'Go slowly, please. Terrible road – winding, and everything.'

'Don't worry. I'll take extra care.'

Anna and I rode down to an unpretentious restaurant by the harbour of Villanova. It was a boxy white structure with a wood-and-glass conservatory jutting out above the water. The fragrance of the sea had seeped into walls and furniture, and tonight it was wafting in through cracks in the wood. No other customers had arrived yet. We picked the table furthest out above the water. I nearly head-butted the elderly waiter in my eagerness to help Anna to her seat – he had positioned himself behind her chair, as had I. He left me to it when he realised I wouldn't budge, but not before shaking his head and chuckling. Anna didn't seem to have noticed, or was kind enough to act as if she hadn't. Between forkfuls of linguine with mussels and salt-coated sea bass, we talked about so many topics that later I struggled to recollect them all. The rare pauses in our conversation were filled by the crashing of shallow waves against the wooden stilts beneath the floor.

'Apparently our fish is so tasty because of the prairies,' I remember her saying while she cleaned her sea bass.

'Prairies?'

'Of posidonia: a plant. It grows in unpolluted parts of the Mediterranean.'

'You mean an alga.'

'No, no, a proper plant, complete with roots, stems, leaves, flowers... It adapted to living in salt water, over millions of years. There are kilometres of posidonia prairies along these shores, teeming with sea creatures.'

'Like mermaids? I bet you're really a mermaid – you have to be: where else does one learn to eat fish so daintily, but in palaces under the sea?'

She laughed. 'Thanks for the compliment, but I'm a terrible swimmer, which rules out life under the sea.' She eyed her fork and knife with a serious expression. 'I never liked the story of *The Little Mermaid*.'

'Why?'

'Because it says: be content with the world you come from and don't venture beyond it, or else. And the tale makes no sense from the start: why put her life at risk for a human being who doesn't even know she loves him? For good measure, her feet feel as if they're being stabbed at every step. She's a masochist!'

'Okay. So you're not a mermaid.'

'Yep: fully human,' she said, raising her hand as if swearing an oath to mankind. 'Maybe that's why what I read about the posidonia stuck: it's a humble plant which adapted to a different world, to become one of the most ancient surviving species on the planet. True-life magic. I suppose that might be why it's named after the god of the oceans. Not bad, for something children call whale dung.'

'That's the one?'

'Yes. The silvery ribbons which litter the beachfront after a storm are the leaves, torn from the bottom of the sea. The brown pellets are made up of those leaves, shredded and compacted by the waves.'

'Well, well... When De André sings that nothing grows out of diamonds, while flowers blossom from dung, maybe he has posidonia in mind,' I teased her.

She rolled her eyes and smiled. 'Sure. That must be what he's referring to, and we're the only ones who know.'

It was my turn to laugh. Yet, as I observed her, I thought: 'You might not be a mermaid, but you are a mystery. How did you become who you are? How did you break the chains which hold back girls from the Città Vecchia? Where did you find the cheek to pursue your dreams?'

After dinner we walked along the harbour, almost deserted without the tourism of the summer months, and with the fishing boats out at sea at this time of evening. I put an arm round Anna's shoulders. She smiled, and we continued chatting, pretending no threshold had been crossed.

The road ended just beyond the only surviving tower of Villanova's castle. We stopped talking, and in the semi-darkness I looked at her. My pulse beat in my temples. I put my hands on Anna's waist and bent down to kiss her, watching her eyes for signs she might withdraw. But our lips touched and remained pressed against each other. And then the body took over – it seemed to know what to do next.

I kissed her on cheeks, ears and neck and felt her frame giving way no less than mine. We closed our eyes and found each other's lips again. It felt as if our whole selves were flowing into that kiss, intertwining in a dimension outside time and space. A soundless bubble sheltered just the two of us. Afterwards we held each other tightly, her face against my chest.

I don't know how long it was before she raised her head and smiled. 'I wish I hadn't fallen in love with you. You're going to break my heart, I know it already.'

'I'll never do that.' We kissed again. Her perfume, flowery and faint, almost made me light-headed. 'My God, you're so beautiful,' I said.

'I hope I'm not your God.'

We both laughed.

Anna might have said it in jest, but that sentence – 'I hope I'm not your God' – has rung in my ears again and again. Anna's love felt like an unparalleled blessing. For her and with her I would have perfected any aspect of myself, though she made me feel loved in my entirety; for a time, she could have said the same. *If* there's a God, love between human beings can bring us as close to Him as we'll ever get. Cynics scoff at the mention of loves like ours, but their arguments sow misery: too many people settle for second best in the belief they're being 'realistic', and before long become cynics in turn. Countless human beings will never experience the kind of love I'm describing, and there it was, being served to Anna and me on a plate. So young. Too young.

How, you might ask, can I have the arrogance of asserting that it wasn't the elation of 'first love', or of the early phase of love, that made ours feel so extraordinary?

The stubborn rationalist I once was – before falling in love with Anna – would almost certainly have answered by listing some facts: the generous dose of interests we shared;

presumably a sprinkling of unconscious mutual needs; a fortunate correspondence and complementarity of qualities... It wouldn't be untrue. But it would deny the magic – the most important, yet most elusive, of all facts. How tragically reductive that would be. All I can do is to leave you with my certainty of how it felt to be loved by, and to love, Anna – and with a thought: the man who concluded that 'the Heart knows reasons whereof Reason knows nothing' wasn't a hopeless romantic but a stern mathematician.

In the days which followed the evening in Villanova, we spent every spare moment together, at and outside school. We dived into our pasts and resurfaced with fragments of memory which the other greeted like priceless finds – stories about our childhoods, our families, friends, old schools, trips... We shared hidden moments – the hilarious, the painful and the most embarrassing ones – without inhibitions. It's difficult to remember examples of them now, to fish them out of what feels like a torrent. But I do recall telling Anna of my maternal grandfather.

He and my grandmother died when I was thirteen. During my childhood, at our customary Sunday lunch with them, he sometimes offered me two one-hundred-lire coins, provided I managed to keep them under my armpits for the whole meal – an old-fashioned method for teaching table manners. At age five I was unable to keep my elbows stuck to my ribcage and the coins dropped within seconds onto the floor; at age seven they slid inexorably down my arms until their high-pitched ding on the ceramic tiles chimed my fiasco. Dad's regular protestations against this practice – a surreptitious cruelty to which I was a willing party, lured by those elusive coins – provoked periods of grudging silences between him and my grandparents. I must have been eight when at another of Grandpa's attempts my father's exasperation spilt over.

'Isn't it bad enough that you... already did this to Emma?'

My grandfather stiffened in his chair. 'Did what?'

'Drummed that pernicious sense of your family's bygone 'rightful place in the world' into *her* head, and – now I understand – even into her movements. You want to do the same to my son? Never.' He poured himself a glass of wine, and took a swig.

Grandma clutched Grandpa's arm. He pulled his glasses closer, the better to glare at Dad.

Mum looked from him to her parents, and back again. 'How can you be so disrespectful?' Her voice was shaky. 'To my father, to me...'

'Darling, I have huge respect for you. More than that. You're the love of my life. But the whole attitude behind such things' – he pointed to the coins on the tablecloth – 'hasn't done *you* any good, has it?'

'Ha!' My mother crossed her arms.

I watched, uneasy. I had never witnessed a flare-up between my parents. Dad's humour, or Mum's fondness for him, normally defused their little disagreements.

'It's painful to watch how hard you have to work to overcome your snootiness – whether towards other guests at a party, or towards the grocer, the...' Dad said. 'Being able to enjoy conversations with perfectly nice people shouldn't require such effort. And that's progress, compared to when we first met.'

'You –' Mum stammered. 'Blowing things out of proportion like this. Father was only encouraging good manners in Tommaso. You should be grateful.'

Grandpa nodded, his eyebrows a scowl, his cheeks hollow.

Dad sighed, and said nothing.

But my grandfather never subjected me to the exercise of the coins again.

So you see? Episodes and feelings of which I had never spoken – presumably considering them unworthy of anyone's interest or maybe fearful of others' judgment – tumbled out of my lips and were met with understanding, warmth and humour. To the example I have given you, I believe Anna quipped she had never thought of coins as torture instruments. I can still see her, shaking her head in sympathy as you have done, while I recounted this and other incidents, or laughing with me when I told her of happier ones. I, in turn, couldn't get enough of the glimpses of the life she had led until then, of the slivers of time that had gone into who she was.

'I wish I had known you years ago,' I kept saying.

'I wish I had known you, too.'

I suppose that, through the sharing of details from our past and present, we were seeking to overcome that impossibility.

I told Anna something which I had never shared with anyone: how I had come to lose my father. I don't know if I'm ready to tell you about it. The thought of it is painful to this day. On the other hand, the full shock of how my mother treated me after he was gone would overwhelm you all the more if you knew of our lives up to that point. I guess I can't expect you to understand why I won't accept my inheritance, if you don't hear the whole story.

But before we start on that chapter, have some lunch.

You must be starving. I am. I'll fix us a *caprese*. Please, do stay sitting in that armchair. See, one of the virtues of this poky open plan kitchen is that we can continue talking while I prepare a bite. I'm afraid the tomatoes and the mozzarella lack the intense flavour they have in Puglia, but they'll have to do. God only knows for how long these tomatoes have travelled before getting to my local Tesco. In Ostuni, Concetta would buy them directly from the farmers, the *contadini*, at their open-air market stalls or at the occasional ones set up before the doorways of their houses. They'd come home in brown paper bags, the tomatoes, be they *fiaschettini*, *San Marzano* or whichever other type she selected – Apulians are fanatical about the aptness of each variety to different recipes in the way that only people living where a fruit is produced in such abundance can be – but all of them, without fail, released an outburst of fragrance. A single whiff of one of those tomatoes carried with it the scent of dark soil, of the brisk green of the plant from which it had been plucked only that morning, of the sunshine in which it and the *contadini* had sweltered.

As for the mozzarella, here in London I can only dream of the texture of the fresh ones made under customers' eyes at the local *caseifici*. The stretched and moulded filaments of the real thing spring back between the teeth with a light squelching noise. But we fare better with the basil leaves: straight off the plant on this window sill. Also the olive oil is as it should be: much as it was on the day it was pressed – a trickle of it, and you're tasting a ray of sunshine.

Nostalgic, you say – I've just proven to you that really I want to go back? No, you've got it wrong. Did you know that the word 'nostalgia' comes from ancient Greek? *Nostos* means a return home. *Algos* translates as pain or suffering. So, I appreciate that nostalgia normally suggests a person's ache for returning home, but in my case, I assure you, it's the inverse: it can only mean the pain I feel at any such prospect. Yes, though I admit to missing the land itself and a couple of people. My friend Giorgio? No, him, I don't miss. A profound disappointment: that's what he turned out to be.

CHAPTER 5

Wouldn't it be wonderful if hindsight were perfect vision? But some questions defy clear answers, irrespective of one's knowledge or experience. It took me a long time to understand it. For years I wondered: if my father had been aware of what lay ahead and steered clear of his first ever big property investment, would it have made any difference?

You should have seen how eager he was about the opportunity. It arose in nearby Brindisi when I was nine. The site of a disused pasta factory came onto the market after a decade of legal wrangles among the heirs. The timing was ideal. My father had been designing and building villas all along the coast for fifteen years. With that track record, he obtained the banks' financial support for redeveloping the site. And the city council expressed a preference for his project as it was the most sympathetic to the architecture of the *quartiere*. He would have to invest all our savings in it and put up our home as security against the loans. These arrangements entailed working under unprecedented pressure. But the venture looked so attractive – he and Mum calculated that the profit would be worth the temporary stress.

The evening he won the bid, the three of us celebrated with a restaurant dinner kicked off with champagne – the real thing, not the usual *spumante*. My father's excitement was palpable: his olive-skinned face had, for once, a reddish glow; he joked more than usual; and he vowed that my mother and I would be the ones to cut the ribbon at the project's completion.

'With some good planning, that date might even coincide with our fortieth birthdays, Emma. We could celebrate with a memorable party.'

'I'd stay shy of tempting fate.' My mother's smile looked tense as if only now that there was no going back had the enterprise become real and petrifying, though she had worked alongside my father on the entire bidding process. 'Keeping contractors and suppliers to the schedule will be hard work – we've built potential overruns into the budget, but you know how quickly any glitch will eat into profits.'

Mum had always taken care of the firm's administrative and financial tasks, which up to that point had been straightforward, occupying her only part-time. She was a qualified *contabile* but not a graduate. In her generation a woman with a secondary school *maturitá* was already among the highly educated. Still, she would probably have attended university away from home, had her paternal grandfather not devoured the family fortune. He lost the vineyards over a game of baccarat, the farmhouses at a roulette table... Not in undistinguished casinos, but in the comfort of Puglia's patrician palaces and villas, where one could be stripped of centuries of wealth by one's peers – and thereafter, if the damage was severe enough, shunned. The only property which survived this piece-by-piece destruction was the one in which my mother grew up: an unremarkable nineteenth-century house crammed with bric-a-brac and dusty books.

Her father earned his living with morose dignity as a municipal clerk bearing the name of yet another family sunk from the ranks of the south's nobility. His craving to re-climb even one or two more rungs on the ladder was channelled into the education of his son, who became an orthopaedic surgeon.

I think I know the reason why my grandparents approved of their daughter's marriage: although my father came 'only' from the emerging bourgeoisie, he was what they called '*un professionista*' – a category consisting of praiseworthy professionals as diverse as an *avvocato*, *architetto* or *ingegnere*, though in their mind none as illustrious as a *dottore in medicina*.

To be fair, I never heard my mother voicing that attitude. My parents' had been a marriage of love. Their first encounter, at a carnival party in Bari, deserved its hallowed place in family lore. Dad had turned up as Harlequin and Mum as Pierrot. She had been dragged there by her brother at the insistence of the host, a fellow medicine graduate – there weren't enough girls, could Eugenio please bring his sister? She and Dad got talking, and then dancing. Dad tried to impress her – or, as he maintained, to have the pleasure of seeing her smile – by displaying Harlequin's famed agility, but his dance move went wrong. Uncle Eugenio ended up in a bedroom in the host's house, with two people – his sister and the young man whose ankle he was bandaging – gazing into each other's eyes.

The demolition of the pasta factory began in late September. My father spent the mornings in Brindisi keeping an eye on the *cantiere* and drove back home to have lunch with us before returning to work, either at his desk in our library or at the firm's office in central Ostuni. At the lunch table I listened to his enthusiastic updates as if they were the news bulletin for children: 'This morning the last remaining section was razed to the ground,' or 'The trucks have carried away the last batch of rubble. Tomorrow the *soprintendenza* will send us the archaeologists for their test-pitting, but they're not expecting to find much – we're not within the Roman town's perimeter. We'll soon have permission to dig for the foundations.'

I watched my mother's features relax with each clip of good news.

A few days after that last 'newsflash', I returned home with Concetta from school – by now we were in October – to find that my father wasn't back yet. My mother was talking with him from the telephone in our entrance hall.

'Alvaro, listen to me. You've got to do all you can to discourage the woman from making a huge deal out of it. Let it gather any momentum and who knows where it'll stop.' She wound and unwound the receiver's chord around her finger as she heard him out. 'Make sure to signal that you'll fight her every inch of the way.'

I left them to their conversation and sprinted upstairs to my room to drop my backpack and take off the white-collared blue *grembiulino* which we boys wore over our clothes – the girls' smocks were white, which must say something about the importance Italians ascribe to neatness in women. When I ran back downstairs, my mother was putting down the receiver.

'Where's Daddy?' I asked.

'Brindisi. A meeting.' She pursed her lips and ran a hand through her dark-blond hair, which in those days was shoulder-length.

'What's wrong, Mummy?'

'Nothing. Well, nothing that Daddy can't charm his way out of, I'm sure.' She smiled but I could see that she was faking.

'Please don't keep secrets from me. You know Daddy will tell me everything, don't you?'

'I can't wait for him to tell me everything too, darling.'

★★★

'Honestly, Emma. You worry too much.' My father put down his thumb-sized glass of *nocino* – the dense, pitch black digestive liquor which Concetta made from fresh walnuts every summer and which he sometimes sipped after dinner – and got up from his armchair. He walked the few steps towards the sofa on which my mother and I were sitting. 'To witness a live archaeological excavation is thrilling, for Christ's sake.'

'Don't blaspheme – in front of Tommaso, especially.'

'Sorry.' He perched himself on the sofa's arm and stroked my mother's shoulder. She shrugged his hand away but he just smiled. 'It'll be all right: the *soprintendenza* is relying on the director of Brindisi's archaeological museum for decisions on how to proceed – and the director is a reasonable woman. This afternoon's meeting with her was reassuring. She won't impose a lengthy suspension of works on us unless it turns out to be absolutely necessary. The shards of pottery they've recovered don't suggest that'll be the case, but given their presence, you can hardly expect her not to request further test-pitting.'

'And if a long delay turns out to be necessary?'

'Unlikely. You know how common it is to come across archaeological remains, when building in the centre of Brindisi. And yet, even there, the *soprintendenza* quickly recovers what wasn't destroyed or looted a long time ago, and construction then carries on. Our site isn't anywhere near the centre of town, darling. In any event, you can't live your life worrying about all the 'what ifs'. But if it came to a long delay, there's a State compensation scheme –'

'– Which is a joke.' My mother sprang from her seat and began pacing up and down the sitting room. 'It should be straightforward, but the bureaucracy can make the claims drag on for years – during which one can go bankrupt. You know it.'

'I'll worry about it if and when it happens, whereas like this you'll dig yourself into an early grave. Also, can I point out that getting into legal battles against the *soprintendenza* is as good as setting fire to a truckload of banknotes – if anything, more excruciating? Best not make enemies of them. So, you might as well enjoy the positive side of things.'

'Is there one?'

'Of course. If they discover anything interesting, I'll be one of the first to set eyes on it. Imagine: if they're Roman finds, they won't have seen the light for around two thousand years. I can't think of many things more riveting. And Tommaso here,' he grinned at me, 'would get a good look at all that. Wouldn't that be an amazing experience? What do you say, young man?'

'Yes, please!' I already imagined the full armour of a famous Roman warrior being unearthed. Brindisi had been a major Roman city. Caesar's and Pompey's fleets had set off from its harbour; at first, Caesar had tried to prevent his rival's ships from leaving it, by blocking its entrance with rocks, felled trees, and rafts. Virgil had met his death there on his way back from Greece – a marble plaque commemorated the very spot. I had stood beneath it with Dad, in the shadow of one of the columns – tall and triumphant – which marked the endpoint of the Via Appia. We had pictured the great poet gazing at the harbour – at quinqueremes and triremes and at merchant ships laden with exotic goods from the Eastern and Southern Mediterranean. Sailors had found safety there since the remotest ages: fragments of Mycenaean pottery bore witness to their passage. I knew all about the Greeks and the Romans: if I asked to be put to bed, Concetta and Mummy told me fairy tales for little girls but my father told me stories of heroes like Hector, Achilles, Diomedes and Aeneas. Legend had it that wise Diomedes, after the fall of Troy, sailed to Puglia and married the king of the Daunians' daughter. The coast of Lecce, just to our south, was Aeneas' first sight of Italy – he and his men made offerings there, at a temple of Minerva. 'Take me with you tomorrow, Daddy.'

'Tomorrow you've got school. And they might not find anything much, anyway. See what you've done, Emma?' He winked at my mother. 'With your worries, you've raised our hopes too high – Tommaso's and mine.'

My mother couldn't contain a smile. She shook her head. 'All right. I guess there's nothing we can do right now but wait and see.'

Lessons the next morning felt interminable. When the school bell rang, I shot out of the door. At the end of the usual short drive home in Concetta's Fiat Centoventisette – a boxy hatchback in a dull shade of orange peculiar to those years – I rushed into the house and up to my mother, who was setting down her briefcase on the console table in the hall, and asked her for news.

'Can't you see I've only just arrived? Have the grace to let me take off my cardigan.'

I straightened out like a soldier surprised by an impromptu inspection. She, in turn, seemed to regret the outburst: she hugged me so tight that I caught the acrid smell of her woollen sleeves. 'Sorry, darling. Mummy had a wretched morning.'

She had been at the office as normal, but this time in the company of the firm's solicitor.

'I'm taking no chances. I asked him to talk me through what we might be facing – *potentially* facing, of course, but I *had* to double-check.' She let out a sigh. 'I probably shouldn't be telling you any of this.'

I grasped merely the gist of what she said, and I don't think she expected me, as a nine-year-old, to absorb the detail, which I understood fully only when I grew up. The *soprintendenza* might demand a temporary stop to the works for sixty or more days, the solicitor had explained. It could also ask for unrestricted access to the land, and for the project's suspension, for however long the archaeological investigations required. The worst scenario was expropriation, should the State decide to open up the site to visitors as a *parco archeologico*: obtaining fair compensation could be nightmarish. Over subsequent months I overheard my parents discussing these threats in emotional, hushed tones. Meanwhile, that day, the lawyer reassured my mother – just as Dad had done – that the *soprintendenza* shied away from drastic measures unless it deemed the finds significant.

'With a bit of luck, they won't discover anything important,' Mum said.

Within a fortnight, as the archaeologists dug deeper, they found more ancient objects and brickwork. The additional test-pitting had uncovered two layers of dwellings and artefacts: a medieval and a Roman one. Both extended to the entire site. Its scale and surprising location outside the ancient town walls made it anything but the 'standard' occurrence faced by construction firms in the city. My father began staying in Brindisi the whole day. He was missing lunch with us, and his sacrosanct afternoon nap, the *pennichella*, though with no visible impact on his vigour: his accounts of the day's events, over supper, burst with enthusiasm, tinged with some apprehension. By late October it was clear that the construction project would be put on hold – the question was for how long. My father argued as before that it was best to co-operate: the *soprintendenza* had the law on its side and anyway he too wanted to see any archaeological finds duly recovered.

'Humanity has managed for long enough without knowing of their existence. And this country can't even keep up the other ancient stuff it's got already,' my mother complained over supper.

'True, but you're being facetious, *bellissima*. To build the apartment blocks, we'd destroy whatever's buried underneath and you wouldn't want that.'

She nodded. 'I'm just worried the archaeologists will slack off and go on longer than they need to, and then...'

'They won't. Come meet the director of the museum and you'll stop worrying. She's perfectly sensible.' He turned towards me. 'Soon enough I'll take you to the *cantiere*.'

'Tomorrow?' I said.

'No, but as soon as there's something more to see.'

'We don't want there to be *anything* more to see,' Mum shrieked, raising her hands to her hair, and letting them fall onto the table with a thump. I winced. 'We should never have taken this gamble,' she added, glowering at Dad.

'Is that what you think it is? Well...!' He exhaled loudly, and shook his head. 'Look, Emma, I appreciate your family history may make you a little irrational about all this – '

'What?' Mum snapped. 'Tommaso – go upstairs and get ready for bed.'

'No,' Dad said calmly. 'Tommaso, please stay. This is just a discussion between adults who love each other – and who can solve problems together. There's no reason for you not to be here.'

'Fine.' Mum made a dismissive hand gesture.

'Honestly, darling, you're being wildly over-anxious,' Dad said. 'It's making things worse for all of us. I don't mind going over and over the reasons for staying calm. But in the final instance, it boils down to accepting things we cannot change and making the best of what's doable. Can we alter the fact that the improbable has happened? No. Nor the fact that the *soprintendenza* has consequently blocked the works. Can we?' He leaned across the table and squeezed Mum's hand. 'Can we, *amore mio*?' he said softly.

'No.' Mum dropped her shoulders.

'But if we're involved in the process, we may stand a chance of influencing it, while doing what's right, yes?'

'I suppose.'

'Getting so agitated about worst-case scenarios that may never happen isn't going to help, Emma. And by the way, even years of delay, or expropriation, don't have to be as disastrous as in your fears. So, let's focus on the situation's good aspects. We're not dealing with the usual few objects excavated here and there, but with enough of them to give a proper glimpse into how people lived. It's an extraordinary discovery – and an astonishing opportunity for Tommaso to grasp concretely his link to those who've come before us.'

'Hmm,' my mother nodded. She seemed calmer, now.

But when, after dinner, my father shut himself up in the library to catch up on his correspondence, Mum beckoned to me to stay in the kitchen, and took me aside. She bent down to face me and placed her hands on my arms. 'I hear what your father says, but still, promise me that you won't egg him on.'

'Uh?'

'Don't let Daddy get carried away with this archaeology

stuff, all right? You and I know him – we love him.' Her pitch rose with each breath. 'Give the *soprintendenza* a hand and, as the saying goes, they'll take off your arm. Your father will volunteer the arm without realising he's done it.'

It was like being pressed between two pillows – fluffy and familiar, but inadvertently smothering.

In the evenings that followed, my father sometimes brought home objects or fragments for me to see, before returning them to the excavations the next morning. The archaeologists, with whom he had become friendly, deemed these trifling. I remember shards of a medieval ceramic cooking-pot. The specialist on the dig reckoned it dated from the time of the Norman domination or possibly from that of the Emperor Frederick II, the Swabian *puer Apuliae*. My father and I sat next to each other on the two chairs by his desk in the library and he placed a fragment in my palm. The grainy, reddish-brown clay was blackened with soot on one side and encrusted with the indistinguishable remains of a last meal on the other.

'There was probably a boy like you there, warming himself by the hearth on the family farm and eating his soup just as you do,' my father said.

I pictured a scruffy lad, home after a gruelling day in the fields and now arched over the pot, breathing in the aroma wafting up in swirls of steam from a minestrone while it sputtered on the fire.

'Why not a knight? Maybe a crusader,' I said. Maybe one of those who had built in Brindisi a small replica of Jerusalem's Church of the Holy Sepulchre. I couldn't count the times I had walked past it or ridden astride the marble lions guarding its entrance, under the gaze of a sculpted warrior gripping a long shield. Above my head, the swallows nesting under the *Tempietto*'s roof tiles never failed to grab my attention with their acrobatic manoeuvres. The white flagstones of the little square amplified their staccato shrieks.

My father scratched his head. 'I see we need to talk about crusaders, one of these days. I guess history wouldn't be *magistra vitae* – teacher of life – if it weren't complicated.' He smiled. 'In any event, the building was outside the town walls and the brickwork is nothing fancy, so it was probably a farm built over the remains of a Roman villa. They're digging up the villa, at the southern end of the site.'

Another evening, he brought home a needle made of smooth bone, and one of copper alloy, green and scratchy with rust. He laid them carefully on the desk on a burgundy napkin borrowed from the stack in the dining room sideboard, and the two of us sat there, trying to picture the women and the girls who, eight or nine hundred years previously, had sewn their family's coarse clothing or the hemp sacks for the olive harvest. I wanted to know the number of generations between them and us, for the years to take on a solid form I could grasp. The calculation proved, at best, imprecise, and I only half-understood it, but the enthusiasm of my father's effort gave me a sense of being taken in earnest, of being let in on a secret. He said there had been long periods during which our ancestors' lives had been shorter than present-day ones, and that they were often very young when they had children. His account of the droughts, malarial coastal marshes, warring armies and earthquakes of centuries past made the early nineteen-seventies feel like an oasis of peace and prosperity even though television was bombarding us with news about terrorism.

Once, my father took the usual wine-red cloth out of the desk drawer – its new home, now that it had been promoted to the function of backdrop to 'our' treasures – and onto it, from a tiny envelope of transparent plastic, he slid a thin coin. 'They're finding all kinds: Byzantine, Roman, Greek... I thought this one would fascinate you.'

The profile of a man – the Roman emperor Trajan, apparently – stood out in relief against the dull silver. 'Have a look at the other side.'

When I turned it over, the coin felt flimsy, like one of the ghosts of shells speckling the waterfront. It pictured a woman reclining against rocks; with the right hand she held a wheel, balancing it perilously over her knee in the effort to draw attention to it; with her left, she clutched a branch; beneath her, a caption read 'Via Traiana'.

'Is it precious?'

'Not in terms of money – it's only a *denarius* and isn't rare. But it was minted when the Appia Traiana was completed. It was an easier route to Brindisi than the old Appia.' He turned towards the door of the library that opened onto our terrace. 'You won't freeze, if we go outside for a minute? I want to show you something.'

'Me, freeze?'

My mother and Concetta would have fussed until I put on a cardigan – but they weren't there. Outside, the cold October evening wrapped my body, but I relished it as a conquest, a right of entry into the ranks of big boys. My father must have noticed me shivering, though: when we got to the railing at the edge of the terrace, he rubbed my arms to keep me warm.

'Look straight ahead. What do you see?' he asked.

'The dark – where all the olive groves are. And a string of lights by the sea – Villanova.'

'Very good. If you had stood on this spot when that Roman coin was minted and you had looked straight ahead, you'd have seen – by day, at least – people travelling on foot, on horses and carts on the Via Traiana, which ran all along the coast between Brindisi and Bari before turning inland. The woman on the coin personifies the road: it stretched at the feet of our hills. That's why she's leaning against them. The coastal road on which we drive to Brindisi runs next to it. And guess what kind of tree the branch in her hand is from.'

'An olive tree?'

'*Bravo*. Now let's get back inside.'

At the desk, I held the coin between thumb and finger. The hands of some of those ancient travellers must have helped to smooth its edges. I imagined the dust raised by their carts and chariots, the rattling of the wheels on the flagstones, and the screeching of the spokes, just like in *Ben-Hur*, which I had watched with my First Communion class the year before.

I wondered aloud if anyone had tossed this coin for heads or tails, and if it had changed everything for them, like when Mummy's grandpa had bet on black – or was it on red? – and lost the farmhouses passed on to him by generations of ancestors. Also the metal ball which had accomplished that feat was tiny. My father ruffled my hair and said that luck plays a role in all lives, even those of people shy to tempt fate. Then he moved on to making up stories about how the *denarius* might have come to be lost or buried, and I joined in.

My mother must have looked on these moments in the library as an indulgence she could not deny us: if bonding between fathers and sons had to happen, it might as well take this form, more patrician than games of football and the like. And although she occasionally still voiced misgivings over my father's eagerness to cooperate with the *soprintendenza*, most of the time she probably admitted to herself the wisdom of his approach. The archaeologists were making rapid progress with the excavations and the authorities had opted for the most benign legal framework. But once I began accompanying him to Brindisi, which occurred maybe a dozen times between the subsequent January and April, the arguments flared up.

'When do you expect him to do his homework?' was Mummy's standard rejoinder if the excursion was to be in the afternoon, and 'I'm not letting him skip school – what a great example you're setting him,' if it was in the morning.

'But Emma, it's an experience worth a thousand books. He can catch up on school stuff any day, and he's got a lifetime to sit at a desk, whereas he might never again have this opportunity. It'd be a colossal shame.' I should see the objects in situ to grasp something about their context while still possible, my father insisted, and catch glimpses of the process by which eventually they might go on display. In January the *soprintendenza* had concluded that once the excavations had recovered all artefacts among the ruins, the building works could commence. The state of the Roman villa didn't warrant preserving it: it had been plundered for building materials in the distant past; the blocks of white marble which once clad it were probably among the thousands used by the Normans in the construction of churches, convents, fountains and hospitals in town. The discovery of so many everyday objects among the rubble – from bronze mirrors to pottery inkwells, and from golden earrings to shards of glass vessels – suggested the end had come violently, though how and why remained a mystery.

The expeditions to Brindisi electrified me: Daddy and I were playing truant together to embark on great explorations. On my first visit to the dig, one of the archaeologists let me hold – his calloused hands cupped underneath mine – a horse of pinkish clay, no bigger than the plastic ones on which toy soldiers used to march into battle on my bedroom floor.

'It was a toy,' he said. 'We've found more of these horses, and cattle, too. And a clay doll, just a little taller than your hand, with articulated legs and a pretty tunic.'

Patches of red paint had survived discolouration, resulting in the bizarre dappling of this likeness of a horse.

'The last person to have touched it was probably a boy like you, nearly two thousand years ago. I suppose you're too young to comprehend what an immense gap of time that is.' He looked at me and a second later at my father, taking for granted a tacit solidarity amongst adults.

'Of course I can.' I understood only the magnitude of the number, but Daddy's evident awe filled in much of the so-called immense gap for me.

My fingertips traced the saddle and ornamental harness sculpted in relief. The clay was rough, as if it were resisting being handled by someone other than its owner. The other objects shown me till then – the fragment of medieval pot, the needles or the *denarius* – had not aroused in me the mixed feelings which this little horse induced. The excitement of holding it – the enormity of its not having been in another child's hands for such a long time – mingled with the guilt of having perpetrated some kind of desecration. When I tried to put this into words on the journey back to Ostuni, my father, at the steering wheel, smiled and nodded. Like all good things, he said, sensitivity came at a price.

CHAPTER 6

Our second expedition was to the archaeological museum, where Daddy had a meeting with the *soprintendenza*'s team. He never missed the weekly update, essential to staying 'in the loop': the threat that the archaeologists might take a different course of action upon the discovery of something unexpected would hang over us until the day they left. But first he and I visited the section on the Messapians, the Hellenised Illyrians who for centuries had inhabited our region before being vanquished by Rome. Daddy joked that the gods had adapted superbly to developments among mortals: Poseidon had simply turned into Neptune, Athena into Minerva...

I remember being amused by the outsized handles of the Messapians' vases – the *trozzelle* – in the display cases, and my father praising me when in two bas-reliefs I recognised a triumphant Heracles and a startled Medusa. Why was he even surprised, he said, considering how dog-eared my illustrated *Myths for Children* had become? When the time for his meeting came, he left me in the care of a thick-set old man with a face so weathered that, but for his museum attendant's uniform, he might have been an ancient seafarer.

'I won't be long. Stay with Damiano. You're in for a treat.'

'*Tranquillo, signuría.*' The strong local inflection in his voice was audible from that phrase. 'The youngster comes with me.' The attendant smiled through a row of stained teeth and beckoned me to follow, while my father, ignorant of the sudden tightness in my stomach, deserted me. I kept my distance, a few steps behind the old man, as we descended the staircase to the lower ground floor. He smelled of cigarette smoke and wouldn't stop talking, as if finally at liberty to release onto me the torrent dammed up by the dearth of visitors. By the time we reached our destination, I learnt amongst other things that he had a tribe of grandchildren. He prayed to Jesus and Mary that they'd grow up to be studious, but to date those *monellacci* set foot in the museum only if he bribed them.

'Not like you, eh? Your father's always talking about you. When he's waiting for the *direttrice*, he sits with me in the entrance and we chat – a good man, he is, not one of those stuck up ones who think they're gentlemen, but they aren't, I tell you. The gentlemen are the ones like your father.'

He jingled the keys on a chain dangling from his trouser pocket and unlocked a door. It belonged to a workshop, little more than a box room, equipped with a table, two chairs, a sink, and crammed with sacks of plaster of Paris and unfamiliar implements. The neon light on the ceiling glistened through four or five stacks of round plastic capsules on the table.

'Here we go.' On closer inspection, the capsules contained coins. 'The *direttrice* says 'take your pick' and I'll help you make plaster casts of them. I suggested it to your father, if I may say so. Tried it with a couple of my grandchildren but those rascals couldn't care less. I figured *you'd* care.' He pointed his finger at me and grinned as at a fellow conspirator. I had a feeling Daddy must have told him of our 'treasure-watching' on the wine-red cloth.

I chose three coins: one with a wreathed, burly Poseidon on the front, a naked boy riding a dolphin on the reverse; another with a helmed Athena on one side and Heracles strangling a monstrous serpent on the other; and finally, one embossed solely with a date, while on the reverse an enthroned Christ raised his right hand in blessing and with his left wielded the New Testament. Days later, when the plaster casts were safely home and Daddy and I were smearing them with bronze shoe-polish to give them the appearance of real coins, I learnt that the first two were from our area when it was still part of Magna Graecia, and the third from Constantinople.

'You just copy what I do, ok?' Damiano said.

From a pack the size of a block of butter, he wrenched two small chunks of a plasticine-like substance. We kneaded them into several disks, into which we pressed the coins, gently, to avoid breaking them or taking off their patina. We peeled back the plasticine from the coins and checked the resulting impressions. Into them we poured the mixture of plaster of Paris and water which I was allowed to stir. It was a bit like helping Concetta whisk whipping cream. Throughout, we did nothing but talk.

'Mighty decent, the *Inglesi* were, with us prisoners of war. But there was nothing to be done about the heat, in North Africa. Not so bad if you were used to baking in our sun. It was the poor devils from up north, and the *Inglesi*, that I felt sorry for.'

'Miss Aiello has started teaching our class *Inglese*. I know how to say my name, and how are you, and I'm fine.'

'That'd have come in useful – the interpreters got cigarettes.'

Finally we poured the liquid plaster into the moulds. 'Next time you're here these beauties will be ready and you can make some new ones, eh?' Damiano said.

'But I don't know if I'm coming back.'

'Nonsense – of course you are.'

He said it with such authority that I didn't contradict him. Some of his certainty rubbed off on me, and for a moment I forgot the row which my presence there that day had set off between my parents.

'I shouldn't be dealing on my own with all the suppliers,' Mummy had said, hands on her hips. 'You think I'm finding all the re-negotiations easy? And now you're using Tommaso as an excuse.'

'You know that's untrue. And how about the need for me to be in Brindisi, to get things moving?'

Afterwards I told Daddy that I thought Mummy was being unjust with him.

'We can all say things we don't really mean, when we get anxious,' he replied. 'And it can take time to ease back into one's gentler self. We all react differently to challenges – sometimes, surprisingly. So we have to be patient with ourselves and each other.'

But his words didn't mollify me. My mother's attack on him still upset me. Hadn't her worries so far proved unfounded? He had been right all along about the benefits of co-operating with the *soprintendenza*. I'd help him prove he was right also about taking me to Brindisi: Mummy would see how much I was learning. She'd be happy. We'd all be happy.

I did return to the museum with my father. Sometimes we explored a new room, sometimes just a display cabinet. Then, during the hour Daddy spent in the weekly meeting, Damiano and I made plaster casts of coins or took a furtive peek around the storage rooms, jam-packed with objects: from red-figured wine bowls to bronze and marble sculptures, from amphorae to oil lamps. The whole museum was an Aladdin's cave, and I the lucky charge of two benevolent genies.

The display case for my coins arrived home on the same after-
noon as the Roman pottery oil lamp. My father brought them.
It was early April. I was in the kitchen doing homework while
Concetta, opposite me, ironed. Mummy was still at the office.

'I have a surprise for you.' He handed me a gift-wrapped
package which I took to the sitting room and opened on the
sofa. It contained a coin collector's display case of tortoise-shell
lacquer, with a red velvet insert and a glass lid.

'Wow – they're going to look real, now.'

My father laughed. 'We can buy real ones, if that's what
you want.'

'No, they'd never be as special as the ones I've made with
Damiano.'

He nodded. 'And they'll always remind you of the last
few months.' His voice was tinged with what today I recog-
nize as a shade of melancholy – I can almost hear it. At the
time, I dismissed it as a hazy impression and ran upstairs to my
room. I returned with the casts to the sofa, and placed one in
each but one of the nine velvet hollows.

'One broke – the *denarius* with the Via Traiana. Damiano
and I had to make a new copy last time I was there. I don't
have it yet.'

'Yes, so he said. I thought it'd be good if you came with
me to collect it tomorrow afternoon, to say goodbye in person
to Damiano for a little while.' My dismay must have shown,
because he put a hand on my shoulder and added, 'We can visit
him and the museum in future, but I'm going to be kept busy
with something else after next week. The archaeologists are
leaving. We start with the construction.'

He looked deflated. The euphoria which that announce-
ment would have aroused the previous October was dampened for us both by the prospect of an abrupt end to those
enchanted months – yes, enchanted, notwithstanding the financial anxieties simmering beneath, and the consequent ten-
sions at home. But an end to it had to come. The strain of the
previous six months had begun showing also on my father in
recent weeks – he was often out of breath and at times complained that his heart was racing. Signs of stress catching up
with him, nothing more, he said.

'The museum director handed me a couple of presents
– for the three of us.' He opened a thick cardboard box filled
with straw and extracted a small Roman pottery lamp. 'This
comes from the villa. It hasn't been catalogued. The museum
doesn't know where to put any more of these, so we're allowed to have it.'

With my fingertips I traced the border protruding along
the top of the smooth, light-brown terracotta, and then the
owl depicted in bas-relief at its centre. Eyes too big for her
feathered body stared back at me with a look both comical and
merciless. From the pointy beak and the talons clenching a
perch, I concluded that she wouldn't have taken kindly to my
hilarity.

'If I lived in Roman times, I'm not sure I'd buy this one,'
I said.

'Oh, I don't know. It's well-wishing: the owl was Minerva's symbol. It stood for wisdom: owls can see in the dark. I
like the thought of this lamp being handed on, so to speak, by
one family to another – just with an unusually long interval
in-between.' He grinned. 'I've got something for your mum,
too.'

Out of the same cardboard box, he took two more terracotta shapes: elongated and cropped square pyramids, each
with a perforation for yarn to pass through.

'Loom weights,' he said.

I picked one up and turned it over in my palm. It wasn't
as heavy as I imagined. On one side of the clay, speckled with
impurities, the anonymous hand which had shaped it or placed
it in the kiln had left a fingerprint, an impression of the unique
pattern of lines which had brushed against the reddish-brown
earth when it wasn't yet dry. 'Look, Daddy.'

'Trust you to spot it. I hadn't. You must show that to
your mum, when we give them to her. Do you think she'll
like them? Loom weights for my Penelope.' He chuckled.

Looking back on it, I can see it was a peace offering – a
token of the longed-for détente, now that the *casus belli* was to
be consigned to family history.

It will sound silly, but I confess that during my first years in
London I walked from time to time into the British Museum
in pursuit of the phantom of those moments with my father.
I was the fool who stood before red-figured vases or before a
Norman sewing needle, chasing a chimera. It was all the more
absurd because I had brought with me from Italy treasures to
which I could return again and again: my plaster casts of ancient coins, and the lamp with the owl. I'll show you. Let me
get the lamp, first. I keep it high up on that shelf for safety
– you'll have gathered that it's precious to me, but I'm also
conscious of my responsibility for keeping it intact. It has survived for nearly two thousand years – I don't want it to break
under my watch.

Don't worry, just hold it in your lap – it couldn't be safer than with you sitting in that armchair. See the details I over-looked as a boy: the denser concentration of plumage on the breast to trick us into perceiving it as darker than the wings; the tousled feathers above the eyes, which give the impression of thick, forbidding eyebrows; the stiff and pointy leaves of the olive tree sacred to Minerva on which she's perching; the delicate beading at the edge of the frame, to hint that any alarm is unwarranted, that the goddess is there to protect. How in-significant each detail on its own might seem, hmm? But how painstaking its execution; how subtly balanced all the parts; and how fitting their subject for a lamp burning with olive oil when darkness falls.

Astonishing, don't you think, that a humble mould-made object should embody an ideal with such apparent simplicity? An ideal of harmony which took centuries and reams of paper to evolve is sitting right there, in the cup of your hand. It nev-er occurred to me till now, but maybe this lamp does for me what Mozart does for my friend Zoe. To her, his scores radiate with the promise that an ideal of harmony is within our grasp, that an equilibrium between depths of emotion and lightness of touch can be negotiated even in the bleakest moments, that restraint and wit – which you British have made one of your strong suits – is as good a coping strategy as any. I'd like to believe that she and her Amadé are right.

And here is the display case with the coin casts. Only five remain. One crumbled on my journey to the UK. Two more shattered a year later, when a nosy flatmate dropped the case from the chest of drawers on which it lay. With time they've all become so brittle. Recently one more broke between my fingers. I've wept, on my knees, for every one I've lost.

But you're anxious to discover what happened to my father. As you'll have perceived by now, life would have taken a completely different turn, with him by my side. The coin casts I've just shown you were there – witnesses as well as players – in the final act you're so impatient to reach. I'll never forget the last conversation my father and I had about them. It took place during the drive to Brindisi to collect the ninth piece. I remember almost every word of it – soon you'll see why.

'I'm so happy that you really appreciate those casts, Tommaso,' my father said. 'Monetary and personal value can be such different things.' He glanced at me in the passenger's seat before re-focusing on the *litoranea*, the coastal road, straight ahead.

'I know. I know,' I said with all the certainty of a ten year old. My hands, on my lap, gripped the display case containing the casts. Showing them to Damiano was the least I could do – he would be pleased to see them treasured.

Olive groves, vineyards, fig trees, oleander hedges, tall blackberry bushes and the monumental paddles of prickly pears flashed past us. New leaves were sprouting on vine stumps and fig trees, while cream and pink buds peppered the oleanders. The four o'clock sunshine swathed the fields with a crispness like silk that in Puglia is peculiar to early April. I wondered what had been the same and what had differed when anonymous travellers had journeyed on the Via Traiana, with in their purses *denarii* like the one whose cast I was about to collect, as I plastered my nose to the window of our blue Alfetta.

'Quite a range of periods you've got there.' My father flicked his head towards the plaster casts.

'I chose coins that looked as different as possible from each other.'

'Funny. D'you know what? If children everywhere did the same – from Cairo to Canberra – the world might be a more peaceful place. Everyone's a mixture, so a notion of all the bloods mingling in our veins, and of the roller coaster of history, might do some good.'

'Silly Daddy.' I mimicked the sing-song tone with which Mummy teased him whenever he surprised her with this kind of observation. 'Going off on a tangent,' she called it.

'I'll tell you what those coins of yours are whispering in my ear.' His tone too was jokey, now. 'Your high cheek-bones are a gift from a shepherd from southern Illyria who settled here – today they'd call him Albanian and try to repatriate him. Your left eyebrow was definitely drawn by a young Greek bride – she used her finest black make-up powder, I can tell.'

'Oh, Daddy...' I rolled my eyes and laughed.

'Wait, I have it all on good authority.' He put on an air of mock solemnity. 'Your forehead was the gift of a Roman *miles* who got his nastiest scars in the war against the great-great-grandchildren of your Greek great-great-etc-grandmother. The wife of a Byzantine soldier-turned-merchant drew your right eyebrow, and a brilliant job she made of it, too – she wasn't going to be outdone by her Greek rival.'

'And my coins are whispering all this?'

'Of course. There's one for an ancestor of almost every origin.'

'Ok. But tell the remaining ones that there have been too many soldiers so far.'

'Well, what do you expect? I'll see what I can do, but this region was a battleground. To be a *porta d'Oriente*, a gateway to the East, might sound poetic, but to those who happened to live here it was often a curse.' He recovered his breath before continuing – his chest heaved and relaxed again. 'You owe your blue eyes to a Norman – a soldier at first, I'm afraid, but a peaceable landowner later. A handsome Arab, maker of damascened shields in Lucera, passed on to you his raven-black hair. That fine nose is from an Anjou young man destined for the priesthood *malgré soi* just by dint of being the youngest son – not all too keen on the vow of chastity, but can you blame him in the circumstances? And finally, to your smooth, light-amber skin: your bequest from a penniless Andalusian bard brought over by a Spanish governor to lighten the load of his foul posting to a malaria-infested Apulian town. How am I doing? That should make eight coins.'

'*Bravo.* That *was* funny.'

His lips formed a wide smile which showed up the dimple in his right cheek. But in a flash his jaw dropped and his mouth screwed itself into a grimace. He emitted a cry of pain. His eyes widened as if he had been winded and stunned. The car swerved left onto the fast lane. I screamed.

'Daddy. Daddy!'

We veered back onto the right, tires screeching.

'Lucky no one was overtaking us,' I said, my spine tensed against the seat.

My father didn't respond. He hunched over the steering wheel. His hands gripped it so rigidly, they might have been claws. He slowed the car down, all the while groaning.

'What can I do? Tell me. Daddy, please.'

We came to a halt in a lay-by. My father now slumped over the steering wheel. The hands relaxed their grip. His arms dropped and then dangled. His face – ashen, almost bluish – was turned towards me.

'Oh my God. Oh my God!' I stared into his eyes, and at his open, contorted mouth. 'I'll go get help. Daddy, I'll get help.'

'No.' All that seemed left of his voice was a feeble thread. 'Stay with me.' The words were slurred.

'How can I? I've got to get help for you. I have to.' I looked into his eyes. He stared back. I waited for another word but it didn't come. 'Daddy, I'll go. We have to get to a hospital.' I opened the car door and lunged outwards but found myself tugged back. The safety belt was buckled – and I was still clutching the coins' display case. Belt unfastened, I dropped it onto my seat and darted out.

'I'll be right back, Daddy.' I looked once more into his eyes, and, leaning towards him, stroked his arm. Then I hastened outside again.

I stood behind the car, facing oncoming drivers so that they might spot me. I waved my arms. I screamed for people to stop. Every second expanded in slow motion. A couple, absorbed in conversation, drove past. A young family approached next, with children in the back; a little girl held a Pinocchio rag doll flattened against the window; its soft fabric stare, fixed in surprise, settled on me for a second and disappeared down the carriageway. Finally a man of my father's age, in a grey suit, slammed on the brakes and swung over into the lay-by, in front of our Alfetta.

He stepped out. 'What...?'

I rushed towards him. 'My daddy...' Tears and sobs gushed out.

The man hurried towards our car, with me at his side. From the window next to my father's seat he could see him now, wilted against the steering wheel. He rushed over to the passenger side with me in tow, opened the door, and looked in. The man put my display case onto the back seats, and sat down. Standing on the tarmac, behind him, I peered inside. My father's eyes were closed. The stranger put his face close to Daddy's to gauge whether he was breathing. He placed two fingers on his neck but must have been unable to detect a pulse because he lifted Daddy's motionless wrist and tried to find a heartbeat there.

'*Dio mio, Dio mio.*' With the back of my hand, I wiped tears and mucus off my face.

The man turned towards me. He looked startled to be reminded of my existence.

'I'm not a doctor but I know we shouldn't move him.' His voice was shaky. 'I'll drive you to the nearest farm. There'll be a phone there. We need an ambulance.'

'I can't leave him.'

He got up and deliberated for a second. Then he nodded. 'All right.'

'Is he...?' I trailed behind the man, who was staggering towards his car.

'Only unconscious, I think. I'll be back as quickly as I can. I promise.'

I got in next to Daddy again, lifted his right hand and, holding it between mine, stroked it with my thumb.

'Please, Daddy, hold on.' I wanted to be brave but there was no stopping the tears and the sniffling. With my fingers I brushed back a lock of hair that was hanging lopsided between his eyebrows; the few strands of white streaking the black glistened in the sun, which came through the windows, indifferent to us. 'A doctor will know what to do.' Maybe, when Daddy woke up he wouldn't even know what had happened and would crack some joke. But still I clasped his hand, and, looking into the sun, I mouthed every prayer I knew.

They wouldn't let me ride with him in the ambulance. Dead on arrival. A hole in the heart.

You'll have heard people say, 'There are no words to describe...' or 'I have no words...' in the face of tragic events. It sounds trite. And yet... For the first weeks after that fateful drive, I felt like the lone survivor of a world once familiar, but now, unrecognisable. Had I been asked to draw it, you'd have seen a ten-year-old boy trudging among glass shards, where cities made of thinnest glass – the people, their houses, schools and offices – had stood until their cataclysmic end. There was only me, lost in this desert of shimmering fragments, under an implacable sun. Could oleanders blossom here? Those who came to pay their respects at the funeral, and at home over subsequent days, met my shell: a brave, self-composed 'little man'.

When, two months later, the missing coin arrived in the post, I placed it in the case with the others and shut it inside the desk drawer. There, inside an empty chocolate tin I had lined with cotton wool, the little owl on the oil lamp also found sanctuary. I didn't know nor care where the loom weights might be – they weren't mine, and by then my mother had become distant and irascible. She seemed to blame me for my father's death, though she never had the courage to say it to my face. If I hadn't responded so eagerly to his enthusiasm, he wouldn't have exhausted himself, and we would not have been on that drive. Millions of people lived into ripe old age with an undiagnosed hole in the heart. I know that's what she thought – and it showed. Within two weeks of my father's death, she was throwing herself into work. But did she ever wonder about her own role in the events? About the stress she had put Daddy under? Not once did I hear her suggest it. And I didn't dare voice it. I remembered Daddy saying we should all be patient with each other – but Mummy wasn't showing much patience towards me.

'*Io lavoro per due*,' she used to say. In Italian that expression is ambiguous but I'm sure she meant that she had to do the work of two people – her own and Daddy's, as if he had disappeared out of malice – rather than for two people. She said it through gritted teeth, if I asked her to help me with maths – never my *forte* – when she had returned from work in the evenings. She fought to restrain a yell if I had stained my school smock so badly that it necessitated trawling around the shops for a new one. She puffed, exasperated, if I confided in her about my distress and bewilderment at the way my schoolmates tip-toed around my loss – it felt like walking around the classroom without a limb while everyone pretended I still had it and expected me to go along with their world of make-believe.

During the first few weeks after my father's death, I often sneaked, unobserved, into my parents' bedroom. I opened Dad's wardrobes, drew to me the sleeve of a suit, a shirt or a sweater, and burying my face in the fabric, breathed in his scent. One sweater – sky blue, dappled with flecks of indigo and aquamarine – had the power to bring him back for an instant. The thick wool prickled my face, but, moistened slightly by my breath, it released the ingredients of my father's unique smell: once, I thought I caught the whiff of the Gran Turchese biscuits we used to eat at breakfast together, and another time, that of his citrusy aftershave. With my eyes shut,

I could see him sitting next to me, sipping his espresso while I slurped my hot chocolate before he drove me to school. Or I could picture us on the dirt road on which we once got lost cycling together. Although finding the way out of the olive groves before nightfall wasn't easy, I was with Dad, so I wasn't scared.

One day I returned from a visit to Fasano's Zoo Safari with Giorgio's family – to whom my mother had packed me off for the weekend – to find my father's wardrobes emptied. It felt like a punch in the diaphragm. Still, I managed to race downstairs. My mother was watching television in the sitting room.

'Where are Daddy's clothes?'

She gave me the misty look of someone who has just woken up. Her answer was delayed, as if it had taken her a while to be certain of my question or to think up a satisfactory response.

'At Caritas. It's a charity. It'll distribute them to people who need them. You and I don't.'

'But... Please, Mummy, get them back.' I fell to my knees and grabbed her hand in both of mine. 'Please, Mummy, please,' I sobbed.

She opened her mouth and closed it without uttering a word. Her lips trembled.

'No, Tommi, I can't. It's better this way. Trust me.'

That was the end of it, no matter how I cried for the rest of the day.

For the next two years I had nightmares from which I could escape only when my howls awoke me. Concetta, whose bedroom was sandwiched between mine and my mother's, would come sit by my bed. She'd caress my hair, my hand, and talk to me. Although by daybreak I couldn't remember her words, they worked the magic of soothing me back to sleep. If Concetta and I had always been close, we became even closer once my father was gone. The only note of discord was her continuous effort to justify my mother: 'She needs to rest. She needs to recover.'

The library became the place where I did all my homework and where I reached for traces of my father's presence: in the casts of the nine coins, in the little owl and above all among his books – he had turned those pages, pencilled comments in them, raised his head in thought, and maybe taken off, unfettered, on what only my mother could have labelled 'tangents'.

CHAPTER 7

Yes, telling you how I came to lose my father *was* hard. I knew I'd end up re-experiencing it all. But it's worth it if it takes us a step closer to our aim, Will. I hope you won't mind if I call you by your first name, but we've talked long enough to warrant it, don't you think? Have you begun to comprehend why I might not want to have anything to do with my mother or with her inheritance? And what I've told you so far is nothing, compared to her subsequent crime.

Aged barely ten, I had lost my father, and effectively my mother, too. I don't know which was worse. He couldn't rise from the grave but I could be certain that his love would have endured, had he lived. She was alive and, though we shared a house, had become numb to me – as good as, or worse than, dead. Why couldn't she comfort me? Why couldn't she accuse me openly of having played a part in the tragedy? Then I could have protested my innocence. Instead the seed of doubt grew inside me: maybe part of the blame *was* mine. But how could any one of us – my father foremost – have known? And was it possible that his heart would have failed irrespective of how he had spent those final months? I remember a doctor, a friend of ours, saying so. Alas regret feeds upon uncertainty.

She, depressed? And severely, no less! Oh please, Will, spare me! The history of humanity is littered with young widows and I bet most of them did not succumb to grief, but clung to their children as to treasure. And my mother hardly seemed melancholy – at least, not for long. Within weeks she was in full control of the company – a real fury. She networked with everyone involved in the industry: engineers, architects, local politicians... As soon as common decency allowed her to call an end to the *lutto* – the mourning period during which the deceased's family wear suitably dark clothing – she redoubled her old efforts to entertain and exchange invitations with members of the narrow elite of Ostuni and surrounds. My father had tended to resist these occasions, so they hadn't been frequent – he cared for friends, not for shallow company.

People talk of the maternal instinct as if it were a given, a mechanism ready to be activated the instant a woman hears her baby's first cry. Think of all those paradigms of motherhood in fairy tales and myths: warmth, patience and self-sacrifice personified; and the embodiment of wrath, if avenging their young. Wickedness is the preserve of stepmothers and witches, right? But with my father gone, it was as if something inside her awoke and overpowered the loving mother I had once known. Of course, she didn't abandon me in a forest or fatten me up in a cage. How blissfully clear-cut fairy tales are.

The fact that I *had* memories of a tender mother made things worse. I couldn't trust they were real: if they were, how could she now refuse me her warmth? I remembered laughter – hers, Dad's and mine – in the kitchen, only a few years before, on the Feast of St. Joseph, which in Italy is Father's Day and was a holiday. I might have been six or seven. That week, Dad had reminisced about the *zeppole* – the traditional cakes for that festivity – which his aunt Rina baked for his family before she got married and moved north to Livorno.

'Baked,' he emphasised, 'not fried like the ones at patisseries. It made them lighter and crispier. They melted in your mouth. Mmm...'

When the day came, we went downstairs to breakfast, and found my mother stirring and scraping a pot. Concetta looked on, shaking her head. Dough as thick as setting cement had begun sticking to the bottom; we could smell it getting charred. A bag of flour had tipped over, spewing its contents over the worktop and floor.

'More water. That's what it needed. But no, she won't listen,' Concetta said, hands on her hips.

'I told you. The whole point is to make Rina's *zeppole*.' Mum stirred with added vigour. 'This is the recipe she gave me over the phone, and it's the one I'm keeping to.'

'Darling, you rang her?' My father reached out to stroke her hair, glued to her forehead by exertion and heat.

'Yes, well, I wanted to surprise you, but...' She relinquished the wooden spoon, letting it fall in the pot, and switched off the hob. '*Che disastro!*'

'No, no, I'm sure not.' He kissed her on the cheek. 'This is *the* recipe, so of course it can be rescued. Maybe the quantity of water was correct but some of it evaporated?'

I saw him motioning to Concetta to leave things to him. She disappeared, stifling a chuckle.

Together, my parents managed to turn the *disastro* into silky dough. They squeezed it through a pastry syringe to form unruly clumps intended to be spirals. I helped whisk the egg yolks and the sugar for the crème anglaise, and Mum allowed me to taste the mixture before she poured in the milk, steaming and sweet-smelling with vanilla. Afterwards, I placed a teaspoon of it, and a sour cherry, on top of each little cake. We then bit into *zeppole* unique for their haphazard shapes and smoky, bitter aftertaste. We laughed so hard – tears streamed down our faces. Afterwards, Dad sat at the table with an arm across Mum's back, the two of them smiling at each other – and at me.

With Dad gone, I increasingly felt as if that memory couldn't have been mine. Even in the little time my mother and I spent together each evening, I didn't merit her full attention – she'd ask me the same question three days in a row. And as each year passed, more aspects of my father which must have irritated her surfaced in me. To those same traits in Dad, she had responded with indulgent smiles and lightly teasing remarks, fooling me into believing she found them endearing. But she can't have, because now she had daily stabs at eradicating them from me. However, their roots were stubborn.

Take an afternoon when I was eleven – I was sitting in our library, leafing through my father's sketchbooks of Pompeii, Athens' acropolis and Rome's forum. She stepped inside. 'Must you sit there reading all afternoon? Invite Giorgio to come and play.' Had she edged closer, she'd have noticed I wasn't holding an ordinary book. Had she shown any interest, I might have asked her the question which had just occurred to me: why, given Dad's love of the classical world, did he design buildings so obviously inspired by our traditional white-washed ones? An answer presented itself only years later, when my first walk with Anna through the medina brought to mind his words about its beauty and wisdom. Now I realise that in his projects – our home, foremost – my father brought both worlds together. Shame he named such a splendid villa after my mother.

You want other examples of her behaviour? Here's one from when I was twelve: 'Did you really have to enter a poem in the school magazine? And of all things about a sewing needle! You'll get teased. No common sense.' If she hadn't sound-

ed so categorical, I might have explained all about the bone
needle my father had shown me from the excavations. But it
was best to avoid talking with her of that period in our lives.

'Must you choose the Classico? The programme of studies of the Scientifico is far better suited to our times,' she said
when I was fourteen. Over the years I complied, the dutiful
son, with most of her requests. But not that one. In fairness to
her, she did not insist, probably sensing that I wouldn't budge.
Una battaglia persa in partenza, goes the Italian expression – a
battle she'd lose before it began.

'Why waste time writing songs? Take up computer programming or something.' At this stage I was sixteen, and did
take up computer programming, to get her off my back. At
the classes, a Commodore 64 taught me that there was something at which I shone not for the usual reasons, but for my
total lack of aptitude.

And now that she's dead, I'm meant to be reconciled to
my mother? That's what she wanted, by leaving me the inheritance. Well, she won't have her way. Money couldn't buy me
when I was young, and money can't buy me now.

I'm not sure why it has never interested me. Maybe because if you've never lacked for anything that can be bought,
you don't develop a hunger for material things? Though there
must be people on whom affluence has the opposite effect. Or
because, though my father stumbled on riches, he never let
them rule him? Or did my mother's craving for wealth inocu-
late me against it for life? Take your pick.

Want to know what's funny? Whenever I told Anna what
my mother was like, she'd listen and signal her sympathy for
me, but still try to find excuses for her. And see where it got
her. Though of course you don't know where it got her. If I

skip to it, I'll confuse you. I'm dreading re-living that part of the story — as make no mistake, putting all this into words is forcing me to re-live everything, even long-forgotten details. Where does the mind bury them? These ones, no doubt, in its remotest chambers.

One moment I'll never forget is the one when I told Anna how I lost my father — the moment when I unburdened myself of the memories which had haunted me for nine years. Anna and I had been going out together for a month or so, and were sitting on the steps of the Gothic cathedral.

The sunshine of the late-April afternoon gave the *pietra gentile* — the bare local limestone — a honeyed tinge, which made the building stand out against the whitewashed ones of the Città Vecchia. From the ledge of the central portal, the statue of an enthroned Virgin and Child surrounded by angels and a pleading bishop looked down on us and on the quiet square. We were interrupted only a couple of times, by acquaintances who stopped by to exchange pleasantries. The attentiveness in Anna's eyes turned to anxiety as I recounted the events leading up to my father's death. Nonetheless, whenever I hesitated, she put an arm around me and stroked my shoulder.

'If only I had paid attention to how quickly he kept running out of breath.'

'You were a child.' She bit her lip so hard that for a moment it was drained of blood. The sight jolted me out of my intensity.

'Don't. You'll hurt yourself — save those beautiful lips for me.' That made her smile.

I tried, but failed, to lighten my account, and kept jumping back and forth in time. I wasn't able to be as restrained as

I am now that over thirty years have passed. Time and again, Anna's mouth opened and her cheeks sank, her perfect oval face elongated like in a distorting mirror as she came close to tears.

'Forget about this,' I said. 'Is this, you know, too much for you?'

'No. Sure you're not finding it too much, though?'

I wasn't. Re-experiencing those events wasn't easy, but it felt safe to open up to her, if she really could withstand it. I was buoyed up by the sensation that with each portion of the story I disclosed, a piece of armour – which only then did I realise I had been wearing – crashed to the ground, and that the layers of clothing beneath it peeled away too, until I stood naked in the gentle sunshine, ignorant of guilt or shame like man before the Fall, Anna my new Eve.

Behind us, the stony stares of the Virgin of the Assumption and the Christ Child suited them well – the sculpted bishop kneeling at their feet could beseech them for all eternity, but I had long ago concluded that if God existed He was indifferent to humanity. Anna, on the other hand, believed in Christ and all His sundry friends and relatives. But she didn't try to re-kindle my faith. We met halfway: she was a sincere Catholic but conceded that God could well be our invention. Remember, she liked Lucretius, though the Church had slandered him for centuries. I couldn't see how God's inexistence could be proven or disproven. It seemed to me that the principles governing the 'good life' differed little, whether you had a faith or not. So religion was hardly going to come between us. Or so I thought.

On that day, we had been walking through the Old Town. We often wandered there, stopping now and then to kiss in one of the narrow cul de sacs onto which a few houses opened their doors. Old Ostuni is a maze – kindly to lovers in search of silent corners and of the shade of low arches, of the bougainvillea's fiery reds against the walls' cool white, of the sound of each other's breathing interrupted only by the distant cries of children from more spacious alleys. It was mostly on these walks that we regaled each other with glimpses of our histories, tesserae of an embryonic mosaic for two, unaware of its eventual design.

I remember particularly well a conversation in mid-May, whilst climbing up through Porta San Demetrio, the thirteenth-century town gate.

'What do your family say about me?' I asked. 'After nearly two months of us being together, they must have some opinion.'

She looked at the tarmac. 'Oh, they don't know you well enough for that.'

I stopped. 'They could get to know me, if they cared to speak with me when I collect you. Your father especially: he shakes my hand, glowers as if I was a thief, and stays monosyllabic. And your sister – she always has a sceptical smirk. At least your mother gives me the hint of a smile.'

'They're uncomfortable. They think you're going to look down on them. Take 'monosyllabic' – they wouldn't know what it means. Remember the first evening we went out in Villanova? I told you my parents left school at fourteen with the *licenza media*, and that Dad is only a *guardia campestre*. He spends his day searching for small-time thieves, patrolling fields and farmers' tool sheds, not in a smart office, like your mum.'

'So? I respect that. It's honest work.'

'Then tell him, one day. As for his glaring at you, if you really must know, he says you can't be serious about me.'

'Why?'

'For all the obvious reasons.'

'And those are?'

'Oh, come, Tommi.' She hooked her arm in mine and steered us both uphill. 'Look – I love you. I believe you. But at home they think you and I are a madness that'll pass, and that soon they'll enjoy wagging their fingers at me and saying 'I told you so'. Give them time to see they're wrong.'

'A madness that'll pass... In other words, a crush? Have you told them what our conversations are like? Or what havoc a kiss sets off inside us? And how your body relaxes when I hold you...?'

'I've tried – though not in those words.' She gazed into the distance before stopping and turning to me. 'Our conversations... Yes... but how do you explain to people who don't care about such a thing how much it means to you?'

'You're right. Sorry for the outburst. If only I knew how to explain to my own mother...' I reached for Anna's hands and squeezed them. Then I clasped her waist and drew her to me. Smiling, we leaned against the wall of a house, closed our eyes and kissed.

We climbed a little further in silence. 'Don't take this the wrong way, but how did you turn out so different from the rest of your family?'

She laughed. 'Careful! What I said about my parents and Barbara is true, but they do love me and I love them.'

'I didn't mean...'

'Don't worry. You don't need to explain. One answer to your question is that the 'culprit' was Mrs. Fischetto. I've stayed so fond of her, that I regularly visit her. She was my teacher throughout primary school. She didn't only teach us at the blackboard and at our desks – she set up exciting projects. We built the model of a Roman town with odds and ends which we then painted. We scoured our neighbourhoods for old women who knew any traditional *Ostunese* nursery rhymes or folk tales; when we had collated and illustrated our booty, Mrs. Fischetto had the whole thing typed up and photocopied for each of us. I still have my copy. Sometimes she took me home for lunch with her family. Her youngest, Clara, was my age – she's still a friend. Mrs. Fischetto spoke to me with a respect I thought only adults had a right to. She lent me books and then asked what I thought of them. Imagine that!'

'What did your parents say?'

'At first they were proud that my teacher had singled me out for attention. But over time their pride turned into resentment – at first of Mrs. Fischetto, then of me. I think they felt indebted to her – have you noticed how often that feeling stirs the opposite of gratitude? – but also left out by my relationship with her. They probably felt judged, too, as if her kindness showed up their inadequacy. Books transported me elsewhere: to ways of being I'd never have imagined. How could they not alter how I saw everything and everyone around me, what I considered valuable, what gave me pleasure and what saddened me, or how I expressed myself? So I can't pinpoint when it started, but soon I had to be careful about what I did or said at home, in case it brought accusations that I was acting 'superior'.'

She carried on. 'Even today, I avoid what might irritate Mum, Dad and Barbara. What else am I to do? There have been times when I've wished Mrs. Fischetto hadn't picked me out. But I know better. She simply recognised the hungry bookworm inside a scrawny seven-year-old, the teeny caterpillar in a hurry to turn into a butterfly. I might have changed anyway. But when I think of the happiness I get from my freedom of thought, I'm grateful she encouraged it. I know none of this makes me any better or worse than anyone else in my family, but try and tell *them* that.'

'Going out with me isn't going to help you persuade them.'

'Maybe not.' She smiled. 'But it'll all work out. They'll see there's no substance to their preconceptions.'

I couldn't resist laughing. 'Substance to preconceptions? How do you say that in Saponaro-speak?'

A scowl flitted across Anna's brow, which made her look even more adorable. Isn't it dreadful? She let me get away so lightly and all it sparked in me was a trite response. Mine was hubris, the arrogance that brings retribution with a capital 'R'. I had read all about it for years in classical myths, plays and epics. I have no excuse.

But what a terrible host I'm being. Where I come from, we have a saying: '*l'ospitalitá é sacra*', hospitality is sacred. It's what the Greeks called *xenia* – you could be Zeus or Hermes in disguise, so if I show you kindness, you might grant my wish. If only! That hospitality is another sign of the past, surfacing in unexpected ways. It reminds you that Greece and Albania are a hop across the Strait of Otranto – Ostuni is closer to Corfu or Vlorë than to Naples. But in London, we are a long way from them all. The voices of the children coming out of school, outside, are as good as a clock. It'll get cold in here soon, now the sun has passed overhead. Look – there's less light streaming in through the window. Not that it was bright to start with, with that cloudy sky. Let me make us some tea – that will keep us warm. Would you mind switching on that lamp? Thank you. A few minutes' break to answer your phone messages? By all means.

Yes, even I have been turned into a tea-drinker by your appalling climate. I love your country, but the weather... I've also picked up the national habit of discussing it. How could I not? I reckon a sense of humour must be a prerequisite for your weathermen – it's impossible to make reliable forecasts on these islands, not like on slivers of earth lulled by the Mediterranean. I do miss the light of Puglia – everything looks so vivid in that sun: the sky, the clambering jasmines... even the clothes hanging on washing lines.

Did you know that Mendelssohn wrote a symphony, 'The Italian', to capture the light and colours of my country? I had not heard of it, till Zoe gave me a recording of it, years ago – a sensitive thought, all the more as she has never pressed me on why I haven't gone back. How she has put up with all my mystery for the twenty-plus years we've been friends, I don't know. Zoe says Mendelssohn was dissatisfied with his Italian symphony till the end, and yet to me – though I'm not a professional musician – it seems he succeeded in his aim.

Well, then. Only a couple of afternoons after that conversation by Porta San Demetrio, I picked up Anna from her home and we rode to Villa Emma. It wasn't the first time, and as before, it was during hours in which my mother was away at the office. Concetta had suggested repeatedly that I introduce Anna to Mum, and I intended to do it soon, but I confess that I also derived a certain glee from the delay. On this occasion, I led Anna to the library to show her the objects I had described to her. I reached for them in the drawer and placed them carefully on the desk: first, my coin collector's case, and then the chocolate tin containing the oil lamp. We sat down on the chairs my father and I had once occupied.

'Who do you think I was with, the last time I sat here with anyone?'

Anna stroked my hand. 'Tommi, if on balance you'd rather not –'

'No, no, far from it.'

I clicked open the brass latch of the case, and, fingers trembling, raised the lid.

'Here,' I said, revealing the nine bronze-coloured disks. 'Touch them.'

'Won't they chip?'

'Not if you're careful. Look.' I lifted one out of its velvet cradle and turned it over. I did the same with the next one. Anna followed suit, the tips of her fingers handling each cast as if the slightest pressure might be lethal to them. 'I did say gently, but it's not nitro-glycerine.'

Of the nine, the one celebrating the Via Traiana seemed to hold her attention longest. She nodded at it in silence. The look on her face brought to mind the statue of the *Addolorata*, the grieving Virgin. It was carried through town during the Easter processions to the sound of the parish band playing Albinoni's 'Adagio'. When I was little, I recoiled at the sight of the dagger piercing her heart, her cheeks gaunt and her eyes imploring. I wanted to flee from the music's lugubrious pounding – but, like all the other children, I stayed in the crowd as the cortège passed, my hand clasping Concetta's or my parents', except for when we had to cross ourselves. For a split second, I still flinched inwardly.

'You'll love the owl.' I took the pottery lamp from the chocolate tin and set it down on the table. 'See the comic expression I told you about? Isn't she a grumpy old thing?'

'She sure is.' Anna stroked the little owl with a finger, and, to my relief, smiled. 'Do you know the tale of the woman taken into slavery by pirates?'

'Of course.' As a child, I had heard it at bedtime from Concetta. 'While she's picking wild *cicorielle* too close to the shore.'

'But before that, she and her husband are given a choice – by an owl in an olive tree.'

'That's right.' The connection between Athena's sacred owl and tree and the ones in that local folk tale had never occurred to me. 'The owl asks if they want their good fortune in youth or in old age.'

'And they opt for old age, when they'd be too frail to fend for themselves.'

'The husband discovers a treasure chest soon after his wife's abduction, but he doesn't find happiness,' I added, 'until he's reunited with her, years later.' I caressed Anna's nape. 'Never get yourself abducted. Not now we've found each other. You are my *tesoro* – my treasure.'

'And you, mine.' She raised her hand as if standing in the witness box, the way she had done in Villanova when declaring herself fully human. 'I promise solemnly not to wander too close to the shore.'

I laughed and clutched her by the waist and shoulders. The playful hug dissolved into a calm embrace and into a lingering kiss. The owl, the brittle coins, and row upon row of my father's tomes, looked on – my faithful guardian spirits.

★★★

The oleanders on the terrace of Villa Emma came into bloom. So did the ones in the oversized amphorae in the alleys and squares of the Old Town. Their clusters of white, pink and fuchsia flowers burst out of the dark-green foliage. From the *contadini*'s doorways, cases of juicy *nespole* released their sweet but slightly acrid fragrance onto the streets. It blended with the grassy scent of fresh fava beans consumed at kitchen tables now that the warm days of May were rolling into one another.

On those afternoons, Anna and I enjoyed conversations brimming with mutual discoveries. You'd be amazed at how everyday actions bring those memories to mind. For example, Anna observed that olive oil linked us to our ancestors and to our land. 'Liquid gold trickling down the slope of history', she called it. Apulians' modern obsession with olive oil was a remnant of how central it had once been, she said. Hadn't it accompanied people every day? From baptism to the last rites, via their dining table, their soap, their lamps and much more? That reflection may not strike you as momentous. Yet now and then, while drizzling oil onto my food, I still picture Anna sharing the thought with me as we sat on the steps of an abandoned house, its flaking wall overrun by an early-blooming scarlet bougainvillea, watching two children walk by with slices of *pane, olio e sale* – bread, oil and salt.

Sometimes I sat with her on the terrace of Villa Emma, guitar on my lap, to sing songs together that we both knew, as well as a few I had composed over the previous couple of years, which until then had been for my ears only. I even wrote one or two especially for her around that time. Our story may have begun with a shared love of De André, but she also took a liking to my inadequate attempts at song-writing. Her pleas of '*Ancóra*' took me aback. I had never imagined my creations meriting enthusiasm. Furthermore, with each 'One more', I had a vision of the child who must have stood open-mouthed before the multi-coloured patterns formed by sparklers on New Year's Eve.

Being able to see the little girl in Anna stung me, as by now I wasn't content with what we had. The open top of a blouse would reveal her slim neck and collarbones, or yield a glimpse of her vest, and I'd wish my hand could slip beneath the fabric and hold her small breasts. I had already formed an idea of their taut softness. I'd ache for my fingertips, my lips, and my cheek to linger on her smooth belly, too.

The rest, you can imagine. What is more natural than wanting to make love to the young woman you adore? Isn't it inevitable that the feelings you corral under the word 'love' should push for physical release? And yet I had a presentiment I shouldn't ask Anna for more, not out of social convention – which still expected her to reach the altar a virgin – but a sense that she was one of those beings dear to the gods, or her God. You might think it laughable for a non-believer to fear committing sacrilege. I did.

But now I wonder: what if some of the myths I grew up with were really timeless warnings against forcing nature – someone else's nature? Apollo could not restore Daphne to human form by cherishing a laurel tree. Nor did turning Callisto into a constellation undo the consequences of Zeus's deceit. I'm conscious the males in these stories are gods, but I'm not bragging: the Greeks were wise enough to form them in our own image – the image of flawed mankind.

You could argue that Anna, too, had a choice. But I

wouldn't be so sure. Maybe none of us is capable of conscious choice when it comes to love.

Anyway, I dismissed my presentiment. I even persuaded myself that my shyness must appear unmanly to Anna. I began with hints like 'We're freer than our parents were,' but they brought only innocent replies. 'In what ways?' she would ask, and I'd beat a retreat. I figured I had to give her stronger clues. An opportunity arose at school in late May during a morning break. We were standing in the corridor with the usual group, when we heard a rumour: Paolo and Federica were having sex. That sort of thing did go on, but being upfront about it wasn't as common as it might be for your generation – and remember, this was Southern Italy.

'Why shouldn't they? They love each other. Just like us,' I said to Anna once I got her on her own.

She looked me square in the eye. 'If you're dropping hints, I'd rather you asked me straight.'

'Ok, ok.' I recognised the intriguing stranger I had upset at my birthday party. 'But keep your voice down.' I looked around. Our fellow students were still chatting in clusters or ambling past. 'Would you – you know – go further?' I whispered.

'I don't know. *Gesú e María*, I never thought that I... Not I, you see?' She shook her head and gaped, as if recognising only then the subject she had rushed to tackle. 'You're not expecting me to answer here and now, Tommi, right?'

'No, *amore*, of course not. I wasn't expecting to have this conversation here and now.'

She screwed her lips up, the way she did when she was nervous. 'Well, I'd rather know the truth. I can still say 'no', can't I?'

'Obviously. I'm not one of those...' I was repulsed by the idea of myself as a cad.

'Oh, I know that, don't worry.' She smiled, and with her hand caressed my cheek. Her touch was so comforting, that she could have held her palm there for eternity, and I wouldn't have moved. 'You *are* asking much. But I'll think about it, I promise.'

CHAPTER 8

By the beginning of June, we were all cramming for the *maturità*, the pre-university exams. The air had the lustre of summer, yet the heat was still comfortable. Together with Giorgio and Lidia, Anna and I decided to take time off. Early on a windless afternoon, we set off in Giorgio's red Golf for Rosa Marina, the holiday village just past Villanova. He flashed the entry pass – courtesy of friends of his parents – at the security guards, and we were in.

I had been inside this exclusive enclave plenty of times, mostly in July and August, when the shoreline and swimming pools became animated by day, and its bars, restaurants and discos by night. But now we came across few cars and pedestrians in the spotless streets flanked by white villas – all modern but reminiscent of Ostuni's traditional architecture – and thriving gardens. We turned into the long boulevard along the beaches. Large houses – some with spectacular glass walls – and exotic trees stretched on one side of it, while dunes covered in vegetation lined the other. The latter's uniformity – its trees squat, its shrubs in darker shades of green – contrasted with the gardens' well-kept lawns, wide variety of trees – from broad-crowned carobs to storeys-high palms – and colourful flowerbeds. It called to mind a legion assembled in *testudo* formation – shields aligned to cover the top and sides – to withstand an attack.

We parked, and, with swimsuits underneath our clothes and a towel each, headed for the beach. From both sides of the narrow footpath through the dunes, wild shrubs of rosemary, laurel, oregano and myrtle enveloped us in their aromas. Ahead of us beckoned the sea, a turquoise ribbon stretched between the light blue of the sky and the pale sand. We walked down the path in single file, Giorgio and Lidia in front. Anna's flip flops dangled from her left hand, and her straw beach bag from her right shoulder. My eye travelled from the heels of her feet to her ankles, and then up her calves to the hollows of her knees, moist from the heat of the car journey. Above them, the hem of her yellow and orange dress rose and fell with each movement, leaving my mind's eye to sketch out her thighs. The bow-strap dress, taut around the bust and then flaring, emphasised her slim waist and exposed her shoulders. The printed pattern of shells and corals swayed with her steps, so that she seemed to float on the sand.

Details of that afternoon have re-played themselves in my mind for over thirty years. I can recall everything about that beach. It was nearly deserted, a far cry from the scene it would offer within weeks. An elderly lady smeared in tanning oil lounged on a sunbed, eyelids beneath protective covers, skin like aged parchment. In the shadow of a beach umbrella, a young woman helped a little boy to build a castle. A teenage couple lay on a beach towel, facing each other and caressing.

The four of us spread our towels close to the water, on dry sand by a rock pool encrusted with limpets. We began discarding the layer of clothing over our swimsuits. I took off my t-shirt and shorts, affecting casualness, though from a corner of my eye I was aware that Anna was watching me. She lifted her dress, but ended up wrestling with it above her head.

'Ouch,' she said. 'A strap's caught in my hair clip. Can one of you help me?'

'Don't move.' I unravelled the tangle and helped her pull

the dress above her head and off her arms, my hands sliding, unwrapping her. We stood face to face, clutching the yellow and orange material.

'Am I allowed to put it away, or would you like to hold on to it?' she laughed.

'Oh, of course'. I let go and she folded it into her beach bag with brisk, elegant movements, while I stole glances at her body in its flowery bikini.

The curves of her waist were sculpted even more delicately than in my waking dreams. Her belly hinted at softness, and diminutive moles, scattered here and there, lured my eye into a game of hide-and-seek. We exchanged looks and a smile brightened her face. I stepped forward, eager to touch her, but Giorgio tugged me by the arm.

'Come on, we're diving in!'

'What?' I could have punched him, but Anna brought a hand to her mouth and repressed a laugh.

'Last one in is a loser. Come on!'

I shrugged and raced with Giorgio. We splashed and screamed like ganders, and then launched into an energetic front crawl. When we stopped and turned around, the girls were stepping hesitantly into the water. We swam back.

'You'd better dive in if you don't want us to splash you,' Giorgio said.

'No, not true,' I reassured them.

'Oh yes it is. I'm counting to three: one, two...'

'Ok, ok.' The girls slid in, pulling faces at the cold.

We swam forward in a breast stroke so slow that three of us could talk without effort, joking that Corfu and the coast of Albania were close enough for us to get there and back. Anna had told me she wasn't a good swimmer, but I hadn't imagined how dire. We must have been less than fifty meters out to sea when she began panting for breath.

'Why don't we head back?' I suggested.

'Good idea.'

Giorgio and Lidia wanted to continue, so we split up, they turning on a course parallel to the shoreline for a long-distance swim, and we towards *terra firma*. When we reached the point at which my feet could touch the bottom, I dived underneath Anna, and, gripping her by the waist, lifted her up against my chest.

'Now you can't escape,' I said.

'Ooh, scary.' She wrapped her arms around my neck.

We kissed — a salty, watery kiss. I was the lucky mortal holding Anna's warm body in the cool water. I could feel two hearts beating inside me.

When we made it to the beach, we collapsed onto the towels and sat next to each other, elbows on our knees, water dripping from our hair.

'Want a *fiorone*?' she said. 'I forgot about them — straight out of our patch of *campagna*. From my mother, to share. I can't return home with the lot.' She reached into her beach bag for a Tupperware box and lifted the lid. The sugary fragrance of the season's earliest figs filled the air. Their grass-green skins were almost translucent, a guarantee that the sun had seeped through them until that morning. They were still so moist that they didn't need peeling.

'Irresistible.' I picked one up and Anna did the same. I watched her bite through the white flesh and ruby seeds. That action had never seemed more sensuous. I gobbled down the fruit in my hand. Anna smiled, unselfconscious, as we helped ourselves to more.

'Another one?'

'Not for me.'

She closed the box and tucked it back inside the bag. 'We must leave some for those two fishes,' she said, pointing at our friends in the distance.

'They're making good pace.'

'On the swimming front. But Lidia says things are cooling off between them – and with no hard feelings. More like friends. Same detachment with which they started off, I guess.'

'That would be Giorgio – not that he has said anything to me, yet.' Strange – normally he'd tell me when he was tiring of his latest conquest. 'He is my dearest friend, but I pity the girl who one day really falls in love with him.'

Anna gazed at our friends' fading shapes, at the spray marking their strokes. 'Poor old Giorgio would suffer no less, should *he* fall in love and find the passion one-sided.'

'He? Passion? I suppose it's always possible – maybe if he came across the woman of his dreams. As I did.' I winked, then slid my arm behind her back and drew her closer. My Nereid, I thought, my sea goddess who can't swim. Her lips, the skin of her neck, and her ear-lobes tasted of the sea.

I was kissing her shoulder, when she whispered '*Si*,' lowering her head and turning it away from me. The way she said it – the tone somewhere between shy and defeated, and the movement at odds with affirmation – unsettled me. I lifted her chin.

'The answer you wanted,' she said, and hid her face on my chest. 'I'll never feel like this about anyone else. Never.' Her voice reverberated inside my ribcage.

I felt dizzy – and realised I had been holding my breath.

Words escaped me. I hugged her so tight that she exclaimed, 'Don't squeeze too hard.'

'Sorry.' I released my grip and she looked up at me. I wanted to kiss her, and hold her, and... and I didn't know what. But I knew we shouldn't let the moment fizzle out. I felt at one with the glorious sunlight and everything it imbued. I cleared my throat. 'Let's go.'

'What? Where?'

'I don't know. Let's just walk. To the next beach? To the one after that? Wherever you want.' My arm swept the full length of the bay, from the ruins of the Spanish watchtower at one end, to the lighthouse of Torre Canne at the other. I got up, folded my towel and threw it across my shoulder. Then I held out my hands and pulled her up.

The old lady on the tanning bed lifted her eyelid protectors as we passed, deigned to glance at us, and returned to her sun worship. We walked along the watermark, my arm around Anna's shoulders, hers about my waist, leaving traces of our passage for the sea to wash away. We fell silent. The sacrament of sorts to which we had quietly pledged ourselves may have lacked the definiteness of a 'when' and the pomp of a 'where', but we compensated by this new solemnity.

Along the foreshore, miniscule crabs scurried in and out of rock pools. We stopped and pointed to schools of tiny fish – iridescent flashes in the water. The sea extended towards the horizon in a progression of hues, from the pale jade at our feet to the ultramarine in the distance. Where sea met sky, the mountains of Albania were hazy mirages, captivating us as if we had never set eyes on them before. Their misty ridges seemed to sway backwards and forwards as if they were floating.

The next beach ended in a crescent-shaped promontory covered in dense vegetation. We headed towards it as if it had exerted the authority of an alpha or omega situated between land and sea. Our progress along the water was impeded by a bulge of sharp rocks – a splinter of reddish brown protruding into the blue – but, next to them, a sandy path stretched through trees and shrubs bulkier than on other dunes.

We entered the thicket, where short oaks and junipers – lashed and bent by the *scirocco* and *maestrale* – vied with rosemary and laurel bushes and with a variety of grasses for a share of the soil. Alongside the main path, narrower trails opened up. We ignored the first, and slowed down as we passed the second, but drew to a halt in front of the third. Turning towards Anna, I caught a faint gasp escaping from her lips, but noticed the warmth in her eyes, too. I smiled back, took her hand and led the way in.

The trail snaked through the vegetation, skirting tufts of *ammofila* – 'sand lover', or, more prosaically, marram grass – and shrubs. Now and then, the track ushered us into small clearings where we struggled to make out its continuation. *L'albero magico* – our magic tree, as we later called it – materialised before us. It was a squat oak – not of the kind familiar in Britain, but a distant cousin rooted in arid earth – whose branches arched downwards, forming a dark-green canopy over a bed of fine sand. It called to mind an apparition out of one of those fairy tales in which nature shields hero and heroine from the villains in pursuit, throwing obstacles – from brambles to boulders – in their way, while offering sanctuary and sustenance to the fugitives.

Anna and I looked at each other. We can never be certain of what's going through another's mind, but I could tell that the same thought had occurred to both of us: this tree was a gift. Yet neither of us could muster the courage to say it. The silence, except for the hypnotic chorus of cicadas, can't have lasted long but it felt endless. Finally I blurted out a 'Now?' and immediately regretted that I hadn't been more poetic.

Anna nodded, but her grip and her flushed cheeks made me hesitate.

'Are you sure?' I said.

'No. But I'm sure I love you. So I guess yes. Yes. I'm not making sense, am I?' She gazed at the oak.

'Give it a couple of weeks and the beaches will be swarming with people...'

'Oh, don't spoil things.' She frowned.

'What did I say to...?'

'Nothing. Kiss me?' she interrupted.

It wasn't long before I felt her shoulders and her back relax. I lifted her up, and, still kissing, carried her clumsily towards the oak. Setting her down before it, I bent low to pass beneath the canopy and stretched out the beach towel. She kneeled down next to me and nestled her chin in my shoulder. Her eyes looked shiny in the pearl-grey light. I slid one hand behind the nape of her neck. Instinct lit our way through the rest.

Funny, what one remembers after so long: the sinuous yielding when I kissed her between the shoulder blades; the sole of her foot caressing the top of mine; her fingertips tracing my spine; her eyes wide open but her mouth tightly shut until she could no longer hold it; afterwards, her smile. If I were forced to let go of all of these memories but one, that smile is the one I'd keep – it held everything, as well as the promise of the happiness before us.

★★★

With Anna, I was astonished by how naturally everything came. Sure, it might have taken weeks to get to the first kiss, but after that, her kisses withheld nothing – nor did mine. And the same was true after that first time making love – we were still lying down on the sand, naked and, in my case, dazed, when she propped herself up on one elbow and smiled. 'I'm so happy, that I could die right now and I wouldn't mind.'

I propped myself up too and caressed her cheek. 'How about 'I'm so happy, I've never wanted so much to be alive'? That's how *I* feel.'

'Me too.' She took my hand between hers, and kissed it. 'But one thing doesn't exclude the other.'

It took me aback that she could strike up an earnest conversation right after making love for the first time in her life – in both our lives.

'Poor old Lucretius.' Her lips formed a pout. She toyed with the sand, scooping up a handful of grains and letting them slip through her fingers. 'To die before he could write the final part of his book – the best bit of Epicurus's teachings.'

'What?' Even by my standards this didn't seem the most obvious moment for philosophy.

'Don't look like that. Please. The bit about how, whatever happens, it's within your power to hang on to memories of happy moments? How no one can wrench them away from you? Well, here's all I meant to say: whatever life throws at me, this moment is the memory I'll hang onto. I'll say a prayer too, of course, but this is where my mind will be.'

'Christ, where do you get such thoughts?' I hugged her,

and with my fingers drew back the strands of hair plastered by salt, sweat and sand to her forehead.

She spoke softly in my ear. 'Pain is inevitable, at some point. But thanks to you, I'll cope with anything.'

She loosened herself from my grip just enough to look into my eyes. In hers I made out a tenderness so unstinting that it awoke my fear: that I might not deserve it; that I might be incapable of the same; and, worst of all, that one day I might lose her.

All I remember of our walk back is a sensation of bliss, and the dry sand under our feet feeling cooler. Lidia and Giorgio were playing volleyball by the water. When they caught sight of us, they returned the ball to the lady with the little boy and strode towards us.

'Where have you guys been? *Imboscati* in the dunes, eh?' Smirking, Giorgio searched my face before studying Anna, who was wrapped in my towel.

'Don't be an ass. We simply lost track of time and ended up on a beach far down the bay.'

Anna's barely sketched smile showed her relief.

CHAPTER 9

You can probably imagine what it was like, when I switched off my bedside lamp that night, and sank my head onto the pillow. Knowing what Anna's 'yes' must have cost her – with her faith and her family – left me in no doubt as to the depth of her sentiments.

'I'll never feel like this about anyone else.' I was certain not only that she meant it but that it was true, for her and for me. When you have the good fortune of stumbling upon love like that, you know it's priceless: every atom in your body senses it. I'm not talking of the sexual aspect, but of how I felt whenever Anna and I were together, and even when we weren't.

Love like this isn't a romantic illusion. It's grounded in a realistic vision of each other. If it's rarer than it could be, it's because it exacts such a price upfront. I'm making it sound like a transaction, when it's anything but. It demands courage: to strip yourself bare; to see yourself through a pair of eyes that recognise your flaws but gaze on you with tenderness; to accept who you are; and to want to draw the best out of yourself.

But back to that night – is it any wonder happiness felt uncontainable? I lay on the bed with my nerves and muscles ready to dance in the darkness. My mind whirred with the day's events, the intensity of all sensations still fresh: Anna's and my moist skin, our bodies one moment pressed and the next sliding against each other; her fingers stroking my chest and then holding on to my arms as to the edge of a cliff; the unfamiliar sounds escaping us; the scent of salt and sea in her hair; the sweetness in her mouth. How could I sleep, when with the re-playing of each instant I felt more and more elated?

Where would we make love next? I imagined us in one of the hundreds of olive groves surrounding Ostuni, beneath a gnarled tree next to a dry wall, for protection from wind and prying eyes. Viewed from the air, Ostuni was a speck of white chalk on a green canvas – the green of nature's impetus flowing through thousands of olive trees. For the first time in my life, I felt that the earth's energy flowed through me too, that I was happy to be alive and to belong to the universe because it contained Anna.

I'd reassure her parents that I wasn't toying with her, that I couldn't conceive of being happy with anyone else. And my mother, perceiving how close the bond between Anna and me was, would eventually understand. I still hadn't introduced them. It was partly out of a certain glee at withholding from my mother knowledge of a relationship which meant so much to me. But it was also because I could anticipate her reaction to my choice of a *guardia campestre*'s daughter. She knew that Anna and I were seeing each other, but as I never spoke of her, my mother had no inkling of how often we met or how strong our attachment. As for Concetta, she hadn't breathed a word of Anna's visits to our home, possibly to oblige me, but, more likely, to spare Mum the hurt of finding out from someone other than me.

When at last I fell asleep, what remained of my night was hardly restful. I awoke from one exhausting dream only to fall into another. I couldn't recall them the following morning, but I was worn out. I wished I was at the Amphiareion, a temple in ancient Greece where people passed the night and had their dreams divined; if only a temple priest had reassured me that mine augured well. Instead, the thought evoked an image which troubled me, and, much later, haunted me.

You see, the Amphiareion priests could tell the time at night thanks to a water clock. The thought of water flowing through the mechanism brought to mind Anna in the light of our improvised alcove, letting sand slip through her fingers. That motion had accompanied her comments about Lucretius. She had maintained there was nothing morbid about them, but I couldn't – still can't – perceive them any differently.

There was one more reason why that gesture caused me alarm. It arose from one of those associations which the mind makes, unprompted, at lightning speed and which then take far longer to put into words. 'Klepsydra' was the Greek word for the water clock; but in Italian *clessidra* more commonly means a sand dial; as art history at the Classico was compulsory, I could not fail to associate a sand dial with Father Time. This wasn't the sort of imagery I was keen to entertain: I was young, in love and loved – there was every reason for a long and happy life ahead of me.

If you really want to grasp why the thoughts rushing through my mind left such a sense of unease, you could step into the Wallace Collection and take a look at *A Dance to the Music of Time*. In Italian, that painting by Poussin has a different title: *The Dance of Human Life*. Enlightening, don't you think? That picture is so famous, we studied it at school.

I've been to look at it – more than once and always with mixed emotions. It draws you to it under the pretence of being an Arcadian scene – all serenity. But once you've had the chance to absorb its details, connect them to each other and view the whole again, you realise it has fooled you.

I'll do my best to describe it. Just give me a moment to picture it. All right: three women and a man are dancing in a circle, holding hands. They look like the seasons, but they're also allegories of the cycle of life's fortunes: the labour which produces riches, which in turn lead to excessive pleasure and from there to poverty. They seem locked in a never-ending dance, oblivious to their own compulsion and to the passage of time.

The fact they don't perceive this – with the exception of Pleasure, who looks you knowingly in the eye – makes their predicament more tragic. They can't help but dance to the lyre played by Father Time; his grey wings are more a vulture's than an angel's. Next to him an infant holds a sand dial, while opposite, another child blows bubbles which only last an instant. A few steps away, a marble statue of Janus, one of his two heads young and the other old, makes time's passage feel as heavy as stone. And if you look to the chariot of Aurora in the sky, you find the hours flying on its back. You see, now, why the sand dial and Father Time couldn't evoke bland associations? Who wouldn't sympathise with my younger self? I had no wish to consider such notions at a happy time and yet their echo reached me.

I was almost angry with Anna. But my annoyance faded as quickly as it had arisen. It wasn't until a long time afterwards that I gave the matter any thought again. There and then I chided myself for pointing the finger at her, when it was *my* mind which had made the leap from her innocent gesture to darker associations. And yet now I believe it was all linked: half-awareness of dangers on which I was reluctant to dwell flowed into the agitated dreams of that night.

★★★

'Slept well?'

'Not really,' Anna answered from the other end of the phone line. 'I was too happy.'

'Me too.' The sweetness and sparkle in her voice dispelled my anxieties. I was pacing around my room, phone in hand, but what I saw weren't the familiar posters decking my walls – the Suzuki motorbikes, the crimson Alfa Spider, the covers of De André and Dalla music albums – or my guitar propped in a corner. No, I was transported to the beach, to the sand beneath our feet and to the water of the sea, to the rock pools and the dunes, the junipers and the oak tree. A sensation of total wellbeing rushed through me once more.

'Curious: I thought I might feel guilty. And I do – a bit,' Anna said.

'I don't.'

'Hmm, it's different for you. But mostly, I feel happy.' She sounded embarrassed to admit it. 'Have you ever felt like this before?'

'No. Never.' I wished she had been next to me. I would have held her tight, kissed her and run my fingers through her hair. For an instant the memory of the scents and tastes of *fioroni*, salt and sea overwhelmed me. 'When will I see you?'

'Around six?'

'So late? That's punishment.'

'Oh. I just thought, with revision...'

'How can you even think about it today?'

'Don't sound so sour. You know I love you. Surely you can survive till six.'

'I don't know. I wish you were here right now.'

'Me too.' I heard her sigh. 'Oh, all right. I don't seem to be able to say no to you, even when it really isn't wise.'

'You mean we should be studying.'

'Well, yes. All those years of hard work…'

'You're right. Six o'clock it'll have to be, won't it? You're a good influence on me, Anna Saponaro.'

'Me? If I had been sensible, I wouldn't have said yes yesterday – I'd have waited at least till after the *maturitá*.' She laughed. 'But I had no idea both of us would be dying to spend every waking moment in each other's arms, afterwards.'

'Ah, so you are?'

'You doubt it?'

'No.'

Her contradictions baffled me. She felt guilty – on account of her faith. And yet she admitted to being overcome with happiness. I knew her well enough to be sure that the cause of the joy wasn't the act of making love – all the more as there had been moments when I feared she was finding it every bit as painful as I had heard 'the first time' could be – but all the emotions flowing into it. It was as if our feelings for each other had become tangible. I don't know which confounded me more: the acuteness of loving her, or the certainty that she loved me. But how Anna might have made her peace with her God, I didn't know.

Nor did I understand how she could show such abandon at the beach the previous afternoon, and now such practical sense. In fairness, she hadn't been unbending: she had offered to see me straight away when I objected. That's probably why I then desisted. The more someone loves you, the greater your power over them. Though I couldn't see it then, something told me not to abuse it. Today I think her abandon was proof of her being totally present in those moments without needing to rule out level-headedness in others: love and healthy self-love. Maybe, if I had asked her about the apparent contradiction, later suspicions might not have taken hold.

It wasn't long before I found out how she had reached a truce with her God.

'He'd see the difference between sex and making love to the one you love, don't you think? He'd know ours is the real thing?' It was only a few days after the first time. We had returned to the stumpy oak in the dunes. That afternoon the breeze ruffled the leaves, opening and closing gaps through which the sun pierced the canopy and dappled Anna's back.

'If He exists and really is as good as you seem to believe, then I think He would.' I kissed her on the shoulder.

'Are you being facetious, Tommi?'

'No, logical.'

She shook her head and smiled. 'Human logic might turn out to be irrelevant. We'll never know, will we? The only thing I know for certain is what a gift you are.'

Anna visited and re-visited the subject that summer, yet always came up with the same answer. No gift as great as me, in her eyes — can you imagine how I felt? She was grateful to her God for me. But I hated witnessing her self-torture. And for the sake of what? Of a religion that exercises its hold by appealing to human weaknesses and fears. I pitied her for it, and was relieved every time the ritual ended with her saying, 'I trust He understands.'

Sometimes I was tempted to shake her and say, 'Of course He'd bloody understand — if He existed. Ours is no casual nonsense. And He's meant to be the god of love, right? With all the evil that goes on every day all over the Earth, why the hell would He want to damn people for expressing love?' But I never did say it, as her words meant much the same thing – minus my anger and plus her faith.

We did manage to study for the July *maturità* and do full justice to the years of work. Thanks to those exam results, I received an offer from Milan's Bocconi University, the business studies Mecca towards which I continued sleepwalking. When I think of that summer, crystal-clear scenes emerge out of a haze. I picture Anna behind me on the Suzuki, her arms tight around my chest, her head against my back, as we rode to Ceglie Messapica along the route flanked by dry walls and olive groves. The wind lashed our faces and made our eyes water – no one wore helmets, least of all on provincial country roads. We shouted over the engine noise to hear each other; her voice reverberated in my ribcage.

It was almost evening when we reached Ceglie. We parked just outside the town walls – so much less imposing than Ostuni's – and ambled through the streets of the centre. The white rendering of many of the houses had cracked into slabs, some of which had disintegrated, exposing the grey-beige limestone. Carefully pruned oleanders, roses and agave plants were matched by weeds breaking through the edges of paved alleys and wild creepers bursting from fissures underneath roofs. Such dilapidation could have triggered sadness: after all, it was the product of an exodus to the factories of Northern Italy, Switzerland and Germany – tourism had spared Ostuni that fate. And yet, Ceglie energised me. Its eerie parallel dimension, so similar and so different from my own, felt liberating.

The aroma of meat skewers filled the air. It came from the stalls set up at the entrances to butchers' shops and trattorie. No one makes *spiedini* like the Cegliesi do. They skewer and grill chunks of red meat, hand-made sausage and *turcinieddi* – heavenly creations despite their unpromising ingredients: morsels of sheep's liver wrapped in sheep's guts and flavoured with parsley and laurel. We bought two portions of *spiedini* from a brusque lad whose stall offered a plastic table and chairs. He placed each serving on a small cardboard tray and supplied us with cheap paper napkins. I watched Anna turn the skewer in her hand, seeking the angle for a bite.

'Why are you smiling?' she said.

'Because you remind me of a cat – the way they tilt their heads and use their paws when they eat. They could be tearing a mouse apart, but they do it so gracefully that one forgets they are carnivores.'

She laughed. 'And you? Are you a cat, too?' She narrowed her eyes and cupped her hands like paws.

'No, more like a dog: uncomplicated, faithful...'

'Faithful, great. But you, uncomplicated? Don't look so put out – nothing wrong with that.'

On the way back, we stopped by Cicinedda, the watermelon vendor on the outskirts of Ostuni. We sat on a bench beneath his gazebo, our palates sweetened and refreshed by slices of fruit. That summer's hits blared from the boombox the old man had for his customers – couples like us, and groups of younger teenagers.

Funny, what happy memories are made of: what you saw, tasted or touched, and what was said. It's the fact that memories embed themselves in the body, in sensations familiar and unique: that's what makes them so painful once your source of happiness is gone. I could recount more scenes, but to what purpose? What will they tell you that you cannot comprehend by recalling your own happiest moments and realising how both ordinary and extraordinary they were?

There was one perplexing incident. Anna and I were eating ice cream with Giorgio and Lidia at a café in Piazza della Libertá. Our seats offered a privileged view of that evening's free show: a medley of acts succeeding each other on stage in front of the nineteenth-century town hall. We felt clever not to be on our feet among the locals and tourists jostling for space on the square in the hot August air. The stand-up comedians' routines made us cringe, but we decided to brave the next item on the programme, a folk dancing performance, for the sake of the pop bands which followed. We had never heard of them, but Ostuni wasn't brimming with alternatives.

The local folk group – teens and twenty somethings in traditional black, white and red costumes – began with a *tarantella*, each couple bouncing to the beat of tambourines, castanets and strident woodwind. They followed with a *pízzica*: a woman in a white nightshirt danced to an increasingly frenzied rhythm, underscored by the clapping, whooping and whistling of the others, until she collapsed. The public broke into cheers and applause.

'They're relieved it's finished,' I said. 'How backward must tourists think we are, with a dance like that? We should be ridding them of stereotypes about the South, and instead we're making it worse.'

'How do you come up with such gems?' Giorgio said. 'Everyone knows the *pízzica* is ancient stuff. Though our women are still the same: fiery.' He pinched Anna and Lidia at the waist. Their yelp turned to laughter, after an instant of surprise.

I managed a polite smile. Such gems. Sure.

Just then, some of the performers left the stage to approach members of the audience. One of them, a girl of no more than sixteen, came up to Anna and me.

'Come dance a *tarantella*.'

'Sorry. No idea how,' I said.

'It's really easy. We'll show you.'

She took Anna's hands.

'Come, Tommi. It'll be fun,' Anna said, allowing the girl to pull her up.

'No way.'

'They'll keep it simple.' She tilted her head, a gentle invitation.

'No.' My tone sounded sharper than I'd have wished. 'I'd trip over my own feet.'

'I'll dance.' Giorgio got up and took Anna's hand. 'We can't let this young lady – what's your name?'

'Me?' The girl flushed. 'Antonietta.'

'Right. We can't let Antonietta go back on stage without her two scalps, can we?'

Anna smiled. 'Absolutely. But Lidia,' she said turning to her friend, 'You'll go with him, won't you, while I keep Tommi company?'

'Of course.' Lidia took Giorgio's arm and they followed the dancer onto the stage. Anna sat down and put her arm around my shoulder.

'You could have danced, if you really wanted to,' I said.

'It wouldn't have been as much fun without you.' She stroked the nape of my neck.

Only about a dozen members of the audience were taking part. Giorgio stood out, as ever: on this occasion by his careless movements, wrong timing and ridiculous faces. And yet, when I glanced at Anna, I saw how she watched him: with affection and wistfulness. Maybe she simply wished she could be up there having fun. Maybe she wished I could be more like my so-called best friend. Maybe I was just being unfair and unkind.

September, and the dread of separation, arrived all too soon. The days were still hot but the radiance of July and August gave way to an autumnal veil. In the garden of Villa Emma, the fig trees were still leafy, and their vivid green had not yet begun to fade, but the last of their fruit had long since ripened and been picked. On the almond trees, the thick grey-green velvet pods swathing each fruit were puckered and shrivelled.

My plan was to fly to Milan towards the middle of that month to secure accommodation before university began in late September. By all accounts, it would be much colder, darker and misty, up north. A year earlier, I would have shrugged and said that such a climate would keep me working hard indoors, but now the prospect of roaming those dreary built-up streets deepened my misery. In the early days of September, every moment I spent with Anna was tinged with nostalgia. I'd hold her hand in mine, or look at her, and try to fix in my mind that instant, conscious that we'd soon be seeing each other every few weeks, at best.

I did not know it but what was about to happen was what a physicist might label something like 'a change in initial conditions eventually resulting in a disproportionate outcome'. They must have a vicious sense of humour, physicists, to coin a phrase as poetic as 'the butterfly effect' for something so devastating. After all, aren't they the ones who dubbed 'Little Boy' that bundle of uranium which melted stones, metal and humans in Hiroshima? On 10 September 1982 I put a match to the fuse of another kind of device.

Anna called me that day. 'Can I come over?' The kitchen clock, as I sat at the table with my *caffélatte e biscotti*, showed barely nine o' clock.

'Didn't we say I'd pick you up at eleven?' I said. 'Is something wrong?'

'I need to see you. Right now. Somewhere private and quiet.'

'All right. Here's good. Mum's out all day. Concetta is running errands but even if she finds you when she gets back, she'll keep quiet.'

'I know. The time to catch a bus and I'll be there.'

'What's this about?'

But she had hung up.

'Are you certain?' I tightened my grip of the terrace railing to stop slumping onto the terracotta floor-tiles. The bones in my legs felt like wax. The familiar valley and the strip of blue in the distance appeared unreal, a replica of the olive groves and the sea, while my blood surged to my temples.

'Yes.' Anna bit her lip and fixed me with wide, anxious eyes.

'But how do you know?'

'I'm sure, ok? The nausea – it made me wonder. It comes on suddenly – and not just in the mornings. Sometimes it's only uncomfortable but sometimes it's really strong – then I have to dash to the nearest toilet to throw up. And my period's two weeks late.'

'Right.' My mouth was all pasty inside, as if I'd taken a spoonful of flour.

'Is that all you can say?'

'I'm sorry – just stunned.'

We stood in silence, leaning against the railing – probably for no more than a minute, but one of those that feel like a lifetime, so densely packed are they with speeded-up reels of alternative futures. Finally I put my arm around Anna's shoulder and kissed her on the cheek and hair. I inhaled her scent – the fusion of her fresh, flowery perfume and honeyed skin – and was surprised that it, just like her appearance, didn't betray any hint of the momentous change taking place inside her body. That was still our secret.

'What do you want to do?' I said.

She hung her head. 'I don't know. I really, really don't.'

'How about we get married, and instead of going to university in Milan, I go to Bari? As soon as you wish, Concetta looks after Baby,' I smiled, still dazed by the news, 'and that way you can continue studying, too.'

She gave me a sad smile. 'Oh, Tommi, Tommi. It's not that simple.'

'Why not?'

'For all kinds of reasons: your mother, your future...'

'Our future. You're in my future, whether we marry in a month or in a year or in five years. So, we might as well do it sooner rather than later. There you go: Baby has simply hastened things – hastened happiness. Well done, Baby.'

She laughed. 'Oh, sweetie! You're being rash. Don't you see that one day you might regret it? That one morning you might wake up and look back at it all as a dreadful mistake? You'll tell yourself: I felt forced to do 'the right thing' and now I'm trapped.'

'No! I'll never feel like that. It's the right thing now and always will be. Call it luck, or Providence, you who believe in God.'

'How can you know for sure?'

'Because I love you. How can you think I could ever resent you? Or do you not love me?'

'No, no. You know I do. I just worry that –'

'Then stop worrying.' I hugged her tight. 'I'll talk to my mother. She'll be angry – no doubt about it – but then she'll take it on the chin. She's tough.'

Anna raised her hands to my face and slid them down my cheeks in a single slow motion. 'But don't turn down Bocconi for my sake. Whatever we decide to do, please don't miss out on it because of me. You don't know where Bocconi could lead – places you and I can't even conceive of, right now.'

'I was going to do it only to be able to manage a family business, not something the size of Fiat, remember? Bari has a perfectly good faculty of *Economia e Commercio*. There's still time to turn down the place.'

'Wait. I couldn't forgive myself if you did that because of me – especially if you make the decision in a hurry.' She sighed. 'Let's take a few days – or weeks – to think it over. Please. Meanwhile promise me you won't act on impulse.'

'Why wait, when I know what's right?'

'Isn't your flight to Milan booked for the day after tomorrow?'

I nodded.

'Then take it, sweetie,' she continued. 'Two days can't be long enough to decide something like this. Go, sort out your accommodation and the university. And when you get back… we'll both have had ten days to reflect.'

'And if, after that, I haven't changed my mind and propose again that we marry?'

She smiled and clasped my hand in both of hers. 'Then we'll go talk together to your mother and my parents.'

CHAPTER 10

During my stay in Milan, I called Anna every day at an agreed time. I squeezed inside a phone booth, inserted a raft of clanking *gettoni* into the slot, and waited for the dialling tone to be cut short by a '*Pronto?*' Her voice almost always answered straight away. She must have rushed to pick up the receiver of the only telephone in the house before her parents or sister.

They knew Anna was talking to me: they did not interfere but I could tell when they were hovering around, as then she expressed herself with terse replies like a 'Me too' or a 'And you, here.' Nonetheless, her delight upon hearing me was audible – the rapid intake of breath, the torrent of news on the couple of occasions when I was lucky enough to catch her on her own – as I expect mine was at the sound of her voice. I leaned back against the scratched glass of the booth, and became wholly absorbed. The constant stream of traffic, the noxious fumes and the smog-stained palazzi dissolved into a blurry background as I pictured Anna in her sitting room. From the few times I had been inside her home, I could recall that the telephone sat on top of a tawdry sideboard of mahogany veneer, close to a sofa upholstered in avocado-green corduroy. I imagined Anna perching on the sofa, with the receiver in one hand and the chord twisted between the fingers of the other.

During my first few days in Milan, those calls re-charged me and enabled me to face the next twenty-four hours, during which I visited now one student flat, then another, weighing up the proximity to the university of the first versus the spaciousness of the second. But being apart from Anna at such a time, and the prospect of four or five years away from her and our child, felt more and more like nonsense. A child! People in Ostuni would point at us and whisper: 'Only students, and married *per rimediare*' — 'to put things right.' But who cared.

I could already see us with our baby — for some reason I imagined a boy — at the seaside: me, holding his chubby little body afloat in the water while he babbled, laughed and stretched his arms towards Anna. I could already see him older, too: a nine-year-old who poked his head around the library door to ask for help with his homework. And I could see myself taking the time — as long as he wished — to explain anything he wanted to know, and then listening to the eye-opening remarks that are children's gift, be they about a book, a school friend, or the walnut desk under our noses.

The timing of Anna's discovery couldn't have been worse: it hadn't allowed me to discuss the pregnancy properly with her, let alone to tell my mother. I could imagine Mum's reaction to the menace to her *bella figura*: the loss of the prospect of a 'more suitable' marriage for me *and* of a son with a degree from Italy's best-known university, all in one stroke. For the time being, I didn't have much choice but to carry on as planned, and then to transfer to the University of Bari once I had talked things over with Anna and won Mum's consent — her approval would be too much to hope for.

When on my fifth day I called Anna, something in the tone of her voice made me uneasy. It was as if its centre had cracked — as if its silvery core had been scratched and dented.

'Cheer up, Anna. I'll be back soon. I might find a flat I can leave at short notice. I don't want to study here.'

'Don't hurry that decision, remember.' If every voice

produces something like a melody, hers had switched to a minor key, with its knack for stirring sadness and unease.

'Something's wrong. What is it?'

'Just tired, that's all. The sickness has got worse.'

The following day, she sounded even more miserable.

'*Amore bella*, it's the uncertainty that's making you anxious. As soon as I get back to Ostuni, we'll talk to my mother and your parents. Everything will be fine.'

'It won't. It's just wishful thinking.'

I could barely recognise this defeatist attitude. Nothing I said seemed to make any difference. Only my return home, a chance to discuss things face to face and with our families, would do the trick.

Over my remaining days in Milan I spent my spare moments searching for presents. At the La Rinascente department store in Piazza Duomo – a temple of luxury, complete with soaring columns and lofty ceilings – I bought Anna a silk scarf printed with cornucopias. They overflowed with plump grapes, wheat sheaves, pomegranates, wild berries and all kinds of flowers. She'd recognise the well-wishing symbol, with which we were familiar from our art history and philosophy lessons, and it might make her smile; and the coral-coloured background would bring out her brown hair and hazelnut eyes. The goddess Fortuna's other symbol – the rudder which Seneca, the old doomster, never tired of saying she could arbitrarily steer towards disaster – was nowhere in sight.

For the first time ever, the baby clothes and toys in a shop window attracted my attention. 'Reach for the stars!' read the lettering embroidered beneath a patchwork spacecraft on the front of a tiny blue sweater. Not that I could buy it: no Italian would buy clothes for a baby until around the time of birth, either through their own *scaramanzía* – the widespread form of superstition not to tempt fate – or, if like me they couldn't abide it, because of others' consternation at the insensitivity shown by breaching the custom.

But no one could crucify me for purchasing nursery-room objects, like the rotating crib-mobile – lions, giraffes, tigers and zebras in vibrant fabrics, chasing each other round and round – hanging in the shop window. Upon opening the door, I set off a tinkling which, when I turned around, I saw belonged to grape-size bells hanging above my head on pastel ribbons. The shop was small, but its white shelves were stacked full of toys, trinkets and meticulously folded clothing. Their colours ranged from pale to garish, but instead of jarring, they produced a cheerful harmony. The room smelt of infants' cologne, of talcum powder and things brand new and unspoiled. A petite lady in a black-trimmed cream suit invited me to browse.

'Though I suppose you might welcome suggestions?' she added. 'Boy or girl?'

'I... I don't know yet.' I picked up a rabbit of pale green plush. At the touch of its soft, longhaired coat, a comforting sensation shot from my fingertips to the rest of my body – I was startled by it, and felt mildly embarrassed.

'Lovely, isn't it?' The woman singled out a grinning monkey from the same series of toys and stroked it. 'But suitable only from three years up. How old is your friends' child?'

'My friends'...? Yes, well, a new-born – kind of.' I'd have to get used to people's assumptions.

'Then these are the ones you should look at: terry cloth on the outside, and the filling in pure cotton. Babies suck and chew anything within reach. But they can't choke on these.'

She wagged her index finger as if proud to be outsmarting the little ones. I couldn't contain a smile; but also, I suddenly realised how much I had to learn – truly an enormity – to keep our child safe. I had never even held a baby, as far as I could remember.

I left the shop carrying a lavishly wrapped teddy bear of white and light-green cotton terry. It wasn't much bigger than my hand – the perfect size for a baby's tiny fingers, and meanwhile, for Anna to hold onto.

By some miracle, I managed to persuade the clerk at the nearest Alitalia ticketing office to let me fly home a day early for only a trifling penalty. I would land late at night, and surprise Anna the next morning by appearing at her house. First, of course, I'd place the presents carefully inside the storage compartment of my motorbike and then I'd ride towards the Old Town. At the ring of the doorbell, Anna might be the one who came to the door, and her face would light up. I couldn't wait.

There turned out to be no need to ring. When I arrived, I found Anna in the little square – in the same open space overlooking the valley where we had stood so awkwardly months before, when I first walked her home. Today was sunny, and the warm air sticky with the smell of *vendemmia*, the grape harvest. Midges swarmed in search of the pulp and skins fermenting in the wineries or being turned into *mostarda* jam inside the homes. Anna was wearing a baggy, plum-coloured dress, and was sitting on the wall where we had often exchanged a last kiss in the dark. She was not alone. She appeared to be crying on Giorgio's shoulder. With one hand he held her tightly, and with the other, he stroked her hair. His head was bent over hers and he was murmuring something in her ear.

I kept my distance. My breath stuck in my chest. What honeyed nonsense was he whispering to her? The most trite of all betrayals – by one's best friend. Of course! Wasn't that how the story went, in real life and in literature? Giorgio had broken up with Lidia barely two months earlier. But why did he have to steal my pearl?

'Tommi!' Giorgio's head lurched back when he saw me standing by the motorbike. He loosened his grip of Anna. She raised her head and gave me a dazed look, as if she had just woken up. While I walked towards her, she dried her eyes, which were red and puffy.

'I wasn't expecting you today.' I recognised the crack that had run through her voice during our recent phone calls. She didn't rush to greet me, but sat there, shoulders and back hunched.

'Clearly not.' I crossed my arms and clenched my teeth to prevent myself from hitting her and my so-called best friend.

Giorgio cleared his throat. 'I'd better leave you two alone.' He placed a hand on Anna's shoulder. 'I'm there if you need me.'

'You'd think he'd have some shame,' I thought, 'but no.' I watched him get up, shoot me a glance, walk towards the alley leading to the old seminary and wave us goodbye before turning the corner. When I spun my head round to face Anna, she was staring vacantly towards where Giorgio had disappeared.

I sat down an arm's length away from her.

'So is this why *I* was meant to take time to think things over? It was really you and Giorgio who needed it?'

'What?'

'I'm no fool. The baby – it's his?'

She gaped. 'How can you think that? No, no, the baby...'
She lowered her head and held it between her hands. 'The
baby...' Her back shook as she wept. There were no passers-by
in the *piazzetta*, but she held her mouth to contain her cries.

I could tell that something awful had happened, and yet I
was, above all, relieved: there seemed to be nothing between
her and Giorgio. Anna dug into the pockets of her dress for a
handkerchief, and with it dried her blotchy face and blew her
nose. Finally, she stiffened her back and drew in a breath.

'I lost the baby'.

It took a few moments to register.

'You mean it's...?' I gawped at the belly hidden by the
plum-coloured fabric. 'Where... What?'

'The other day,' Anna said in a whisper.

I tried to fight off visions of her and the baby in a pool
of... what? Don't think of it as a baby, I told myself. Where
did you let your imagination take you? It was still a shapeless
thing.

'By last night... No control over the thoughts rushing through my head, last night.' She clutched her arms and
looked down at her feet. 'You'd think it's more than enough
to cope with. But no, now my parents have discovered I was
pregnant, they call me such names...'

'Oh, Anna.' I edged closer to her and put an arm around
her shoulders. 'And your sister?'

'Barbara's idea of comforting...? Worse than being on my
own.' She rocked quietly back and forth, like a wooden shut-
ter with a hinge loose, at the mercy of the wind.

'You weren't here, and... I couldn't tell you over the
phone.' She shook her head.

'No, of course not.'

'I called Lidia and Giorgio. They listened. Giorgio rushed over, this morning. But no one can help. Not even you.' She whimpered, and dabbed away fresh tears with a scrunched-up handkerchief, bright orange and printed with daisies which seemed to wilt with shame at the cheery colour. I rubbed Anna's arm, while the two of us stared at the ground.

'It's not all.' She curled her shoulders over her chest, as if trying to make herself smaller or disappear.

'You don't have to tell me the rest.' I lifted her chin with my hand, and managed a smile. 'It'll only upset you more.'

She turned away. 'You don't understand, *tesoro mio.*'

'I... I can try to.'

'I'd feel like a fraud if I didn't tell you the truth,' she said with a choked voice. Her shoulders rose and fell as she inhaled and exhaled. Then she turned to face me. Still sitting, she straightened up and took another deep breath.

'It wasn't a miscarriage,' she said, burying her face in her knees.

I froze, open-mouthed. 'How... How c-could you?' I finally said, rising to my feet. She remained huddled on herself, without meeting my eyes.

'You, of all people?' I shouted, planting myself in front of her, feet apart.

'I... I thought I had to leave you free.' She wiped her eyes with the backs of her hands.

'Free? To do what?'

'To... To make your decisions.' She looked up at me with eyebrows and lips pinched into a plaintive expression, like the beggars who set up shop at church entrances around Christmas and Easter time. 'I had to. So you wouldn't feel forced to marry me.'

'Forced? Me? I was happy to marry you: happy, happy, happy. What was wrong with 'happy'? Why the hell didn't you talk to me first? Didn't I have a right to a say?'

'I... I thought that... that maybe you couldn't tell whether it was a free decision... really free, I mean.' Soggy handkerchief now discarded on her lap, she wrung her hands so hard that her knuckles went white, bones showing through the tanned skin.

'Me, free to make decisions, or you? Is it my love you doubt, Anna, or your own?' I couldn't stop my rage from gushing out. 'So you did decide to swap me for Giorgio. And a baby would obviously have been an obstacle. Is that why you wanted me to stay as far away as possible? Were the thousand kilometres between Ostuni and Milan sufficient?'

'Stop it! It's not like that.' She squeezed her eyes shut and gripped two fistfuls of her dress's fabric. 'I honestly thought only of you,' she said, her pitch raised by a full octave. 'God, if only I could –' She left the sentence unfinished.

'Could what? Are you sure that even on the afternoon of our first time, on the beach, Giorgio wasn't the one you really wanted?'

I remembered vividly how she had chided me for suggesting he wasn't capable of real love. Something had been brewing. That must be why he was so curious about whether we had 'done it' in the dunes. And then there was that yearning look as she watched him clowning his way through a *tarantella* before hundreds of spectators. How slow had I been to spot their veiled dance around each other, with me in the middle?

'Tommi, please. It's me you're talking of.' She was shaking and a tremor was in her voice. 'You know me.'

'I do, now.' Chest out and arms crossed, I looked down at her. 'You broke your principles for me. Why should I be surprised if you've done it again when an abortion suited you, and if now you want to try out someone new? Giorgio is no doubt more experienced than me. I expect sex – sorry, I won't call it 'making love' – is more fun with him.'

'Dear God!' She cocked her head and gaped. 'I told you the truth because I didn't want any dishonesty between us. I'm telling you... all I'm able to.'

'You call what you did 'honest'?' I let go of a laugh, savouring its mocking tone. 'And as for your faith in God: I'm not falling for it anymore. All that self-torture about making love... Isn't abortion a thousand times worse for your book-keeper in the sky?'

She got to her feet, using hands and arms to push herself up. Hobbling, and biting her lips as if in pain, she walked a few steps and halted in front of me. 'I was wrong – horribly wrong. I can't sleep, I can't bear to be awake...' she said, tears on her cheeks.

I took a step back but she grabbed my arm. 'My reasons weren't the... the foul ones you're imagining,' she said, crying. 'The way I saw it, I had to do it – for you – though it cost me far more than you seem to understand.' Her eyes looked feverish: redder, wide and too bright.

I shook off her hand and backed away. She stayed where she was, but leaned forward, hands on her thighs, with a pained grimace. 'Please, Tommi. I've told you the truth. I could add to it, but... That truth alone has turned out to be much worse to live with than I could ever... You have no idea. Please try to understand. I can't believe you'd let jealousy... I love you.'

'Really? I thought we had agreed to break the news to your parents together – and off you go and tell them.'

'I didn't. Listen...'

'And,' I interrupted, 'off you go and 'lose' the baby. I love the euphemism.'

'I told you, I thought –'

'I should have figured from our first encounter that you weren't what you seemed. So plucky, that evening on the terrace.'

She shook her head, fury rising from her raised shoulders and clenched teeth to her eyes.

'Maybe it hasn't occurred to you, Tommi, but you're... God only knows, I couldn't help loving you – taking you as you are: so self-obsessed, and so harsh with people that... that... sooner or later you'd turn on me too. I should have figured that you were the odious creature I met that first evening on the terrace, and never given you a second chance.'

I sneered. She gaped. We stood opposite each other, searching for signs of the beloved.

'Yes, look at me. Look at me!' she screamed, her voice hoarse. By now the neighbours all around the square must have been peering through their net curtains and wooden slats. Good. They could look at her all they liked, and get to know her for what she really was.

'A... monster,' she said. 'I've turned myself into this... The baby... What have I done? For you. And you're not even worth it. Christ... Christ in Heaven forgive me.' She put a hand through her hair and shook her forehead, like a professional mourner on an ancient Greek urn.

'This is all too much to take in,' I said. 'I'll fly back to Milan tomorrow. Even today, if I can. To think I –' It was too much, too much. I strutted towards my motorbike.

I heard Anna behind me.

'What horrible things we've just said, Tommi. Some true. Some not. Horrible. As if I wasn't already drowning. I hope that once you're in Milan you'll see how wrong you are – and forgive me for... don't make me say it.'

I didn't turn towards her, but opened the Suzuki's storage compartment and extracted the two presents. 'Here.' I swung them at her, nearly slamming them into her belly. Her mouth opened. Arms dangling at her sides with the two little packages, she edged closer.

'Please, Tommi. All I ask for is some level-headedness – not easy for either of us, starting with me. Both of us can be wiser, from now on.'

I turned away and mounted the motorbike. I gripped the handlebars, pushed my foot hard on the kick-start and revved the engine until its roar filled the little square. Then I shot off, aware of Anna's gaze fixed on me to commit my features to her mind.

I reasoned that my mother would soon come to hear the whole story, distorted by 'Chinese whispers', so I might as well come clean immediately. I didn't want to have that conversation at home – any room in which it took place would ambush me with the memory. So I went to the company office in central Ostuni, an airy first-floor conversion in a nineteenth-century *palazzo*. I dragged myself up the marble-paved staircase, stroking the smooth sandstone balustrade, wishing it were possible to acquire its solidity before facing my mother.

Elena let me in. Intimidating as ever, with rust-coloured hair pulled into a bun, and her desiccated figure shrink-wrapped in one of her black suits – all that her wardrobe had ever seemed to contain – she surveyed me over her tortoise-shell reading glasses. She pointed to her wristwatch. 'Ten minutes late. I told you she could see you at 11:30. She has already cancelled an appointment for you. I hope this really is urgent.' She sat back at her desk in the lobby. 'Well? You know your way.'

I was tempted to ape Elena and her tone, but contented myself with walking at a snail's pace – that was sure to wind her up – towards my mother's office at the far end of the corridor. I nodded politely to all the people whose doors I walked past, from the young apprentice draughtsman, to *Ingegner* Forgalli. When I reached my mother's, I took a deep breath, and knocked.

I had prepared myself for emotional pyrotechnics, dampened only by Mum's sense of decorum – as, for once, she was sure to lose her self-control. My colossal blunder was bound to trigger an explosion, loaded with pent-up resentment.

Instead, she listened to the whole story with unnerving composure, sitting up straight and still, her lips thin slits, as if the geometry underpinning the construction business had seeped into her person. She hardly interrupted me, so I carried on talking without knowing which words were making things worse for me, a man hastening his own drowning by struggling to disentangle himself from a net.

'I'm sorry I didn't tell you how serious it all got – the relationship, I mean. I thought you'd never approve,' I said, and admitted, 'I guess we weren't that smart, if Anna ended up pregnant.'

'No point in rebuking you,' my mother said when I finished. She got up very slowly, like a statue coming to life. I followed her with my eyes. Any second now, surely she would turn around and vent her fury, hands firmly on the desk, voice strident. But she merely stepped towards the window behind her and lowered the white Roman blind. The sun's rays, which had been streaming through the window – just to heighten my discomfort – dissolved into a milky light. I sagged into my chair, relieved by this surprising gentleness, but wary.

She sat down again and I braced myself for one of her wounding remarks. What would it be this time? My total lack of common sense? My unworthiness, compared to my father? Her thankfulness that he had been spared such a disappointment? Whichever of these, it was surely about to be delivered with a new power.

She leaned towards me, elbows on the desk and hands knotted as if in prayer. 'You've clearly learnt your lesson. In future you'll be more careful in your choice of girlfriend, that's for sure.' She nodded sympathetically.

I gaped.

'I was much too hard on Anna, though.' I let out a long breath and winced at the mental image of the distressed young woman I had left behind in the square.

'She'll recover. You'll go your separate ways and get on with your lives.' My mother reached across the desk and patted my hand. 'For both of you, eventually it will feel like a story set in the distant past.'

'I can't believe she decided to abort. The least likely person... I'd have sworn it.'

'I expect her parents pressured her into it for the sake of her reputation – and theirs. She ought to keep her mouth shut instead of blabbing to Lidia and Giorgio and God knows who else. Frankly,' she said softly, 'thank your lucky stars. For all you know, she's a gold-digger who thought she had her future all wrapped up, until her parents intervened – and quite rightly: *they* figured I'd never let you marry her.' She crossed her arms and smirked.

'No, no. She's not like that. She's the sincerest person I've ever met.'

'Not sincere enough to tell you what she was about to do, was she? And you said it yourself – the little doe-eyed innocent was probably cheating on you with Giorgio.'

'No, I told you: I was furious, so I said things I shouldn't have. It can't be true.'

'I adore Giorgio, but I wouldn't put it past him to consider even your girlfriend fair game. Would you?'

'I don't know what to think.' I let my hands drop onto my lap, and looked at her. Tiny particles in the air flickered between us like white noise on a television screen. 'Could I have got Anna and Giorgio so wrong?'

She gave the desk clock a sideways glance. 'You never can be sure with people.' She got up and came round to where I was sitting. 'We can delude ourselves of others' goodness because the truth would hurt too much,' she said, stroking my shoulder. 'If it's any consolation, others can't see inside your mind any better than you inside theirs. Just put this experience behind you.'

'I don't know...'

'Yes, you do. The idea of heading straight back to Milan sounds very sensible. You shouldn't miss the start of your course. A new beginning. It'll take your mind off this affair. And who knows? At Bocconi you might meet a lovely girl.'

'I... I suppose.'

'And now I'm afraid you'll have to go.' She patted my arm

and gave me a small, efficient smile. 'My next appointment must be here already.'

I spent the afternoon packing, having managed to book myself on the evening flight. Should I take my music albums with me, and my guitar? No – too many memories of Anna were attached to them: Anna holding the cover of De André's latest, and pronouncing herself and me out of joint from those around us, like the native American on the cover; Anna's fingertip tracing the Moorish pattern of the guitar's rosette; Anna's fingers twisted and stretched around the instrument's neck to produce the F-major chord I was teaching her, my hand cradling hers.

Each time I glimpsed the phone on my bedside table, it prodded me to call Giorgio, but each time, something stopped me. At first, I was again certain that my suspicions about him and Anna that morning had been correct, in which case I never wanted to see or speak to him. But then I wondered if my conjectures had been folly. I kept swinging between the two extremes. Finally, barely half an hour before I was due to leave for the airport, I resolved to call him: no one but he would be able to confirm or dispel my fears. He might lie, of course, but I hoped that my newly acquired diffidence would help me detect any falsehood in his tone, in his choice of words or in uneasy pauses.

'You know what amazes me?' he said when I tackled him with my question, 'Not that your opinion of me should be so low – *that* is seriously offensive, but amazes me a lot less than your doubting Anna. Christ, she adores you – how can you not know that? And she's hardly the 'easy' sort. What does she see in you? You don't deserve her.'

'Then explain to me why she...' I couldn't finish. I couldn't dam the thoughts flooding my mind, or put them in order. 'She can't love me enough. That's what I've figured. If you love someone, you'll defy the world for their sake. I would have, for her.'

'Please, Tommi, give her another chance to explain. Don't leave her like this.'

'My absence will give us time to think.'

'She doesn't need time. She needs you.'

'I've got to go, now. Taxi's here.'

CHAPTER 11

I threw myself into my studies with all the vigour of a man trying to escape his thoughts. I delved into abstruse permutations of demand and supply elasticity – far beyond anything the economics syllabus required. I even completed the optional exercises in the statistical methods textbook. I let the strategy case studies absorb me as if they were thrillers. Although I lived only a few minutes' walk from the university, I left the flat early in the mornings to study in the library to avoid all distraction.

With the exception of the time spent in lessons, I stayed there until late in the evenings, while my flatmates sampled the gigs and jazz bars of the Navigli district. To Livio and Roberto, I was the stranger who had taken up the third room in the apartment, an anonymous set of walls and cheap furniture which had seen dozens of previous *Bocconiani* and would see others afterwards.

I remember waking up one night to the stench of burning, the clanking of metal, and laughter. I rushed into the kitchen.

'What the...?' I said, seeing thick smoke escaping from the oven. Livio was laughing as he tried to pull a baking tray out with a kitchen towel, but he was too unstable on his legs and too butterfingered to fold the cloth thickly enough. This seemed to be the cause of his cackling.

'Give it here.' I snatched the towel and extracted a pizza so charred that the smoke scratched my throat. Coughing, I placed the tray on the worktop and opened the window. Roberto, sipping a glass of milk at the table, followed my movements with an inane smile.

'Can't you guys even heat up a pizza? Idiots.' I spat out the words. 'With you, it's just fun, fun, fun every bloody night. Ever heard of the grasshopper and the ant?'

'Have you ever heard of being young? And enjoying yourself?' Livio said, pouring himself some milk and spilling a good part of it onto the floor. 'Freak.'

I stormed out. Afterwards, lying in bed, I couldn't help feeling guilty and unsettled. Why had I been so aggressive? Next morning I apologised to Livio and Roberto but they set off for their lectures without seeming to care about what I was saying. I knew I had earned their indifference.

I must have stood out, on the other hand, for my professors. I expect they thought me one of the most dedicated students in the year, the kind who from the age of twelve sifts through the company news and stock exchange pages of the salmon-pink *Sole 24 Ore* while everyone else likes comics, pop music and football.

Yet loneliness rushed towards me like an out-of-control truck the moment I lifted my head from my notes and textbooks and surveyed the shelves and people at the library desks around me. Being cut off from Anna – not merely her immediate absence, but the prospect of a life without her – felt like being buried in a vault where air was running out. Who was to blame: Anna, Giorgio or me? In the evenings, whenever I grilled myself a steak, the sound and aroma of the sizzling beef sparked memories of our evening in Ceglie, of Anna next to me, biting her *spiedini* and playing along when I said she resembled a cat.

How full of warmth her brown eyes were – I pictured

them, wide open and limpid, as if they were staring at me. With each day that passed, I believed less and less that they could have been insincere. When I had refused to turn back as we parted – when already she lamented the 'horrible things' we had said – she had probably gazed on me with love. And sadness. Nothing could make up for being without her. My studies gave my mind some respite, but they seemed meaningless: increasingly, there seemed little point in filling my day and my brain with knowledge about business and economics, when I wasn't sure I wanted to continue existing in a world I couldn't share with Anna.

I skipped a breath whenever I caught a glimpse of someone I thought was her. One drizzly evening, as I left the library, I saw a familiar-looking figure on the opposite pavement. She had her back to me, but her shoulder-length brown hair and the beige mac tied at the waist made me think it was Anna. I darted across the street, dodging the traffic.

'Anna! Anna!'

When I reached her and placed a hand on her shoulder, a startled stranger turned around. 'There's some mistake,' she said. She didn't look anything like Anna. Same build, same hair, but small, piggy eyes looking out of a round face.

'I'm so sorry,' I said, withdrawing my hand. 'I thought you... Well... A mistake, as you said.'

I walked away, my spirits sinking. If only, returning to my flat, I would find Anna there. If only she were the one brave enough to take the first step in the reconciliation for which I had begun to long.

At night, images would flash through my mind like random film clips. One moment I was kissing Anna in a remote corner of the Città Vecchia, the next she was clinging to Gior-

gio in the square before her house; now her eyes were all tenderness, a second later, they were blood-shot and rimmed by
shadows as she begged me to hear her out. Giorgio was right
– there must be a full explanation for her actions. She had giv-
en me an idea of what it was: fear that I'd feel compelled to
do 'the right thing' – and I had been incapable of listening
to another word. But what lack of faith in me! The thought
made me want to punch something, but now I didn't doubt
the selflessness of Anna's reasoning, however misguided it had
been.

Harrowing – an abortion must have been nothing short
of that, for her of all people, and yet she had gone through
with it. If she was already remorseful and distressed when I
surprised her in Ostuni, how had she coped with my reaction?
There were moments when panic seized me. Every so often,
the thought of De André's 'Marinella's Song' haunted me. But
no, in the version I had re-written for Anna, all ended well.
Yet memories of her sensitivity – her eyes filling with tears
during my account of how my father had died, for example
– set off a chain of terrifying conjectures. My heart galloped
and my muscles and nerves tensed up so badly that I couldn't
breathe; it was like having a lasso tightened around my ribcage
and knotted between my shoulder blades. The twinges made
me want to rush to the phone to make certain that Anna was
alive and to reassure her that I loved her, before it was too late.

What was this conjuring up of melodramatic scenarios,
I chided myself. I had read too much literature, and attended
too many operas at Bari's Petruzzelli Theatre. Anna was no
Dido, who had killed herself when abandoned – and I was
certainly no Aeneas bound for glorious deeds. Nor was she
some eighteenth or nineteenth-century heroine who dies of

heartache. Who did that in real life? No, deep down, Anna was strong. Gentle, but strong. I had got my stories mixed up. Epics and tragedy were so often based on absurdities. Instead, I should have been thinking of Aesop's fable of the mighty oak and the wispy reed in the storm – the reed was the one that survived. Surely, now that nearly three weeks had passed, Anna could see that my first reaction was perfectly understandable. Or might another man have behaved differently?

I don't know how many times I swung between panic and self-possession, until the thought of Anna's state eventually troubled me so much that even clinging to my studies as a haven of calmness didn't work anymore. I could ring her. The sound of each other's voices might restore us to serenity – a new kind of serenity, as recent events could hardly be erased. I'd be able to draw an easy breath again, and my heart would revert to its normal ticking. If Anna too was ready to understand and forgive, mutual reassurance would be a kind of baptism from which we'd emerge ready to start afresh.

But what if, when I rang, it wasn't her who picked up? Would her father or mother pass her the phone? Would they listen to me, or assail me with a barrage of accusations? Worse, might they simply hang up? And if they did call Anna, wouldn't they cluster around her as she spoke to me? Then, there would be no chance of a spontaneous conversation, and our stilted sentences might do anything but reconcile us. What if she refused to hear me out, and walked away?

A letter – that was the answer. It wouldn't matter if her parents read it too. At least, it would give me a chance to be heard: she would read and re-read what I had to say and reflect on it before responding. For two days I skived off lectures and stayed at home, trying to find the right words. I remember the final draft well. I was to end up re-visiting those words time and again until I had learnt them by heart and finally transcribed them – my defence witnesses – onto a sheet of paper:

Amore mio,

I failed you just when I should have shown you my love. Please don't tear up this letter without reading it. I beg you to hear me out. I don't seek to justify myself. I can't understand the emotions that overcame me, but I don't need to, to feel guilty and ashamed for having plunged you – I've no doubt of that, now – into misery. I know you thought you were acting for my good. I'll always love you. Please call or write to me at the address at the top of this letter, to tell me you're willing to see me – even once, so that we may part friends, if that is what you want. As for me, I would renew right now my proposal that we marry, were it not presumptuous to hope for so much. Please, Anna. Please.

I kissed the envelope before slotting it into the rusty-red post box at the bottom of my street.

For the first three days after posting the letter, I felt oddly light-hearted. I imagined Anna sitting down and holding the sheet of paper. At first, she would resist my words, but then she would let them heal us both. On the fourth day, I rushed to the flat after my morning lectures, convinced that she must have received the post and be rushing to call me straight away. I made myself a couple of fried eggs, and while they sizzled in the pan, listened for the phone in the hallway. But it did not ring. She probably imagines that I won't be home until later in the afternoon, I thought. But the phone remained silent when I returned from the afternoon lessons, too. 'Ah, the Italian post...' My letter was probably crushed among hundreds of others in a sack on a regional train chugging through Puglia.

For the next few days I swung between anticipation of Anna's call, and the instinct to rein in my hopes, with the balance shifting towards the latter. When after ten days I still hadn't heard, I reasoned that I had lost her. No doubt I'd be receiving a message telling me she couldn't forgive me. I had brought it on myself.

That morning, I couldn't find the strength to get up for lessons. It felt as if my heart were giving up. I lay on my unmade bed, disordered thoughts alternating with stupor. Eventually I roused myself to sit on the chair by the desk, my head between my hands. I stared at the textbooks and folders piled up on the oak-effect surface, at the chewed-up tops of biros and pencils, at the wrappings of the previous evening's cheese and crackers and at the adjustable lamp with its claw-like arm. I shoved it towards the wall and twisted its head to the ceiling so that it looked like a crumpled-up marionette. I almost felt sorry for it.

There was not a memento of Anna anywhere – I had brought none. That's when I realised that I had none in Ostuni, either: nothing that had been hers, only possessions of mine which she had touched and places that held memories of the two of us. Before I knew it, I was sobbing as I hadn't since I lost my father. Had my flatmates been in, they'd have imagined someone had died. In a way, they'd have been right.

Sleep eluded me: thoughts of a future without Anna crowded my mind. By morning, I knew there was only one way to avoid losing her. After forcing myself to wash, dress, and make myself an espresso, I stepped into the narrow hallway, picked up the phone and dialled her number. The ringing tone sounded like an echo of my heart beat. The eventual click at the other end of the line made me jump. My mouth and the back of my throat went so dry that I nearly choked.

'Erm, may I speak with Anna?'

'*Bastardo!*' said Mr. Saponaro. 'It's all your fault.'

'I want to put things right.' I struggled to make myself heard through the abuse.

'*Figlio di puttana!* Don't come anywhere close to my house or I swear I'll wring your spoilt little neck.'

I heard Mrs. Saponaro shouting to her husband, from a distance, not to hang up, till the row was muffled by what could only be a hand pressed against the receiver. Then, she seized control of the phone.

'Anna's not here.' Each word was sharp.

'Please, Mrs. Saponaro. Let me speak to her. I want to put things right.'

'I wish you could. But she's gone.'

'Where?'

'No idea. I had hoped you might know... *Gesú e María*, why us?' I heard her blow her nose into a handkerchief and begin to weep.

Heat rushed through my body. My head spun. I sat down on the floor, my back against the wall, my legs stretched out. I flattened the palm of my free hand against the floor tiles, but their coolness offered no relief. Sweat trickled down my temples as I waited for Mrs. Saponaro to stop crying.

'I read your letter,' she finally said. 'Two days after she had gone – that's when it arrived. Couldn't you have sent it earlier?' A misshapen cry, like a high-pitched hiccup, escaped her, but she pressed on. 'You stupid boy. Stupid, the two of you,' she screamed. 'So smart and so stupid!'

Nausea gripped my stomach. 'You must have some idea of where she is.'

'None. If you hear from her, promise to let us know. Promise.'

'I do, but...'

'Good.'

She hung up. I felt so sick that I nearly retched.

'Disappeared?' said Giorgio.

'You sound shocked,' I replied. 'I thought you knew – and you hadn't told me because you were still mad at me.' I paced up and down the meter of hallway to which the telephone cord tied me.

'Grow up. I reckoned you'd soon realise you had gone off your head.'

'Sorry. I should have called you before. To apologise.'

'Never mind about that now. You're sure Anna's parents didn't invent a story on the spot, just to keep you away from her?' Like me, he was speaking with such urgency that each word nearly tripped over the next.

'It did cross my mind. But the argument between them, his anger, her crying... Too real. I hoped you might know more.'

'No. Weird, though, to have kept it so quiet. I guess they want to avoid people talking – especially if they hope she'll come back. I don't get it. I thought she was getting better.'

'How do you mean?'

'I saw her – just once. But we spoke on the phone a couple of times. You were being a jerk. And I felt responsible, too – for having taken her along to your birthday party, for starters. When you came back from Milan and saw us in front

of her house – that was just because she didn't know who else
–'

'I figured,' I interrupted. 'Late, but I figured. Go on.'

'Her parents were calling her all kinds of things: *puttana*, *assassina*... Can you believe it? A sweet girl like Anna. The worst thing is, she thought maybe they were right. After you had gone, I rang her a few times to check how she was doing, but they wouldn't put me through. And then one day – maybe a couple of weeks after you had left – I called and she picked up. She was alone – not for long, she said, as there was almost always someone to keep an eye on her. Anyway, she was...'

His pause alarmed me. Searching for a precise word would have been a first for Giorgio. I knew him too well. He was the one with whom I had hidden under my parents' bed when we were six, making Concetta hunt for us throughout the house and the garden until I took pity on her panicked cries. He was the one for whom I 'covered' when we were sixteen by assuring his parents that we were slaving away at some homework, when he was at their summer villa with Samanta, the well-endowed *bona* from the year above. I could tell that something was stopping him from finishing his sentence.

'Well...?'

'Shit. I didn't think Anna would ever do anything so stupid.'

My nausea welled up again. 'You're scaring me. What did she say?'

'It's not what she said, it's how she said it. She was hysterical. She said she had killed her baby and that no one could forgive her: not you, not her parents, not God, so she was alone, alone, alone.' He let out a sigh. 'Now those words feel like three bullets. At the time, I thought: it's early days, soon enough she'll manage. That's what I believed, I swear. But maybe I shouldn't even be telling you this?'

'No, no, please carry on.' I leaned my head against the wall, closed my eyes and drew in a breath.

'Well, the second time I managed to speak to her, it wasn't much different. But the next – only about ten days ago – she finally sounded calmer. She gave me a day and a time to come by. I had to collect a letter for you, as... she wasn't intending to see you again.'

'Open it and read it to me.'

'I haven't got it. I went to her house, and she did give me it – at the door. We didn't speak much, but she looked better than the last time I had seen her – which was the same time you saw her. She was paler and thinner, but otherwise, her usual self. Do you understand why I thought she was finally coping ok?'

'Yes, yes. But where's the letter?'

'I went to your house and gave it to Concetta. She put it on the post tray in your hallway. I didn't want to get in touch with you – you had to calm down in your own time. But Tommi,' he paused, 'Call it instinct: I wouldn't ask Concetta to read you the letter from all this distance. Can you get yourself over here?'

CHAPTER 12

I have no recollection of buying an airplane ticket or of board-
ing a flight, though I must have done both things that very
morning. And I don't believe I packed a bag. Once in Bari or
Brindisi, I must have taken the train to Ostuni, which would
have stopped at every small town en route. Each station would
have looked much like the next: the stark lines of Fascist architecture softened by the building's minute scale and by Mediterranean pines and magnolias; the neon signs of the bar and
tabacchino; the patrons consuming espressos on the platform;
the tacky wares on pedlars' trays; and passengers scrambling
onto and off carriages. And yet all I remember is standing in
front of Anna's house. It must have been around five in the
afternoon, as the air had the spectral veil of that hour in late
October.

I'm sure I was wearing a leather jacket, because when Mr.
Saponaro answered the door and lunged at me, he grabbed
both sides of my collar. He held them so tightly while shaking
me that the twisting of the leather burnt my skin. Afterwards,
when I saw the streaks on my neck in the mirror whilst shav-
ing, or traced them with a finger, I accepted them as a warrant-
ed public branding. The Romans had marked fugitives with a
hot iron; criminals had shared that fate in other eras, too. My
marks, however, remained visible only for a few weeks.

I didn't try to refute the obscenities Mr. Saponaro was
yelling at me. Yes, I thought, I am an arsehole, a fucker, and
whatever else you say I am. You have every right to broadcast
it to the world. I wonder, now, if the commotion drew neigh-

bours to their windows and balconies. I expect it did, but in that moment only Mr. Saponaro and I existed, in a time warp which had swallowed us and where reality unfolded in slow motion. I had become an empty sack, all contents dispersed through a rip in the fabric.

I put up no fight, but stared into his narrowed dark eyes and at his flaring nostrils, his grey stubble, his clenched teeth, and at a tomato sauce stain on his unbuttoned shirt collar. I was gasping for breath, but that wasn't the reason for my passivity. His ferocity could only mean that something dreadful had happened to Anna because of me – something worse than running away from home – and if that was the case, I didn't want to go on. So I thought: if you want my life, it's yours to take. There, yours are the last pair of eyes I'll ever see, and I don't mind – it's as simple as that.

But he let go. I fell on all fours, with a thump of the knees on the paving stones. I drew in gulps of air on which I choked and wheezed. I don't know how long it took until my breath flowed unimpeded. Only then did I become conscious of the presence of a third person who now stood between me and Mr. Saponaro. I realised who it was even before my eyes travelled up from her feet to her head. Mrs. Saponaro was gripping her husband by his arms.

'Have you gone completely mad?' Panic had raised her tone to a screech. 'You want to kill the boy?'

Mr. Saponaro was not much taller than me, but he had a sturdy build next to which his wife and daughters had always struck me as insubstantial. He could easily have freed himself from the woman's grasp, but looked too stunned to respond.

'He's killed her,' he muttered.

'Don't say that. You don't know. She might be fine. Maybe he can help us find her.' She turned round to face me just as I staggered to my feet. The houses around me swayed. Mrs. Saponaro held me up by sliding her shoulder underneath one of my arms and grabbing my waist.

'*Signore Gesú*, what have you done?' she said to her husband, and looked at me again with a startled expression. 'I'd better take you inside.'

With her support, I lumbered indoors. Mr. Saponaro followed a few steps behind, grumbling indistinctly. 'Not you,' his wife said. 'You stay away.' She slammed the door behind the two of us.

'I'm going to get you, you bastard, you hear me?' Mr. Saponaro screamed. 'If Anna is dead, you're a dead man.'

Dizzy, I propped my back against the wall. At my side, Mrs. Saponaro stood immobile, sea-green eyes wide, listening out for her husband's movements. Now that her cheeks were drawn in and her jaw clenched, her face appeared angular and hard. I braced myself for more shouts and banging from the other side of the door, but after an interminable minute I heard Mr. Saponaro's soles shuffling on the flagstones and then the sound of his steps receding. I took a deep breath and exhaled; the sitting room – onto which the house door opened – seemed to expand in unison with my lungs. It was not large, but the traditional vaulted ceiling made it feel airy. I took another breath.

'You need to sit down.' Mrs. Saponaro's face had softened slightly. She made an offhand gesture towards the avocado-green couch at the centre of the room, and offered me her arm. We walked past the dining table reserved for big occasions, a lugubrious piece of dark furniture decked in an embroidered white cloth. At its centre gleamed a bowl of

Rossanas, crimson-wrapped sweets I had found sickly even as a child. I didn't know they still made them. Their scent added tartness to the room's usual odour, an acrid melange of cooking, round-the-seasons preserving of vegetables and jam-making, soil-stained boots, laundering and ironing, all saturating the limestone walls, from which humidity could never be fully expunged in this, as in so many other houses of the Old Town.

The foam inside the corduroy sofa had lost its elasticity but I was glad of its softness. I sank into it. It was like lying in bed when ill, propped up by pillows. Only now did I real-ise that my knees hurt and that my hands were scratched. My neck felt sore and ablaze. I rubbed it with my palms.

'Don't do that,' Mrs. Saponaro said. Her lips were pursed and her forehead furrowed in what I took to be pity, disgust and alarm. She pulled up a chair and settled opposite me. 'Maybe it needs ice. *Signore santo*. No, best leave it until it's not so raw.' She smoothed back her light brown hair with both hands.

For a moment I could almost see Anna in her, but that flash of resemblance had the effect of emphasising their differ-ences. It wasn't just that Anna's physical features were gentler – the arc of the eyebrow, the height of the cheekbones or the curve of the chin. The delicacy in the daughter's character was evident at first sight from her movements and speech. In the mother, hints of it merged with a rougher manner.

No less striking was the difference between the woman who had waived Anna and me off on the evening of our first dinner in Villanova and the one now before me. I remembered her appearance as being modest but neat. Today, her hair was a dull mass streaked with greasy tufts and her eyes bulged out of dark rings.

'Say something. Or does it hurt to speak?' she said.

I cleared my throat. 'What do you want me to say?'

'Bless God you haven't lost your tongue,' she said, clasping her hands. 'You hear of that, in the news. From shock.' She took a quick breath. 'You won't press charges, will you?'

'Charges?'

'Don't play dumb.' She covered her eyes with a hand and shook her head. 'Please don't report Pietro. It's bad enough not knowing where Anna is. Don't make me lose him, too.'

'Don't worry. It's all my fault, anyway.'

She lifted her head and observed me. 'Yours? Yes. And hers, his, mine... Pietro and me, we were tough on her, these last few weeks. We had to be: with the stuff the two of you had got up to. And with what she did next! But afterwards, she couldn't take it, could she? Must have been more upset than she let on.'

She rose slowly from her chair. 'You might as well see her letter,' she said, without meeting my eyes, and walked the few steps towards the mahogany sideboard behind me. On it, I glimpsed the grey Bakelite telephone Anna must have held in her hands whenever I called – the same telephone I now longed to have rung just a few days earlier. Why hadn't I plucked up my courage before? From one of the drawers, Mrs. Saponaro took out a sheet of paper folded in half. I recognised it from the grainy ecru of the reverse.

Anna and I had spotted it in the window of a bookshop, on a May afternoon in Brindisi, and had exchanged knowing grins. A little owl was sketched in sepia on the bottom right-hand corner of each sheet. They came in a handsome wallet of tawny cardboard embossed in white with the same drawing.

'Ah! I must buy it for you,' I said.

'Why for me?'

'Because I have a little owl already, whereas you don't. So, for luck?'

'You don't believe in luck.'

'Maybe I do now. You are my luck and my wise friend.' I straightened up in mock solemnity and stretched out my arms as if holding an offering. 'I'll make sacrifices at your altar, O divine one.'

'Good job you're joking.' She laughed. 'I bet that someone who's quick to put you on a pedestal is just as quick to knock you off it.'

'Never,' I said, and, taking her by the hand, stepped into the bookshop. We left with a gift-wrapped packet of the writing paper dangling in a carrier bag from her wrist.

'I've looked for clues in it – something that says where she is,' Mrs. Saponaro said, jolting me back to the sitting room, to my bruised knees and neck, and to her tensed up features. 'But there's nothing'.

She handed me the note. I began shaking and clenched my teeth to stop them clattering. I unfolded the letter:

Dear Mum, dear Dad,

Sorry to have given you such pain. Forgive me. The only way out now is for me to leave. Don't look for me.

Anna

'Is this it?' I said aloud, to myself. I flipped the paper onto its reverse, hoping it contained something more, although I knew it was blank. What did it mean? Was the real message unwritten – and for me rather than for her parents?

'That's it,' Mrs. Saponaro said, her back to me. Her restless hands picked up and rearranged some of the objects displayed on the sideboard: a pair of porcelain figurines in eighteenth-century dress, typical souvenir of a wedding; a snow globe containing a statuette of Padre Pio which by being lifted found itself in a blizzard; and a fading photograph of a girl – perhaps one of Anna's great-grandmothers – on the day of her First Communion.

'Much good it did, to show that letter to the police – *bastardi*,' she said, turning around and snatching back the note. 'As far as they're concerned, it proves she has chosen to leave, so she's not a missing person. Over eighteen. As if that made her an adult. They won't look for her.'

'Didn't you tell them what happened?'

'We did. I'm surprised the shame didn't kill us: having to air our dirty linen in public, for love of the little slut.' She scrunched her hands into fists and clasped them to her chest as if wanting to punch or hug her daughter, I couldn't tell.

'Anyway,' she continued, 'we show them her note, and this fat old *poliziotto*, who while taking down our details has been looking like he couldn't give two hoots, suddenly lifts his face from the typewriter and I think, 'Ah, now he gets why we're dead worried – ripe time!' But no, the porker gets up, plants his hands on the desk and leans towards Pietro, who is a good head shorter than him.

'This letter isn't genuine, is it?' he says. At first, we don't get what he's driving at. Then he calls a colleague – a younger man with a sharp, gelled-back hair cut. They move just far enough for us not to manage to make out what they're whispering. When they return, they take us into separate rooms. I end up in the one with the smug young peacock. There's only a table in there, with a chair either side; the window has bars and the paint is peeling off the walls; there's a smell of disinfectant, like in hospitals, which says what kind of scum gets dragged in.

'I know it's difficult,' the *poliziotto* says, putting on an understanding tone I don't fall for. 'But if your husband has harmed your daughter, you must denounce him.'

'Harmed Anna?'

'Do you know or suspect of anything?' he continues. 'You'd be an accessory to a crime if you were trying to cover up for him.'

'Cover up for what?'

'Well, with what he's been calling your daughter, I wonder. Let me make it easier for you by suggesting what you might be finding hard to tell me. Did your husband hit your daughter so badly that she ran away? Or in his rage might he accidentally – which only makes it manslaughter, you understand – have killed her?'

And I say, 'No, no, a thousand times no! We came to you for help and this is the help you give? *Disgraziati!* Pietro's no criminal. And he has every right to call our daughter any name he likes – because she has turned out to be a *puttana* and an *assassina*. But she's our daughter and we want her home.' And we *do* want her home – or at least we need to know she hasn't gone off to crown it all with the worst of all sins. It's not for us to know the Lord's ways: even Judas might have been saved if he hadn't hanged himself.'

'But so, how can you...?' I stared at her. 'A whore and a murderer?' I could picture Anna moving among the furniture and objects in this very room, just days earlier, and being sucked into the vortex of condemnation.

'Don't get on your high horse, *giovanotto*. She said you had accused her of it too, though not in the same words. You use posh language and that makes it all right, eh?'

I opened my mouth to reply but couldn't. She was right. I leaned back into the sofa and closed my eyes. Darkness spun inside my head, and the nausea of earlier welled up once more. 'Alone, alone, alone.' Anna and Giorgio's voices, intermingled, echoed in my ears.

'Surely this can wait,' my mother said. She didn't shift her gaze in the direction of her bedroom door, where I was standing, but finished doing up her beige cardigan, paying such attention to each shiny button that you'd have thought they were made of real gold.

'Give me a second to tidy up and we can talk calmly downstairs,' she added. From the bed, she picked up the navy blue suit jacket out of which she had changed and placed it on a wooden hanger, adjusting the shoulder pads and stroking the cloth to smooth it down. The mirrors of the wide open wardrobe doors reflected back her image from different angles.

'No. I want to know right now. What do you mean, you've never seen the note?' I said.

'Well, as it must have been addressed to you and not to me, I presume I might have seen it but taken no notice.' She shrugged. 'How am I to remember it now?'

'It sounds odd. It's not as if letters addressed to me arrive here every day.' I stepped outside the bedroom and called out, 'Concetta!'

'In the kitchen,' she shouted from downstairs.

'Please come up. It's urgent.'

'So is your dinner. It's not going to cook itself.'

'It's much more important than dinner.'

She came muttering up the steps, while my mother, imperturbable, hung up her suit trousers and folded away a silk scarf.

'It'd better be important,' my *tata* said when she emerged from the stairs, carrying with her the aroma of *braciole al sugo*, the meat parcels she had been preparing. She re-arranged her apron, tugging at the blue gingham and flattening the skirt with her damp palms. 'What's so urgent?'

'Ten days ago Giorgio brought you a letter for me. He says you put it on the post tray in the hall. But it's not there and Mum doesn't remember seeing it. Where is it?'

'I... I don't know.' Her gaze shifted rapidly from me to the floor and then back to me again.

'For goodness' sake, it can't have evaporated.'

Concetta looked behind me at my mother. I turned to catch Mum's expression, but her thin-lipped smile gave nothing away. As for her light brown irises, I might as well have stared into a porcelain doll's. I strode towards her, followed by Concetta.

'For Christ's sake, give me that letter. It's my only hope of finding Anna. She has run away from home.'

For once, my mother's eyes widened. She took two steps backwards. 'What?' she said. 'I didn't know.'

'I've already seen her parents.' I instinctively raised a hand to my neck – the scarf I had put on was successfully concealing the weals. 'She has left them no clues. Whatever's in that letter is... vital.'

Concetta clasped her hands together so tightly that her fingers turned sallow. My mother stiffened and looked anxiously at her. I clutched my *tata*'s arms, staring into her face.

'Please. Anna might do something terrible – if she hasn't yet. And it'll all have been my fault.'

I turned towards my mother. 'I shouldn't have listened to you. When I spoke on the phone with her, and she sounded so distressed, I didn't imagine... And I made it so much worse when I met her. But you, Mum, you...'

'Are you blaming me, now?'

'Yes.' I stepped closer. 'You, with all your talk of how she was some gold-digger and how my suspicions of her and Giorgio might not be all that ludicrous and how she'd just get over me. Well, she couldn't and you know what? I can't get over her.'

'*Bravo*, yes, blame me.' Her composure regained, she managed to make me feel looked down on from on high. She held herself in a signature pose: shoulders level, arms only seemingly relaxed, hands in her lap, head tilting upward – a loss to royal portraiture.

'All I had to go on was what you told me,' she continued, her tone impassive. 'You didn't have to accept my advice. You've got a fine brain – funny you didn't use it that day, or on subsequent ones, to reach a conclusion of your own.'

'I trusted you,' I shouted.

'Keep your voice down – we aren't heathens. I'll tell you what's going on: with hindsight, you think you should have acted differently. Well, now don't pin your decision on me. As for the letter, I expect it ended up in the bin by mistake. For that, I'm very sorry. With the heaps of post I have to sift through every day... It's extremely unfortunate, but I can't think what else might have happened.'

I threw my hands up. 'I don't believe you. But I haven't got time to waste.' I stomped past Concetta, who trailed after me to the staircase and kept calling out my name until I slammed the house door behind me.

Outside, I rested against the wall, eyes to the evening sky. Why was the scent of the first fallen leaves from the fig and almond trees in our garden so stomach-churning? And how could the light pollution from our small town blot out the stars?

'Think, Tommaso, think', I told myself. 'Where would Anna have gone, if feeling abandoned by everyone?'

It occurred to me, with a twinge, that on the night we had first met, on the terrace, I had told her we can never feel lonelier than in the company of people who don't understand us. We had spoken more than once of that encounter: of the mutual sensation of being wholly known. And now she must think that the mysterious connection between us had been an illusion. There was no one left: not Lidia, not Giorgio, both of whom she loved but whose ways of being in the world were alien to her; and certainly not her family.

God – there was God. Surely, Anna would find some comfort in the merciful God of her faith. For once, I wanted Him to exist. But a moment later I recalled Giorgio's words – had our conversation really taken place only that morning? I broke into a sweat and unwrapped the scarf from my neck. 'Alone, alone, alone,' because she thought neither I, nor her family, nor God could forgive her.

What is there to lose by cutting your life short if it's become unbearable and you're one of the walking damned? Why not cease suffering, and hope there's nothing beyond? If there is, what difference will a few more years on Earth make, when compared with eternity? I shivered – the perspiration covering my body had turned to ice.

The parish priest – maybe Anna had spoken with him before disappearing. Her mother had probably taken her to see him after learning of the abortion – as she definitely had learnt of it, judging by the fact she called her daughter a murderer. Anna would not have lied to her parents, just as she hadn't lied to me. She would have wanted them to love her as she was – her, not a fake. Why live a lie and then feel that others love not you but a phony image? Far better to do without.

Maybe that's another reason why I haven't let things get too close between Zoe and me. I'd have to deceive her, as I couldn't bear facing regularly a woman who knows the story I'm telling you. It'd be like having a mirror held up to me time and again.

On the other hand, she has probably imagined countless scenarios as explanations for my past and already forgiven me each of my conceivable crimes. I admit it: now I realise she loves me and that she'd probably still love me if she knew what happened. But it is I who can't forgive myself. So it's best not to tell Zoe anything and to try living in the present – forgetting the past as much as possible. Just like Anna, I've no desire to be loved for someone I'm not. Better to do without love.

I haven't been to confession since I was ten, but this conversation with you can't be all that different. Not that I'm ever likely to do that again: the proverbial lost sheep returning to the fold – not me. But I've always thought that Mrs. Saponaro must have dragged Anna to confession the moment she found out what had happened. I suspect Anna repented of the abortion but not of our having made love because her love was too real to renege on it. I'll never know for sure, of course. But I strongly suspect that she made her peace with God in that respect – it might mean that she could aspire no higher than the lowliest sphere of Heaven, but it was the price of integrity.

As I leaned against the wall of Villa Emma, on the evening of my hasty return to Ostuni, I pictured the parish priest in his confessional, aghast at unexpected resistance from this devout girl. He had probably known her since birth – christened her, smiled benevolently at her and the other children playing hopscotch as he passed them in the cathedral square, and, later, even taken pride in her achievements when her mother rattled on about them. To him, they were signs of the Lord's grace – it was He who distributed talents and He who eventually called us to account. And now it fell to him, to the parish priest, to save this young woman's soul as it tottered on the brink of eternal damnation. I could almost hear him giving her a lecture brimming with visions worthy of Dante's *Inferno*. Poor Anna. And how had I – I, of all people – ended up inflicting the coup de grâce? A difference of a few days, and we would not only have been together but engaged.

The best I could do was not lose any more time. I rushed across the garden to the parking shelter, threw the grimy waterproof cover off my motorbike, opened the gate, and rode as fast as I could towards the Old Town.

CHAPTER 13

I had to ring the bell twice before someone came to open the parish house door.

'Have patience,' a male voice said while the lock clicked once, twice, three times, revealing a short, lean man with a round face. A thick napkin tucked into his white shirt covered the front of a brown sweater. The grey hair at the sides of his balding head and the lines around his mouth suggested he might be in his fifties, though the lively dark eyes searching me from behind a pair of John Lennon spectacles hinted at a younger man.

'What can I do for you at this hour?' He wrinkled his forehead.

I glanced at my watch: eight o'clock. Was this the cathedral's priest or his lay sacristy assistant?

'I need to talk to the *parroco*. Is that you?'

He scrutinised me. Then he stretched out his hand, 'Don Luigi. Parish priest – for my sins, no doubt. Do come in.'

I shook his hand. 'Tommaso.'

I followed him through a dark corridor, at the end of which a light shone from a room. It turned out to be the kitchen, a 1950s time capsule with the units in pale yellow plastic, with handles like those of old American gas-guzzlers.

'I was almost done with my supper,' he said. 'But you look like you could use some food, son. Are you ok?'

I wasn't his son nor his God's, but his kindness didn't deserve a fractious retort. And his question flustered me. I probably did look out of sorts: the day had been interminable and it wasn't finished; but though I hadn't eaten since breakfast, I wasn't hungry.

'I take it you'll have a bite,' the priest said. He opened the door of the unit above the sink, and from a draining rack pulled out a dry plate, two glasses and cutlery, which he laid at the head of the table on a PVC tablecloth. 'There. While you eat you can tell me how I can help.'

I sat down, and he opposite me, where a half-eaten slice of bread and cheese was waiting. He passed me the bread basket and a wooden board with fresh *scamorza* on it. Then he poured me water from a jug, and red wine from an unmarked bottle.

'I'm not one of you,' I blurted out. 'I'm an atheist. You should know.'

He smiled. 'What – in case you have no right to the food?'

'I'm not hungry.' I moved the wooden board close to him. 'Have you seen Anna Saponaro? About a week ago? Did she come to confession? Do you know where she is?'

'Slow down,' he said. 'Which Anna Saponaro?'

'She's nineteen... Assunta and Pietro Saponaro's...'

'Ah – thought so.' He brought a hand to his chin and nodded. 'Her boyfriend...?'

'Yes.'

He sighed. 'I'm not allowed to tell you – or anyone – if she came to confession.' He pushed up his spectacles and squinted.

I leaned forward. 'But you can tell me if you've seen her.'

'Yes. Unfortunately I haven't.' He opened up his arms, palms upwards.

'I'm worried. I'm worried she might have... I can't even say it. D-do you think she could have?'

He pressed his lips together. 'The type to run away from home? I didn't think so. It's unbelievable. But the type to... to... No, definitely not, son.'

'How do you know 'the type'? How do you know what might drive someone to it?'

'It's not as if anyone can be sure. But Anna has strong faith.'

'It didn't stop her from having an abortion. Would you have imagined her doing that?'

'No.' He traced the edge of his plate with a finger. 'She was the very last person I'd have imagined doing that.'

'But if she has surprised you twice, she could surprise you a third time, right?' I grabbed my wine glass and half-emptied it.

'No, no.' He shook his head. 'What you're thinking about is different. Everyone baulks at that threshold – Christians especially. Final. There's a kind of holy terror...' he said, gesticulating. 'Heaven knows how many lives it has saved. Afterwards, most people are grateful they didn't go through with it.'

'And if she has gone through with it? Surely, your God wouldn't punish her? If unhappiness drills so deeply that...' I tightened my grip on the glass.

'I... I don't know.'

'But you must know,' I said, banging the glass on the table without meaning to. A purplish-red stain spread over the tablecloth. Don Luigi jumped back in his chair, but recomposed himself.

'I'm so sorry.' I hung my head.

'It's nothing. Don't worry.' He cleared his throat. 'About

your question – I know what the Doctors of the Church have written, but...'

'But?'

'But God's mercy may be greater than we can conceive of. His ways are not our ways.'

'Heard that one before.'

'Then for once let it comfort you.'

'I told you, I don't believe.'

'You talk as if you do.'

'Well, I don't. I'm asking for Anna's sake. She deserves a God who'll show her compassion – the compassion the rest of us lacked. If your God exists, He must know that. You do understand?'

'I do.' He nodded. 'But please, don't leap to such... morbid conclusions. I still don't think she's done what you're afraid of. She'll come back, you'll see.'

'I hope you're right.' I stood up and offered him my hand. He held it in both of his. 'I'll pray for the two of you.'

'Don't bother praying for me. I wish you had prayed that Anna would never meet me, months ago.'

I stepped into the dimly lit corridor and made my way to the exit, walking ahead of the priest.

'I hope you didn't mean that – about never having met each other,' he said at the door. 'There's much to be said for hope – despair unleashes all manner of evils.'

Pushing my motorbike for the last two hundred metres of the steep road to Villa Emma was tougher than I thought. My arms and legs hurt, but I kept the engine switched off. My mother mustn't hear me arriving.

Our iron gate didn't give me away. Its lock slid open and shut with only a faint hiss. I manoeuvred the motorbike noiselessly into the parking shed. Across the garden stood Villa Emma, the ghost of its daytime self, its white form blurry in the glow of the lamps among the grass. A gush of light shone through a parting in my mother's bedroom curtains. All was silent in the garden: no crickets at this time of year, and no passing cars. Even the scent of rotting leaves, which had made me queasy less than two hours earlier, now seemed dormant.

I trod softly on the paving stones leading to the house, then tiptoed towards the kitchen at the rear. Concetta, with her back to me, was taking clean plates out of the dishwasher and stacking them on the worktop. I tapped on the window pane. When she turned, I pressed a finger to my lips and gestured to her to open the kitchen's back door.

'There you are – your mother's in a state,' she whispered. 'Run upstairs. Tell her you're back. Make peace.'

'Never mind my mother.' I walked over to the door between the kitchen and the sitting room, and closed it softly.

'She didn't even want dinner. She's gone to lie down with some drops of *calmante*.'

'Oh, poor Mummy. As if. I saw the way you exchanged looks, the two of you. You wanted to tell me something, didn't you? And she was scared.'

Concetta bent over the dishwasher, pulled out the cutlery basket and plumped it onto the worktop.

'Please. I'm afraid...' I stepped closer. 'If Anna... It'll all have been my fault.'

'Why?' She emptied the cutlery basket with a clanking of steel onto granite, and began sorting forks, knives and spoons, still without glancing at me.

'Because it's true.' I stared at the cracked ceramic jug crammed with wooden cooking spoons, next to the hob. The traditional local motif, a colourful cockerel striding forward, riled me. I was tempted to throw something at it.

'Maybe it isn't true.' Concetta put down a fistful of forks, and placed her hands on her hips. 'Great position, your mother's put me in. I don't deserve it. I don't know which of you to...'

'To what? To be loyal to?'

She nodded and let go a full-cheeked huff.

'Then just tell me the truth.'

She studied me, a concerned expression on her face, and nodded again.

'Not much else I can do, is there?' She paused, as if she were thinking better of it.

'So?'

'I saw your mother picking up that letter.'

'And opening it?'

'Yes.'

'I knew it.' I punched the air and made for the kitchen door.

'Wait. Wait.'

I turned around.

'She... She burnt it.'

'What?'

'Right here.' She motioned to one of the cooking rings.

I gaped at her, then at the hob. I pictured my mother setting the match to the little sepia owl in the corner of the writing paper, watching the fire spread and consume the sheet. A flame scorched me inside.

'No. No,' I said.

Concetta opened her lips, and pressed them together.

I rubbed my forehead. 'At least, it means Mum knows where Anna is. She's got to tell me. And then I'll have my Anna back, and we'll... Thank you, Concetta.' I hugged her, squeezing her fleshy arms. She smelled of the parsley, garlic and pecorino cheese with which she had stuffed the meat parcels now simmering on the hob.

She didn't return my hug with her customary warmth. 'There's more,' she said, in a monotone.

'Oh?'

'Your mum... I heard her talking on the phone with Dr. Ruggero, the obstetrician.'

'When?'

'The first time must have been about a week after you left for Milan.'

I guffawed. 'Oh! It has nothing to do with Anna, then.'

'Of course it does.'

'Impossible. A week would make it, what? The nineteenth of September. And Mum didn't know Anna was pregnant until I told her. Which wasn't till the twenty-fourth – that's the day I was back in Ostuni. And by then... no pregnancy... anymore.'

'You can be as sure as you like of your dates. But signora Emma knows more than she's letting on.' She shifted her weight onto one hip, and sighed. 'Do you think this is easy for me? You and your mother – you need to talk.'

'Yes. Mum had better explain herself.'

'You had no right to destroy it. What did it say?' I asked through gritted teeth.

At least my mother had admitted to opening the letter

and burning it. A victory of sorts. Still seated, she glared at me through the mirror of her dressing table. She scrunched the cotton wool pad with which she had removed her make-up and chucked it into the wastepaper bin. The clinical light of her beauty lamp exposed the wrinkles around her eyes and mouth.

'Sentimental stuff.' She peeled off her headband and slung it onto the table surface. Her hair fell back in a bob. She brushed back a tuft which had fallen on her eyebrow.

'It can't have been only what you call 'sentimental stuff'. She must have said where she was going.'

'On the contrary.' My mother raised herself abruptly from her stool and turned around to face me. I shrank back, repelled by her reek of chemical concoctions.

'She said not to look for her – she was getting out of your life for good and without a grudge. The girl has read too many novels, if you ask me.'

'Oh, shut up.'

'How dare you? After all I've done for you.' Her voice was steely.

'Exactly what do you think you've done for me? It was you, wasn't it? You made her have the abortion.'

'Yes.' She looked me in the eyes. 'And you should be thankful.'

'Thankful? Oh my God.'

'Don't say that.'

She could have been speaking to a toddler, not me.

'I'll say as much as I like. I mean, you... you... and then you care about the name of God?'

I chortled and was so overcome by laughter, that I had to hold my stomach. Tears rolled down my cheeks. Laughing, or crying – I wasn't sure – I tottered towards the wardrobe and leaned against it. My mother remained standing by her dressing table, watching me with a troubled expression. She didn't speak until my fit died down.

'It was the only practical thing to do. God forgive me,' she said in a quiet voice. 'But you're both so young.'

'Not too young to make up our own minds. What the hell did you say to make Anna do something so...?'

'Never mind what I said. It worked.' She took a couple of steps forward, then halted, keeping her distance. She tilted her head.

'Look, Tommaso: yours was an error of youth, but now you're both free. You'll get over it, so will she.'

'She won't. She has disappeared, I told you.'

'A bluff. Must be.' She nodded to underline her certainty.

'You don't know her.'

'Whereas you do?' She edged a step closer and opened her arms. 'If she loves you, how can she do this to you? A bluff and a punishment – great love, that shows. No, darling, you fell for the oldest trick on earth. A serious girl would have waited until she was married, before... well... you know.'

'You've got her so wrong. Giorgio said she was in a terrible state. She must have thought I had abandoned her. It was too much, on top of...' I held my head in my hands.

'Oh, please.' She placed her palms on my shoulders. 'This is just the kind of response she was aiming for. And you've fallen for it.'

For once, her tone was warm, and her face the picture of concern. She actually believed her own words.

'You know what?' I locked eyes with her. 'You're deluded. Completely. Anna might be killing herself right now, if she hasn't done it yet. You're the one responsible, and you can't bloody see it.'

I shook her hands off me. She stared. Her lips trembled.

'No.' She backed away.

'Oh yes. When I came to see you, you pretended you didn't know anything.'

'It was for your own good.' She swallowed.

'I can decide what's for my good and what isn't. If you had told me that you were behind an action... so unlike Anna, I'd have understood everything. I'd never have left for Milan.'

'And what, then, would have been the point of it all?' She sounded hoarse now, as if her throat were parched. 'Why couldn't she just tell you it was a miscarriage?'

'You still don't understand her reasons, do you? And you had no qualms making me believe that Giorgio betrayed me too.'

'You were the one who suggested it first.'

'But you knew it wasn't true. It just suited your plans, right?'

'It was all for your future, Tommaso.'

'Your idea of my future, you mean. And for that, you were willing to sacrifice my best friend, too? Then I'd really have been left alone.'

'You have me. I might not be one of those effusive mothers who have to keep saying how much they love their children, but love is made of deeds.'

I interrupted her. 'I've seen your deeds, and if that's what your motherly love is made of, I can do without it.' I shook my head and walked towards the bedroom door. 'You disgust me.' I turned back to face her and with slow, deliberate emphasis, said, 'I am not your son.'

'Where are you going?' she shrieked, rushing after me.
'Where do you think? To find Anna.'

CHAPTER 14

My motorbike leaned far into the curves of the road into town, hugging the contours of the hill. I raced past the few cars in my path, heedless of what might be coming around the hairpin bends. If I found myself staring into the lights of a juggernaut, so be it.

The engine's vibrations rushed through my legs and arms. Its scream blared from ear to ear inside my helmet. The darkness, broken by the beams of the occasional vehicle and roadside lamp, swallowed me up. On the adjoining hill, the windows of the Old Town sparkled like fairy lights in a nativity scene. Most people were in their homes, finishing off late suppers or watching television shows whose chief attraction was skimpily clad soubrettes.

The inconsistency involved in dreaming that their daughters would one day become starlets on such shows didn't seem to strike most Ostunesi, let alone bother them – I wouldn't have been surprised to learn that Anna's parents were no exception. How many of my schoolmates, and their mothers and grandmothers, were called Assunta after the Cathedral's patron saint? The name referred to the absurd dogma of a virgin mother beamed up to Heaven so that her body would remain uncorrupted even in death. The idea of young women named after the Assumption cavorting in titillating outfits on television was almost funny. But the mentality behind the inconsistency wasn't. Without fear of their neighbours' judgment, might my mother and Anna's parents have behaved differently? Might they have been less self-righteous? Cowardice was the mother of cruelty.

Of my own cruelty towards Anna I was only too aware. 'I want to put things right,' I repeated to myself like a mantra as I entered Via Pola. I had said it to Mr. Saponaro and wished I could say it to Anna, face to face. If only I could find her. I rode past the turning for the Liceo Classico. What if she were wandering near it, imagining that I'd look for her there? With a U-turn, I screeched into the side street.

In front of the school, I dismounted, took off my helmet and placed it on the seat. I stepped towards the gate – closed. I gripped its white metal bars and shook them. The eucalyptus and pine trees in the school forecourt rustled with the puff of a cold breeze, releasing their gentle scent.

'Anna!' I called out softly. Then 'Anna!' I shouted.

I marched around the perimeter, calling out her name. A middle-aged man, walking his Dobermann, eyed me guardedly while his beast fouled the pavement.

'No, I'm not the one who sprayed the latest graffiti on the school wall, but I might just start, if you keep looking at me like that,' I thought of saying.

Back on Via Pola, I slowed my motorbike at the bus stop where Anna had refused my lift, back in March. No trace of her there, now – only the memory of my overconfident 'Jump on' and her awkward 'No, thanks' while her class mates sniggered.

'If only you hadn't given me a second chance,' I thought. 'But please wait, now. Don't do anything stupid. I'll find you. Help me find you. And everything will be all right.' I had never believed in telepathy, but for once I was willing to allow for the possibility.

I carried on down the boulevard until the corner where

Cicinedda, the watermelon vendor, would have been open at this time, were it summer. I stopped. The gazebo where Anna and I sat on our return from Ceglie, surrounded by other young couples and the radio's blare, was boarded up for the night. Too cold, now. Only two days to go and it would be *I Morti*, All Souls.

One of the metal beams holding up the gazebo glinted. I looked for the source of the reflected light. A full moon had emerged out of a cloud cover so thick that in the darkness it had been invisible – until it had illuminated the misty forms encircling it. Not for long – within a minute the clouds' outlines shifted and merged into one another. The moon disappeared again. It seemed impossible that the vision had been real.

I sped down the hill towards Piazza della Libertá and turned into Via Cattedrale. 'I bet up north you'll miss our bakeries – and more,' Anna had said the first time we climbed that street together.

'It's you I miss,' I thought.

I took a deep breath, seeking out the comforting aroma of fresh bread, *tarallini* and biscuits which permeated the street in the daytime. But the doors of the bakery were shut. All I breathed in were the fumes of my Suzuki. Under the street lamps, the humidity-clad flagstones glistened. I pushed on.

'*Mi manchi*' – 'I miss you' – I repeated in my head like an incantation.

When I reached Piazzetta Cattedrale I wasn't surprised to find all the doors locked: those of the church, the diocesan centre and library, and the souvenir shop which in summer would have stayed open late, luring tourists in with the colourful array of traditional ceramic whistles in the windows.

A young couple who had been kissing under the baroque passage linking the seminary and the bishop's residence scuttled away when I got off my motorbike.

I plumped myself down on the steps of the cathedral, spreading my hands over the cold, wet stone. The chinks at the edges were smooth under my fingertips. My palms settled inside faint depressions – white against white – unnoticeable to the eye. Anna and I had sat right here as she listened to my account of my father's final months. How I wished for her hand on my shoulder now – now that I felt more bereft than ever.

I turned to the bas-relief of the enthroned Virgin and Child above the church's portal.

'What good could ever come of making an idol out of you?' I thought. 'Can any woman approach the ideal of a virgin mother, of a demi-goddess without flaws, ever obedient? Real human beings are creatures of... embodied feeling. If the ones around Anna and me didn't equate chastity with goodness, our child might still be alive in *her* womb, and she'd be with me.'

I got up and kicked the step where I'd been sitting. The cold humidity of the night seeped through my leather jacket. Rubbing my arms, I wandered off in search of other places which held memories of Anna. The scarlet bougainvillea at whose feet we had often sat, by an abandoned house in a cul-de-sac, was now a web of dried up, dark brown branches. It clung to the wall with roots like fangs and was shorn of everything but spiky stems. The air reeked of dank walls and the putrefying foliage of the bushes growing through the floors of the roofless house. I could see it through slits between the shutters. In the other alleys and squares through which I roamed, the oleanders had lost all flowers and many had been pruned, so that they had a portly, constricted appearance.

I didn't know what agitated me more: the unaltered wayside shrines of our love, where I half-expected Anna to appear at any moment and where her absence was a physical, petrifying fact; or the ones which had changed so greatly that the loss of their spring and summer guise was a bereavement.

At this time of night I'd never get a proper look at the most sacred site in the topography that was all our own. She might be there. And if not, she might have left me a clue to finding her. I'd be there at first light.

The day's events, the sleepless night and my empty stomach were making my head woozy and my legs rickety. Time to lie down for a few hours. I trudged back towards the cathedral to pick up my motorbike and ride back to Villa Emma. It might no longer feel like home, but it promised a mattress and a pillow. I'd slink in and out of the house, to avoid my mother. And if she heard me? If she lay awake, with her ears primed for the sound of my steps on the staircase, and opened her bedroom door demanding we speak? I'd tell her I was too exhausted to talk – it'd have to wait until morning.

I had never seen the colour of the sea shifting between moss, slate and ash. But then, I had never been on a beach when the sun had barely risen and dense clouds hovered above the water. The first autumn storms had washed away swathes of sand, exposing serrated, liver-brown rocks and leaving behind mounds of tangled algae – posidonia, among them. A cold wind carried their pungency to my nostrils and coated me in spray. Shivering, I trod on moist sand, following the sea line, my ears filled with the heaving and sighing of the waves.

The crescent-shaped promontory hadn't changed. Its dense vegetation seemed to emerge out of the water. The sharp rocks surrounding it bore the brunt of the waves' lashing. My steps quickened when I reached the sandy path through the trees, the shrubs and the grasses. My pulse throbbed in my neck. The familiar sight and scents of the juniper and *ammofila* and of the oregano, laurel and rosemary bushes stirred my hopes. Yes, Anna could be here.

Our kind oak, our magic tree, appeared before me as if I had stood in its clearing only yesterday and it were still summer.

'Anna. Anna. I'm here.'

I listened – only the swishing of leaves and grasses in the wind, the shriek of a seagull. I edged close to the oak. My legs felt boneless, my body hot and clammy. I swallowed before going on all fours to peer through the opening in the low-slung canopy.

But *l'albero magico* harboured no one. I sank to my elbows, winded, my forehead against the ground. I raked in handfuls of sand and clenched my fists until the grains in my grip stung. When I raised my eyes, they had adjusted to the shade. I crawled deeper inside and caressed the sand where Anna's head had rested; where my fingers brushed through her hair as I raised her face to mine and we kissed; where she looked at me with such trust that her eyes seemed both deeper and transparent, like the sea. In them I was free and safe. In them I could lose myself only to find myself a better man. When we last lay here together I had imagined a lifetime of losing and finding ourselves in each other's eyes. Now there was only cold sand. Out of the corner of my eye, I saw a small right-angled shape, half-buried. Brushing the sand away revealed a tawny cardboard wallet. For a moment, I was unable to breathe.

The wallet held 'our' writing paper: the one with the little owl sketched in sepia in the right-hand corner. Trembling, I lifted the flap and took out the sheets. I leafed through them. A biro fell out.

'Please, Anna, tell me where to find you.'

All the sheets were empty, bar one. I scrambled into the dawn light to make out the writing. There were a couple of scribbled lines, both crossed out. I didn't waste time getting up, but sat on my knees with the piece of paper stretched between my shaky hands.

'Our happy memories cannot be taken from us,' read the first line, followed by 'So much to say, that however hard I try, it keeps defeating me: nothing I write seems to do it justice.' She had substituted that 'it' with an 'us', then reverted to 'it', and finally scrapped the whole sentence, with two slashes of ink.

I read her words again and again, at one time taking them in and the next gazing at them without absorbing a single one. In front of me, a black beetle crawled on the sand, sliding in a flurry of grains down each hollow, and then stubbornly clambering up despite the failure of hold after hold.

'Our happy memories...' I remembered clearly what Anna had said after we first made love. So happy, she wouldn't mind dying there and then. Lucretius. Epicurus. No fear of death. Whatever happened, that magical moment in the shade of our oak would remain eternal.

Hadn't Lucretius supposedly killed himself?

What was this message Anna had reserved for me? A note to hint at what she was about to do – what by now she must have done? When? How? Oh, God, oh, God. This way, her parents could still hold out hope. Not I. If her body were found, they could still believe it had been an accident. Not I. They could delude themselves it hadn't been their fault. The absence of an unambiguous note – was it an act of compassion towards them? But the hint left behind for me – the hint that was bound to overwhelm me with the memory of when she had uttered those words and leave me in no doubt as to their meaning – was it my final sentence? For me, no pity? Still on my knees, I held my forehead in my palms and leaned over until my head touched the sand. My vest and shirt clung to my skin, drenched in sweat.

What if she hadn't wanted me to find her message? After all, she had buried the cardboard wallet and its contents. And the two lines of writing were crossed out; they said she didn't know how to express all she wanted to say. If she had wanted to condemn me, she wouldn't have found the task so difficult, right? A couple of bitter words would have done the trick. And my darling Anna was never a harsh judge – not of me or anyone. In no one else's company had I ever felt so thoroughly known and loved.

What had I done?

What had we all done?

Whose step – which one? – had made the difference?

For my part I pleaded guilty. I should have known. At some level I already knew, when anxiety gripped me in Milan and I pushed it away. If a human being couldn't be driven to suicide, why else did Dido's plight still move readers of the Aeneid?

For all my guilt, no one was to blame as much as my mother: without her meddling, none of this would have happened. I hated her. Yes, regardless of my love of the classics and their insistence on the control of emotions, I now hated her.

I folded Anna's message and placed it in my jeans' pocket. Then I got to my feet and tramped through the bushes.

'Anna! Anna!'

At each turning, I hoped to find her breathing and relieved that after all I had arrived, though I believed the search to be hopeless. The mewling which, after much fruitless trudging, raised my hopes, turned out to be a dangling branch of myrtle snapped by the wind. In the hissing and rustling of the leaves, I strained to pick up a human sound. I tottered on the rocks jutting into the sea, looking for her there and in the water, mindless of the spray. Soaked through, and with salt and sand sticking to me from head to toe, I sank to my knees.

Should I put an end to it all, too? Giorgio's father had a hunting gun – it wouldn't be difficult to get my hands on it and then... foolproof and swift. But what if she was still out there? If she was alive, we could explain everything and forgive each other and ourselves. The slimmest chance of that was worth staying alive for.

I trudged for hours on sandy strips, along rocky stretches, past coffee bars and restaurants boarded up at the close of summer, until I was calmer. By the time I returned home, I had formed a plan. As my mother had been so scheming, for once I would prove her worthy heir.

'Gesú, you're a sight!' Concetta said, clasping her hands to her chest. I hadn't closed the house door yet, but she had already rushed towards me.

'A hot chocolate. I'll make you a hot chocolate. I told your mother not to worry. Go tell her you're OK. Then have a shower. No, actually, have a shower first. I'll tell her what you're doing. You don't want to frighten her, do you?'

'Don't worry about the hot chocolate. I'm all right,' I said, avoiding her gaze. 'But you're right, I do need a wash.' I kissed her on the cheek and rushed upstairs.

A simple jet of hot water couldn't loosen the tension in my shoulders and back, but it refreshed me. My mind cleared and felt ready for the step ahead. I was still in my bathrobe when there was a knock at my bedroom door.

'Did you find her?' My mother sounded exhausted. Unusually, she was still in her dressing gown and her face wasn't made up.

'No, I didn't.' I shook my head and, without looking her in the eyes, added, 'Look, sorry about the things I said last night. I shouldn't have.'

'No, you shouldn't, but...' The relief in her tone was unmistakable. 'You'll see – she'll turn up.'

'I think so too. But the shock, yesterday... I wasn't thinking straight.'

She hugged me. 'Thank God you've come to your senses. Come, have some breakfast.'

'Sure. I'll be downstairs in a minute.'

I dressed and joined my mother and *tata* in the kitchen. It smelt of hot chocolate. Concetta switched off the hob as the nut-brown froth rose to the rim of the milk boiler, and poured it into two cups.

'Drink up. Get some strength back, both of you.'

She set down the steaming drinks and pushed a tin of breakfast biscuits closer to me. I dunked the large *biscotti* in quick succession, with the hunger of one who hasn't eaten for over a day. They had never tasted so comforting. Their aroma of vanilla, lemon zest and wood-fired oven transported me to the bakery where I used to buy my daily piece of focaccia for the school break. The familiar roughness of the caramelised sugar on their surfaces sparked a sense of wellbeing, a connection with the thousands of mornings when I had sat at this table with a lighter heart. But it also felt as if those mornings not only belonged to a past life, but that the door to re-enter it was barred.

My mother cleared her throat. 'I'm glad you've an appetite.' She held her cup in both hands, seemingly to warm them up rather than drink. 'What are you planning to do? Or I guess you don't know yet?'

'I do, actually. I'll fly back to Milan and wait for news. We're powerless, here – all of us. Until Anna decides to re-appear, we're not going to find her. In the meantime, I'll get booted out of Bocconi if I don't turn up for lectures and exams.'

She took a sip and eyed me suspiciously. 'Hmm. But you will stay for *I Morti*, won't you? It's only in a couple of days. Even your professors have to take a break for that. I expect that plenty of them aren't from Milan and need to travel far to get home. It's not for nothing that it's a national holiday.'

That was true, and I hadn't forgotten the festival of All Souls. Like every year, cemeteries would be swarming with visitors carrying fresh flowers and votive candles to graves.

'It's an appointment I've never missed,' I said. 'I'm already here, so of course I'll stay.'

'Funny,' my mother said. Her hand flew to her mouth. 'I mean, you don't believe, but you respect that date.'

'I do it for Dad – it's him I honour.' I caught a look which asked: what are you implying with this hint of the fourth commandment?

'Might as well do it on the day other people honour their dead,' I carried on. 'Or don't you like going with me?'

'Of course I do. And Concetta.' She turned towards my *tata*, who nodded at the acknowledgement, whilst continuing to scour the milk boiler.

I had always shied away from visiting my father's grave on my own. Today, I can see that I was unable to put a finger on what it was I feared. Not that I was close to recognising any such fear: the thought of venturing to the cemetery on my own never ripened into an intention, let alone action; provided I kept it at a distance, my dread remained suffused. I told myself that the concept of 'visiting him' meant acquiescence in a bunch of superstitious nonsense: like the notion that my father's spirit resided in or around the piece of earth where he lay buried; that on the Day of Judgment it would be re-united with his mortal spoils and rise up to Heaven; that our praying for his or anyone else's soul had miraculous effects. No. For me, going to my father's graveside on All Souls' Day was a due honouring of a good man. He did live on, but only in my memories and the tangible tokens of what he had loved, which still surrounded me in our home.

But now I wonder: could the real reason for my venturing there on that single day of the year have been different? On that day the little alleys of the cemetery became crowded with people, who went about their business as if visiting the kind of living friend or relative who demanded that you be well turned out and on your best behaviour. No funereal clothing. No crying or wailing. Much bumping into extended family and friends, shaking of hands and kissing of cheeks, at once affable and restrained. Without strangers and acquaintances around me, who knew what depths my emotions might reach?

★★★

The rest of that day and the next passed in an alternating flow of action and distraction. I revisited familiar corners of town – and there wasn't one that didn't evoke Anna. The road in from Villa Emma had seen us on my motorbike, her chest against my back and her voice in my ears. The streets behind the Liceo Classico had hidden our first kisses from our school mates. The newsagent's kiosk, with the daily headlines posted in its windows, had set off our chats. It was impossible for me to set foot in Ostuni without being ambushed by her absence. I hesitated before entering the Old Town, so crammed with memories, but eventually I resolved to search it for clues which might have escaped me in the dark. In vain. In the afternoon I fell into a deep slumber. It made up for my lost sleep and replenished my stores of energy. Little did I know, but I would soon need them.

Isn't it funny, how our bodies seem capable of intuition? Lucretius was on to something when he said that body, mind and soul aspire to perfect harmony. There's so much we know – deep truths about ourselves and others – without being conscious of it. Much easier to espouse the crude doctrine of mind over body than open yourself up to the complexity of reality and to doubt.

Not that I had done that until today, I suppose. What need was there for me to reconnect with my old life, before you gatecrashed my new one? Maybe it was time. I couldn't avoid it forever. And it doesn't hurt as much as I expected, now my mother is dead. Could it be that anger loses its sting, once its object no longer exists?

★★★

Chrysanthemums are among the few flowers which smell unpleasant. There's a whiff of decay to them, a physical kinship to things dying or dead. The white and yellow ones in my arms made me hold my nose. Petals stuck to my jacket sleeves. My mother carried the bag containing candles encased in red lanterns. Concetta's bunch of red and white carnations bobbed on her bosom as we marched along the cemetery's main avenue.

At ten in the morning we were early visitors, but the streets were already crowded. By the more modest burials, in the soil, relatives were busy replacing old flowers, lighting new candles and shining up gravestones plainly inscribed or adorned with angels and Madonnas. Along the edges of the *cimitero*, the sunshine of that chilly morning bounced against the white marble of the columbaria, walls of coffin-size chambers stacked on top of each other. The alleys were lined with family chapels of varying opulence. Ours, just off the central boulevard, bore testimony – even in the city of the dead – to our one-time social prominence.

It was for my mother's family, but my father was buried there too. I was glad not to believe in the hereafter, as the prospect of being stuck with his in-laws until Judgment Day would have been my father's idea of Hell. His position on the chapel's equivalent of the *piano nobile* was the result of negotiation between my mother and her brother. In exchange for putting his grave at eye level, my uncle got the promise of the equivalent slot opposite; eventually my great-grandparents would be shifted up two storeys, out of reach; my mother and her sister in-law accepted second place, above their husbands.

Great-aunts would be relegated to the ossuary below ground. Even death didn't put an end to family politics.

We picked up the cleaning tools from the back of the chapel. My mother brushed dead leaves and insects off the floor; Concetta mopped. I rubbed clean the brass-framed photographs staring out from the marble slabs. How young my father was when he died – each year, I was struck by just how young. This time I noticed that my hairline was becoming like his: low over the forehead, close to the temples at the sides. My eyes were the same shape and colour, but our expressions differed. He seemed to smile even when his lips didn't.

'Goodbye, Dad,' I said silently as I polished the glass over a formal snapshot in which he wore a dark blazer and tie against a light shirt. 'I can't promise to be back. It'll depend on Anna. If your spirit lives on and you know all that's happened, you'll understand.' I smiled at the irony of a non-believer like me addressing a ghost. 'Well, just in case,' I added.

The taxi to the airport was due. I had better make my way downstairs. The open bag on my bed was fully packed with my warmest jumpers, the pottery lamp with the owl and the case containing my casts of ancient coins. At the very top, I had managed to fit the shoebox Concetta had insisted I take, filled with fresh plum tomatoes because 'They don't have 'em like these, up north.'

For lunch she had cooked a *tajedda* of potatoes and artichokes.

'Eat up. You're not likely to have artichokes as fresh as these in Milan.'

I smiled to hide my guilt and ate in silence. I wanted to let her into my plan, but it was too risky: torn between loyalties, she might betray me. Besides, it'd be cruel to put her in that dilemma.

'It's the effect of the cemetery this morning,' my mother said in a soothing tone.

Concetta shrugged. 'Enjoy being alive and well. That's what the dead would tell us if they could.'

Now, as I pulled the zip of my travel bag shut over the boxful of tomatoes, the same twinge of guilt made itself felt. 'I'm so sorry, Concetta,' I thought. 'But I've no choice.'

CHAPTER 15

The train had been stuck at Ventimiglia for twenty minutes when the *gendarme* finally slid our compartment door open.

'Documents, please.' His monotone matched the dour expression on his face. Middle-aged and wiry, he exuded the air of someone who wouldn't allow an extra gram of nourishment into his system. The same applied to letting another foreigner into his country.

A bespectacled old gentleman seated closest to the door put down his book and presented his passport, which was swiftly inspected and returned with a light bow of the head. Next was the young man opposite me by the window. The officer studied him, a stubbly, curly haired twenty-something in a pair of jeans and shabby trainers, and compared him with the photograph.

'Where are you headed?' He spoke Italian with a faint French accent – a native of that border region or possibly the son of Italian immigrants.

'To England. To work. My brother's there already.'

'Ah, *bien*.' Maybe second-generation immigrants were as snooty with new arrivals as the newly rich with humbler relatives.

When he turned towards me, I disguised my tension by confidently handing him my passport. No reason to be nervous, I told myself. My mother and Concetta weren't looking for me. Why would they? I had rung them upon arriving in Milan the previous afternoon. My passport was valid. And the bank clerk at the branch nearest Bocconi had instantly obliged my request to withdraw my full account balance that morning. The amount wasn't large enough for questions. It might last me two or three months.

'This photo needs to be replaced,' the gendarme said. 'How old were you? Twelve?'

'Fifteen.' I felt blood rush to my brain, but tried to keep my voice steady.

'I know for sure because it was issued for a trip to Greece,' I added, as if being specific might carry some weight. Mr. Santoro had managed to assemble a group of students for a tour of ancient sites.

'Don't your *questura* tell you people to update the photos once you're not a child anymore? What am I meant to do with you? Where are you headed?'

'England.'

The attention of the elderly gentleman in the compartment had by now shifted from the story in his book to the one in front of him.

'May I ask,' he interjected, 'how far you've already travelled?'

'From the Salento.' I kept just enough presence of mind to reveal only an approximate origin. The Salento comprised the provinces of Lecce and Brindisi, and part of Taranto's.

'That's a long way.' He exchanged an understanding glance with the gendarme.

The officer returned my document. 'I'll let you through, but no idea if the British will. Up to you. If you'd rather leave the train, tell me now.'

'I... I'll take my chances.'

'As you wish. Good day, *messieurs*.'

The moment the door shut, I sank back.

'Don't worry,' the elder of my companions said. 'Unless you've changed beyond recognition, they'll let you through. Going there to improve your English?'

'Yes.'

'Where in England?' the younger man asked in a southern accent I couldn't place.

'London.'

'First time?'

I nodded.

'Me too, but my brother's told me loads about it. Huge place.'

'Sure is.' That was why I had chosen it: the biggest capital in the European Community. No visa necessary. And vast enough for me to disappear, one anonymous human being among millions.

'Where're you staying?'

'Not sure,' I said, unprepared for all the questioning. 'I suppose at a youth hostel, to start with.'

'Well, as we're going all the way together – Alfredo.' He extended his hand.

'Tommaso.' Giving out my first name couldn't do any harm. I'd have to come up with a surname soon. A few days to have thought everything through would have come in handy.

By the time we approached London's Victoria Station – two trains and a ferry later – I knew a great deal about Alfredo, and he very little about me. He didn't seem to mind but rattled on good-humouredly, as we took our bags off the luggage rack and made our way down the carriage. The corridor was packed with passengers raring to leave the train as soon as it came to a halt. Meanwhile it was passing through a lengthy stretch of artificial lights – I made out houses, offices and industrial buildings – in the darkness of early evening.

'Can't wait to hug Pasquale.' Alfredo beamed. 'Two years, it's been. It won't be long before our sign goes up: *Ristorante Fratelli Ciriello*.'

I smiled. 'London beware.'

'Oh, yes. London get ready for real pizza, and buffalo mozzarella... Apparently people here think mozzarella is that long-life rubbery stuff in little plastic bags. Wait till they taste the proper thing.'

'It's great you've got it all sorted out.'

'We haven't, really. But we will, bit by bit.' He shrugged. 'It's not like we've got the money yet. But we know where we want to get to. And anything's better than being stuck in Campania with a high school diploma in hospitality and no job.'

For all my carefree replies, as we approached our destination a fear which until then I had reined in grew: had I done the second most stupid thing in my life? How terrifying to be totally alone and, for the first time, without a clear aim. London was a faceless metropolis: I knew no one, and no one knew me. And yet wasn't that what I wanted?

Despite the throng, Pasquale spotted his brother as we streamed through the platform gate.

'Alfré! Alfré!'

They exchanged vigorous hugs and talked fast in their Neapolitan dialect. I stood waiting to wish them well and head off. Pasquale had the same curly dark hair and colouring as Alfredo, but was heavier set. I reckoned he was in his late twenties, though his confident manner gave a first impression of someone older.

Alfredo turned towards me. 'This is Tommaso. We travelled together.'

Pasquale winked. 'I hope the sprat behaved.'

Alfredo laughed. 'I've come all the way to London to get abused like this.'

His brother patted him on the shoulder and looked at me. 'Where're you headed?'

'Right now, to the information office.' A nervous chuckle concealed my deepening gloom as I took in the unintelligible signs of the station shops, the stench of frying oil and stale coffee, and the clouds of vapour when I exhaled – and it was only early November. 'To find out about youth hostels – till I can look around properly.'

'You here for long?'

'Don't know. Maybe a month? Maybe more? Could be years.' If Anna didn't turn up, it could be forever.

'Not sure this'll be of any interest,' Pasquale said, taking in my expensive sports jacket, 'But we've got a spare bed. One of our flatmates left a couple of weeks ago. There'd be six of us, all Italian, four in your room. Bunk beds. Like a youth hostel, minus the merry-go-round of strangers coming in half-drunk. But you're probably after a posher place?'

'No. It sounds great.' Anna would have called it Providence, I merely a stroke of good luck. Unless being among Italians made it easier for my mother to find me? But no, she didn't know I was in England. Even if she ever discovered that I had crossed its border, there were tens of thousands of my countrymen in London. The police would be loath to search for me, for the same reason they weren't looking for Anna: we weren't under age. I had made certain to leave behind evidence that I left of my own free will – my flatmates in Milan had a note to open only in a week. It stated clearly that 'as a citizen guilty of no crime under the law', I had every right to disappear and not be pursued.

The flat on the Harrow Road turned out to be the first of many encounters with a peculiar phenomenon: the unification of Italy outside its borders, more thoroughly than within them. As far as I can tell from here, North and South remain as distrustful of each other as ever, more than a hundred and fifty years since deciding to form one nation. There are those in the North who maintain it was a merger exploited by the South to leech off the former. There are those in the South who maintain just as staunchly that it was a deceitful colonisation by a North now lacking historical memory.

Abroad, however, Italians band together whatever their origin. They give each other a helping hand in a new country. And they create opportunities to enjoy what they treasured 'back home'. They know better than anyone that the very idea of a monolithic South is fiction.

Their Christmas celebrations, for example, are a riot of regional contrasts. The Abbruzzesi must end the feast with *caciunitt*, sweet ravioli filled with chickpeas, chestnuts or Montepulciano grapes rooted in Apennine earth. The Campanians, meanwhile, are dunking in wine their rock-hard *roccocò* biscuits, the name a corruption of the French *rocaille*, a reminder of their medieval origin in the Naples of King Robert of Anjou. The Apulians will offer you *cartellate*, honey-dipped rosettes identical to the *xerotigana* of Crete and to the *diples* of parts of Greece, betraying their birth as ritual offerings to Demeter, and later to the Virgin Mary. The Sicilians will bring along *nucatuli*, whose aromas of dried figs, nuts, honey and cinnamon evoke the island's Muslim past and their ancient Arabic name, *nagal*.

My new flatmates hailed from disparate corners of Italy: the Veneto, Marche, Sicily, and the two brothers, of course, from Campania. I shared a room with the other three: Carlo, Franco and Pino.

Pino pointed me to the top bunk. 'I hope you don't snore.' The pine was scratched and chipped. Hopefully the slats wouldn't sag under my weight.

'But if you do, don't worry,' he continued. 'I'm below, so I'll kick you hard till you stop.' He looked me in the eye so seriously that I couldn't tell whether he was in jest. His fair hair and green eyes reminded me a little of Giorgio – a scrawny version of my old friend.

'And if you carry on, we'll be forced to boot you out the way we did with Enzo,' added Franco, raising his fleshy hands to indicate his helplessness to do otherwise.

Carlo grinned. 'Lay off, guys. He isn't used to your jokes yet.' He was so lanky, surely he couldn't fit in one of these beds?

Pino looked at him 'Oh, come on. Humour beats reality any day, no? Fine. Have it your way. Truth is we're so pooped by the time we get to bed, that we fall asleep in seconds and snore like old hogs.' Pointing at my face, he spoke to the others. 'See? Panic. My first version was better.'

I laughed. 'I just need a job that'll make me as tired as everyone else, then there won't be a problem.' I was yet to discover the aptness of this, given that sound passed through the plasterboard walls like water through a sieve.

'You really need a job?' Pino asked with a disbelieving tone, motioning to my shirt and pullover, cords and sturdy moccasins. 'It's just that... You look more like a daddy's boy who comes here for a language course, all expenses paid.'

'That's what you think. Actually, I haven't got a father. I've got to pay my own way.'

My answer wasn't meant as unfriendly, but it caused an uncomfortable silence.

'If you need a job, ask Pasquale. He's been here longest,' Carlo said. 'He knows people – decent people.'

Signor Luciano surveyed me. Ringed by shadows, his dark eyes stood out against the pallor of his olive skin, which was starved of sunshine. A receding hairline and a small beak of a nose made his forehead seem too large. However, his remaining hair was still brown and he had few wrinkles.

'You'd be good with diners – such a nice manner,' he said, looking wistfully around the room, all tables empty but for one at which an old man sipped his espresso while browsing the *Corriere dello Sport*. It was too early for lunch, when, according to Pasquale, the restaurant filled with people living or working in Putney.

Along the white walls, photographs in bright red frames displayed some of Italy's famous sights: Piazza San Marco, the tower of Pisa, a view of Castel Sant'Angelo, the bay of Naples... The tables were already set with sturdy white crockery on red gingham mats. Bottles of popular *amaro*, *grappa* and *marsala* occupied the shelves to one side of the counter which separated the cooking from the dining area.

'As you barely speak English, all I can offer you is the kitchen: loading the dishwasher, scrubbing pans and helping the chef and his assistant any way you can. But that won't be good enough for you – with such proper Italian, you can only be from a *buona famiglia*.'

'Please, Signor Luciano. The kitchen would be perfect. I won't be able to do much else until I've learnt the language.'

He gestured at my hands. 'You don't look as if you've done a scrap of work in your life.'

'Not manual work, that's true, but I've studied hard and the attitude is what counts. Why don't you take me on and see for yourself?'

'Everyone in my kitchen is Italian. If you've come to learn English, what good is that?'

'I can study when I'm not working.'

'Your hours would be from eleven in the morning till midnight, six days a week. Not much study time.'

'Plenty. Please.'

He shrugged. 'All right. If that's what you want.'

Scouring pots, filling and emptying the dishwasher, checking cutlery for watermarks, wiping tables clean – during the restaurant's busiest hours, I dealt with my tasks like a man on a white-water raft: too busy handling currents and rocks to think of much else. But at quieter times, when only the occasional customer wandered in for an afternoon cappuccino, I couldn't help asking myself if my mother had already become aware I had left Milan, if Concetta was too hurt I hadn't trusted her, if Giorgio now thought me a fool. Above all, I ached to know if Anna had reappeared, and if not, where she was. What if my fears were justified and she really had walked into the sea?

'Been here only a week and you're already running your hands through your hair?' Signor Luciano spotted me in a corner of the kitchen, hands over my eyes, in a moment when thoughts of Anna and Ostuni overwhelmed me.

Gianni, the cook, laid the two carving knives he had been sharpening onto the worktop. 'Take a break.' He turned to our boss. 'At the rate he works, I can spare him between three and five, no problem – as long as he still gets everything done.'

Aldo, his assistant, stopped chopping up bacon into little cubes for that evening's carbonara and crossed his arms. 'How about me?'

Gianni, with his height and girth, loomed over him. It would have been impossible to guess they were cousins. 'No way,' he said.

Aldo made a face and brought down the chopper on the pancetta with a bang.

I was surprised to be fussed over. 'I was just lost in thought,' I said. 'No need for a break.'

Signor Luciano put an arm around my shoulder. 'Home-sick, hmm? Everyone is, at first. When I came over, twenty years ago, I wanted to rush straight back to Portici.'

Gianni widened his arms, forgetting he was clasping the carving knives again. 'Me too. Everyone's the same. And if Aldo doesn't shape up, I'll put him on a train back to Salerno myself.'

'You learn to love this city,' Signor Luciano said. 'Though it helps if you speak the language. How're you planning to learn it?'

'I saw there's a public library near here. They might have some language books.'

Signor Luciano looked amazed. 'You're not going to take a course?'

'Difficult, with a restaurant's working hours and the time it takes to get here from the Harrow Road.'

Had I wanted to, I probably could have found alternative accommodation and a daily one-hour course, but that was out of the question. I'd be asked for an identity document, which I had not had to produce until now. And if my mother managed to persuade the police – which was on the cards – to search for me abroad, the enrolment registers of language courses would be an obvious starting point. The Classico had made me well versed in the words of the dead, not of the living. It occurred to me that, ironically, it was one of the reasons why my mother would have preferred me to study at the Scientifico, where English was taught for the full five years, instead of the first two; no wonder my vocabulary now stretched little beyond 'hello' and 'goodbye'. Even so, I wouldn't have chosen a different education.

Signor Luciano scratched the back of his head. 'See what books you find. If you're stuck on the words, you're welcome to ask me, whenever we aren't busy.'

The public library turned out to contain plenty of suitable texts. I couldn't take them out, as I didn't have a card; to obtain one, proofs of identity and residence had to be presented and I had no intention of risking that. So far I didn't exist for the British authorities. Like my job, my accommodation was a 'strictly cash' affair. Until I learnt how to get hold of fake ID, I'd have to avoid falling ill: the need for a doctor or a hospital would scupper my anonymity.

Over the subsequent months, I made a habit of sitting at one of the library desks for an hour before work and another in the early afternoon. I started out with a set of graded readers designed to teach Italian to English speakers. I studied their pages in silence every day, learning the expressions in reverse and itching to test their sounds aloud. I moved on to illustrated texts for students of English as a foreign language, and then to brutally abridged classic novels with levelled vocabulary.

I wandered into charity shops on Putney High Street in the hope of coming across books I could read on my own, but, with my meagre pay, every pound was precious and few made the cut. When they did, I took them with me to work and Signor Luciano corrected my pronunciation of words whose spelling seemed devised to confound. Before going to sleep at night, I lay down on my bunk and read my treasured finds with a dictionary and a torch.

My small but growing library would have looked eclectic to an observer, yet there was method in it: each title reflected my knowledge of English at the time. I leafed through the paperbacks on the shelves of Oxfam and gauged whether their vocabulary would be a useful stretch or too dispiriting a challenge. That's how Joseph Conrad sat next to Jane Austen, E.M. Forster to Aldous Huxley, and George Eliot to Graham Greene.

I have long since discovered through teaching Latin and Greek to my pupils that the harder English vocabulary is for native speakers, the more likely it is of Latin origin, and easier for Italians, the French or Spaniards, who remain ignorant of the similar Anglo-Saxon term. So in those early days, 'selflessness' and 'storm' sent me rushing for the dictionary while 'altruism' and 'tempest' didn't; by the same token, Thomas Hardy or Henry James offered me an easier read than some recent authors.

There's no pride in this assertion. More than thirty years on, I'm still dumbfounded by the number of idiomatic phrases in your language. It is extraordinarily rich. That it should have incorporated words from all over the earth – Celtic, An-glo-Saxon, French, Navajo and Swahili, to name but a few sources – testifies to a society that has absorbed much from other histories and cultures. Language holds up a mirror to its speakers, though many seem not to pause and reflect on it.

Signor Luciano was right that I would learn to love Lon-don – and your country as a whole. Today I smile at the mem-ory of his English pronunciation: at the Italian vowels that turned 'bag' into 'beg' and 'fit' into 'feet', or the accentuated double consonants which lengthened the 'p' in 'apple'. But don't get me wrong: I have only gratitude for him.

Within months he entrusted me with serving diners. From time to time Pasquale pointed out vacancies for wait-ers at restaurants closer to our flat. But 'closer' meant largely around Notting Hill and the Portobello Road, an area popu-lar with Italian tourists. However small the chance of being recognised by someone from Ostuni, I didn't want to run the risk. And I had grown fond of Signor Luciano and the spar-ring cousins.

I retained one link with Ostuni: Giorgio. Coin-guzzling payphones kept our conversations brief. I first rang him a cou-ple of weeks after my arrival to ask for news of Anna.

'No one's heard anything. But where the hell are you? Your mother's going nuts. Apparently you left a note with your flatmates in Milan? Don't be stupid, Tommi. Come home.'

'Whose side are you on, then?'

'I just want you to be ok. We're all worried about Anna, but running away and being totally on your own can't do you or anyone else any good. And your mother...'

'My mother deserves this and worse. Promise me you

won't tell her I've called.'

'Why?'

'Promise, or I won't ring again.'

'Fine, fine. I promise.'

'On your life.'

'For Christ's sake, don't be so bloody dramatic.' He sighed. 'Ok. On my life. But keep calling me, will you? I'll tell you when Anna turns up.'

I rang him every couple of weeks for more than two years. For a few minutes, a bright red phone box was my cage, and I, hurtling from side to side, the trapped bird: whenever I dialled his number I braced myself for news of Anna but there never was any. I nursed a miniscule hope that she was alive. Yet sometimes I wished for an end to not knowing, even if it meant learning that she was dead.

The sole means of escape from my own anguish were my menial tasks at the restaurant, my books, and a few words with flatmates – who like me worked hours too ungodly for sociability. I suppose it was an ascetic life: but how could I deserve a better one? Not until – if ever – I expiated my share in the crime against Anna.

No doubt my mother would have called my self-negation shameful and self-indulgent. If only she could witness how low I had fallen. How it would hurt her to see that her scheming had made her ambitions for me less attainable than ever. Her parents must be turning in their graves.

As Signor Luciano had predicted, my manners endeared me to customers. With tips, I could afford a few luxuries: a couple of new shirts from Marks & Spencer, unlimited second-hand books... On warm spring and summer days I strolled to Putney Embankment and spent my afternoon breaks reading. The rowing boats entranced me. Sometimes the cox-swains barking their commands jerked me out of the pages. The crews' fluid, rhythmic strokes and the syncing of the blades' height and angle reminded me of flocks of migrating birds circling and soaring above the Adriatic. I could almost hear their cries. My eyes followed the boats until they turned the bend towards Barnes or disappeared towards Wandsworth Bridge.

The humdrum cadence of my new existence made my first two years bearable. Most of the time, going through the motions of life produced the numbing effect I desired. The rupture which was about to ensue caught me off-guard.

March 1985, afternoon break, eve of my twenty-second birth-day. Ashy clouds low over London. Gusts of rain flailing the streets. Not even a hundred meters separated the restaurant from the public phone box but when I reached it and shut its door, my parka dripped water onto the floor.

Giorgio and I had a sort of code: I rang for a couple of seconds, then again. If he wasn't the one who picked up, I put down the receiver and tried later.

'*Pronto?*' he answered, accompanied by a jangling of coins at my end.

'The blasted thing is bust. It's eaten up all my money. Ring you tomorrow? Same time?'

'Ok. Just wanted to ask you –' The line went dead.

The next afternoon, as grey and damp as the preceding one, I dialled his number from another phone.

Giorgio answered with a wistful tone. 'Happy birthday, my friend.'

'Nothing to celebrate, is there? Any news?'

'I'm afraid not. But you've been away almost two and half years. Isn't that enough?'

'No.' My best friend should have known better than to try to persuade me to return. After his last attempt, I had not rung him for a month.

'Staying away won't bring Anna back. It won't make any difference.' Giorgio waited for a reply. 'Tommi, still there?'

'Yes. Won't make any difference. I heard you.'

'But it'd mean so much to your mother and Concetta... Even if you don't care about yourself... Wherever you are, come back.'

'No.'

A long sigh crossed a thousand miles of cables. Silence followed. Then another voice – one I recognised all too well – came through the receiver.

'Tommi, darling, please,' my mother said in her finest pleading tone: tremulous, high-pitched and yet hushed, as if she could barely breathe out the words. I pictured her face, a tragic mask of torment and concern, supposedly for me, but really for herself.

How dare she? How dare Giorgio? He should never have told her I was alive. Blood rushed to my face. My hands tightened around the receiver. Words became broken strings of letters floating across my mind. The urge to lash out at the walls of the phone box almost overwhelmed me but even in my trance-like state the idea was risible. I remained immobilised, speechless. My mother went on speaking but now she was only noise coming through plastic. As if in slow motion, I put the receiver back in its place.

Have you ever seen pictures of rope bridges hanging over

chasms? I walk past one almost every day on Queensway: a poster in the window of a travel agent. 'Peru', it says. A native man with a multi-coloured cap and green shirt looks straight at the camera and invites you to follow him. He is already halfway across the bridge, which is so narrow and rickety that only one person can pass. Feet on the sagging, plaited fibres, he keeps a firm grip of the woven grass cables either side of him.

For me, Giorgio was a rope bridge between my two worlds. When the grass fibres frayed and snapped, I swung to safety on the unfamiliar side of the gorge. I was finally free to explore it without being pulled back. At last I could admit that Anna was never coming home, that in all likelihood she had disappeared into the sea, trusting that it would never give her up.

I've asked myself so many times: do I wish I had never met Anna? The answer is: for her sake, yes. I can't forgive myself. Nor do I delude myself that anyone has the power to relieve me of my guilt. Anna alone had that right. But for my own sake, no, I cannot wish I hadn't met her. In the end, you see, she was right: our moments of happiness together have remained eternal. No anguish can outweigh them.

So will you leave me in peace, now? Can you finally grasp why it's impossible to accept my mother's attempt at reconciliation, even in death? The fact that until the end she thought money could buy me is the ultimate proof of how little she understood me.

Convinced at last? Really? If I were religious, I'd praise God. But why do you want to hear what happened after that phone call with Giorgio? Pure human interest, you say – is that the latest name for curiosity? Fine, though I'll be brief.

There's nothing noteworthy about my life since then, I assure you. It's exactly how I have wanted it to be, and how it can continue, if you'll only leave me alone.

But it's already eight o'clock. Will you have a bowl of pasta with me? It'll take no time to prepare. Then we can carry on talking.

CHAPTER 16

I didn't know that a bowl of pasta could have wine's power to loosen the tongue. You've done well to tell me what happened to you. I suspected something of the sort. I had been wondering whether the real reason only you had tracked me down was that you understood me because of your personal experience. Now I know it.

I see why your father is so bitter about the way things turned out, though I wish that he had treated you differently. A police sergeant for thirty years, he must have been incredibly proud of you when the Crown Prosecution Service made you an offer before you graduated, and when you earned your first-class degree. Only for you to ruin your future by running over a cyclist.

It must feel so unfair: to have volunteered to drive after the graduation party because you were the most sober among your mates, then end up with a conviction for drink-driving and the remorse of having put another young man in a wheelchair for life. You must think yourself stupid, to have got into that driving seat. I needn't tell you how well I know that feeling. But time cannot be rewound. I hope you won't let your father's fault-finding add to your burden. Guilt is crushing enough on its own.

As for me, I'll keep my promise to tell you what happened after that last call to Giorgio. It wasn't long afterwards that I discovered a special second-hand bookshop. On an afternoon in late March I strolled aimlessly up the High Street and then into a side road, instead of wandering down to Putney Embankment. The spire of a church and the green of the surrounding trees stood out against the dreary sky. As I approached, the road narrowed into a path flanked by a row of white cottages behind pristine hedges.

It was like stepping out of the city and into a picture post-card of an English village. Now and then a cyclist pedalled past. Two young mothers chatted while pushing prams. An elderly woman with a shopping trolley even said 'Hello' to me.

I ambled around and sat on a bench at the edge of the church's lawn, taking in the high windows and pointed arches. The open space drew gusts of wind which ruffled the leaves; they broke into flurries of whispers. As always, I had a book with me and the reading of it was so tranquil that I lost track of time. I had to sprint back to the restaurant.

Returning there the next day, I noticed a bookshop on a corner of the street leading to the enchanted path. I pushed down the handle of the door, but it stuck.

I peeked through the glass panels. A man, white hair combed back over a high forehead, came towards me from the far end of the shop. With one hand he gestured to me to be patient.

'You have to give it a nudge,' he said as he let me in. 'Needs sanding. I'll get round to it one of these days. Feel free to look around.' Grinning through a silver-white beard, he flattened the creases of his shirt over his paunch and hobbled back to his desk.

The shop was a single large room. Natural light came through a wide window in which a selection of volumes, some marked 'first edition', were displayed. Along the walls, bookshelves of dark, polished wood rose to the ceiling. Lower ones, reaching my waist, crammed the middle of the room in parallel rows. Wooden labels in gilded letters marked the sections: history, travel, art, fiction...

What a selection, after the limited fare of the charity shops! Here, the titles were arranged in meticulous alphabetical order. It looked more like a private collection, run by a professional librarian, than a display of used books. I caught a whiff of musty volumes blended with a faint fragrance of citrus, most likely an old-fashioned cologne for men. It must have come from the shopkeeper. I recognised his check shirt and pale moleskins as the kind of clothes worn by a particular kind of customer at the restaurant: impeccable manners, but at the same time friendly and down to earth, the kind you could rely on to leave a fair tip.

Here were hardbound editions of Herodotus, Tacitus, Homer, Virgil, Plato, Aristotle and other old friends from the shelves of my father's library. Here were all the Shakespeare plays I wanted to read when my English improved enough. The 'Fiction – General' and 'Fiction – Classics' sections took up an entire wall and spilled over onto the lower bookcases. If only I could find the time to read the biographies whose subjects – Pascal, Poussin, Churchill – also intrigued me.

The man left his desk. 'Searching for anything in particular? You must have done the full round twice already. May I be of help?'

'It's not that. It's – '

'Too much choice?'

'Yes. Exactly.'

He nodded. 'I thought that was likely. You look like a child in a sweet shop, if you don't mind me saying. Do take your time. There's no hurry.'

'Maybe... Maybe you can recommend something?'

He beamed and straightened himself up. 'You'd be surprised how rarely people ask that. Are we talking fiction, philosophy, history...?'

'Anything.'

He broke into a laugh laced with cough and wheezes.

'You obviously like books but you'll have to give me something a little more specific to go on, young man.'

I shrugged. 'I like to read all those things. And the ancient classics, but my English isn't good enough yet.'

'Ah, an avid reader. That makes two of us.' His gaze travelled round the four corners of the room before coming to rest on me.

I cleared my throat. 'This time maybe fiction? With the English not too difficult.'

He nodded and took a pair of reading glasses from his shirt pocket. 'You're from Italy?' He adjusted the spectacles carefully on the arch of his nose and began inspecting the shelves.

'Yes.'

'That's a long-winded answer. Are you always this chatty?' He set a paperback aside on a nearby stool. 'Sorry. It's not easy in a foreign tongue, I expect, even if you're quite advanced. I shudder to think how the French must feel when I mangle their language – and I started learning it long before you were born.' He took out another book and leafed through it, but returned it to its place. 'I'm not joking. Unlike you, I manage to maul even a language as musical and charming as French. Count yourself lucky I've never attempted yours.'

'It's so obvious I'm Italian?'

He surveyed me through slate-grey eyes. 'You could be

from anywhere between Spain and Greece. But from the accent, yes, Italian.' He resumed his perusal of the shelves.

I spoke to his back. 'I've been learning English through books. Mostly. I live with Italians, work with Italians... In a restaurant near here.'

'Nothing wrong with having an accent.' He lifted the small pile of books he had picked out and put them on his desk. 'Here's a few possibles.'

I can't recall all the titles, but I remember him talking me through the stories and their authors, one by one. In some cases, he remembered at which house clearance, auction or library sale he had picked them up.

'I sift through everything myself. I sell immediately to the trade anything that doesn't belong here – sometimes it's the bulk of what I've just bought.'

'Why?'

'I haven't got the space to hold three copies of one title. I keep only the books that will widen the choice. And people come here because they know they'll probably find what they're looking for – and in good condition.'

'But what matters is what's inside – the words, no?'

He fixed me with his eyes and scratched the back of his neck. Then he laughed his breathless laugh again. 'That's a little strong, isn't it? But yes, what's inside has to pass my test – it may be a little subjective, but I'm broad church.'

'Church?'

'A manner of speaking: it just means assorted opinions are welcome. For example, Mr. Hobsbawm and his fiercest critics sit next to each other on my shelves.'

I didn't need to know who Mr. Hobsbawm was to grasp the idea. 'I'm all for that, too.' I had a brief vision of the shelves of our library at Villa Emma and was almost surprised not to see almond, carob and fig trees beyond the window pane.

In the end I chose Orwell's *Nineteen Eighty-Four*, more because of the shopkeeper's enthusiasm for it than for any other reason – though the appeal of the central character's struggle against an all-controlling authority might have played its part. The idea that the year of the title had only just passed was amusing.

The man accompanied me to the door. 'I hope you enjoy it. Come back and let me know.'

I did go back – regularly. Instead of spending my afternoon breaks solely by the river, I headed more often for the church lawn. I read on the bench beneath the tall London planes and, on my way back to work, called on the bookshop owner. His name, I soon learnt, was Edward.

We discussed the weather, the end of the miners' strike, the success of 'We Are The World', and, of course, books. He often set aside one or two for me. At first I bought from him, but within months things changed: once I was done with a title, he let me return it to him and exchange it.

'Costs me nothing,' he said when I protested. 'My way of saying 'thank you' for your company.' But I could tell he didn't want to take money from a youngster on a waiter's wages.

He had an amusing system for grading a text's vocabulary: a 'foal' was accessible, a 'fully grown horse' a stretch and a 'Pegasus' best reserved for later. It was always gratifying to find myself able to read a work which had once been in the hardest category.

'I like your system,' I said, when he first set it out. 'Horses – very British.' We were sitting on the two leather-cushioned chairs by his desk, where we usually talked.

'I didn't come up with it. My late wife did. A paediatric physiotherapist. She helped children walk again after accidents and operations. She'd say: 'Now you're a colt, trotting slowly inside the paddock, but keep practising and before you know it you'll be a horse, galloping so fast that you'll grow wings.' I've often thought one could apply that to all kinds of things. She'd have made a wonderful mother, Sarah: so easy-going... We'd have enjoyed retirement together.' The crack in his voice belied his stoical tone. I looked down at the brass handles of the desk drawers and didn't raise my eyes until I was sure he had regained his composure.

This must have been in May or June 1985, a couple of months after I made it a habit to drop by.

As the summer wore on, Edward confided more.

'Sarah couldn't have children and in those years IVF wasn't on the horizon.' He sighed.

'Maybe working with them was the best thing, then.'

'Most of the time. Sometimes it was the worst. Got her down. Got us down.' He shrugged. 'Life. But you've got yours ahead of you – I don't want to weigh you down. All the more as we were happy, Sarah and I – not without our tough moments, but which couple doesn't have its share? Your parents too, I imagine?'

'Told you: dead, both. Still too painful to talk about.'

'So sorry. I understand.'

'It was after Sarah's death – cancer – that I opened this shop,' he revealed weeks later. 'After the wake, when the last of the guests left, I roamed through our house. What hap-

pened to all the dreams we had, Sarah? I asked. Where are all
the varieties of roses you wanted to grow in the garden? And
the Piranesi prints I was going to collect and deck our walls
with? Holidaying in France – we made *that* dream come true,
almost every summer. But learning to play the piano and the
violin to make music together? Reading the complete works
of Charles Dickens? Researching his biography? Children and
grandchildren – nothing we could do about that, but the rest?
How did we let ourselves be dragged along by the everyday?'

'As long as Sarah was there to talk to, even to sit with,'
he continued, 'I didn't feel the weight of all those dreams.
But now they reappeared. They filled the void of our home.
Why spend what's left of my life trawling through companies'
invoices and drawing up their accounts? There was enough
money in the bank. Piranesi? A passion I grew out of. Learning an instrument? Not without Sarah – it was for the closeness in making harmonies that I once had that dream. But literature, yes: I was too worn out to attempt writing, but now
was the time to pick up all those books I'd been saying I'd get
round to reading. Maybe I could even make a modest business
out of it, if only to keep active.'

He smiled at me and patted the pile of newly acquired
titles which he had been cataloguing when I stepped into the
shop. 'That was nearly fifteen years ago, son.'

I gave Edward a hand whichever way I could. I helped
him with stock taking, I learnt to write catalogue cards and to
find what clients requested on the shelves. Many of the books
were affordable paperbacks, but there were also plenty of expensive editions and complete series, often hardbound.

The clientele consisted partly of locals who wandered in,
browsed and left with a title they had chosen there and then,

partly of people who telephoned first and then came quite a distance for something specific. I soon found myself answering the phone if it rang while Edward was busy, and taking note of requests, whether for scholarly studies of Elizabethan furniture or 'how-to' guides to backyard treehouse-building.

In April 1987, a couple of years after first setting foot in the bookshop, I switched to working there in the mornings and early afternoons and at the restaurant in the evenings. Signor Luciano didn't mind. He was happy I stayed at all: Aldo and Gianni had long moved on, their places taken by others who left in turn; he had no illusions about how long the current set would last. It was the norm at that end of the restaurant trade.

Also my original roommates at the flat on the Harrow Road had gone – years earlier. Pino had bequeathed me a memento. On the day he left, he must have rummaged through my drawer and opened the box of coin casts. That night, on my return home, fragments of a shattered plaster coin stuck to my feet and wedged themselves between my toes. He hadn't even bothered to brush away the shards. They turned to powder in my hands. I still clench my fists at the thought.

Over the next three years a succession of roommates followed. If our working hours already stood in the way of socialising with each other, my awareness that for them the place was a revolving door put me off getting to know them properly. Pasquale and Alfredo were the exception: they stayed. They had saved all they could, obtained the backing of a cousin who had arrived a decade earlier; and finally opened a handkerchief-sized pizzeria at the northern end of Notting Hill, past All Saints Church, a neighbourhood where you were offered ganja by a sickly-looking stranger while taking a walk on a Sunday morning. Nonetheless, 'up and coming' was how my two friends described it. When I expressed reservations, they laughed and said, as usual, that I was being Eeyore, the gloomy old donkey who was a favourite with their cousin's four-year-old daughter.

Pasquale nudged Alfredo with an elbow. 'He needs a woman to cheer him up.' The two of them teased.

'Yeah, yeah,' I said. 'Like the ones you guys keep company with?'

'What's wrong with them?'

'One-night stands picked up at a pub? Not for me.'

'No, of course not: you talk to your dates and keep them waiting for you to make a move – until they tire and leave. Still saving yourself for 'the serious thing'?' Alfredo said. 'Thought you'd have given up by now.'

'This is the time for fun. First make your money. Then find a wife,' Pasquale added.

Their social life wasn't as dynamic as their banter. They worked even longer hours than when they had been hired by others.

I strove to do my best at the bookshop now that Edward employed me for half the day. I visited potential sources of stock, took over most of the cataloguing, emptied and varnished the bookcases... Even so, idle time was inevitable in an activity so dependent on people walking in or telephoning. By this stage the Classics section was well within the reach of my English. I worked my way through it: the great epics, plays, histories and philosophical treatises; commentaries on them; studies of life in the Greek and Roman worlds...

'I'm delighted to have you, Tom, but I can't help thinking you ought to make more of your life. If your folks were still alive, I'm sure they'd want you to.'

I tensed, almost hearing my mother saying, 'Make more of your life.'

'You could go to university.'

'No, thanks.' I moved away from the set of shelves where I had been sorting some books and turned my back on Edward. He stood where he was.

'If it's a question of money, I can lend it to you. You can repay me after your degree. No hurry.'

I shook my head.

'Then carry on here and go to university in the evenings. There's a college, Birkbeck, where you can do that.'

'No, thank you,' I repeated.

He shuffled towards me. 'Don't be too proud.' His tone was stern.

I turned to face him. 'I'm not. I'm happy as I am, that's all.'

'But you're very academic. And there is a right time for everything. I couldn't forgive myself if I didn't insist: can't think who else will but me.'

'In that case, Edward, I solemnly absolve you from your duty.' I raised my hands in mock blessing.

He took a step back and straightened. 'No need to get testy. I'm only telling you what I'm sure your father would.'

'No, he wouldn't. You never knew him.'

Edward took a deep breath and exhaled. 'Hear me out, Tom. Or have I not earned that right?'

I nodded. He had only shown me kindness.

He cleared his throat. 'Now then. When my wife died, I found it difficult, well, more like, very difficult. It won't feel as hard in a month or two, I told myself. But the first month or two passed. And then another. Finally, a friend suggested a bereavement counsellor. With hindsight, I wish I had seen her sooner. Time does heal, but when there's someone who can help us get there faster... There's no shame in it.' He waited for my reaction.

I crossed my arms and spoke slowly. 'You want me to see a counsellor?'

'I'm just saying they're there to help you – any of us – move on with your life after one death, let alone two.'

'I'm absolutely fine. Let me find my own path. Ok?'

He sighed. 'As you wish.'

It was weeks before the atmosphere between us recovered.

Over ten years at Edward's shop I read at least as many books from and about Ancient Greece and Rome as Classics undergraduates might. Unfettered by curriculum demands, essay deadlines or faculty politics, I was free to be a genuine lover of learning – 'amateur' means 'lover', after all. So I 'travelled' with Tiresias, the blind seer, through his life and those of others on his path, all pawns in the hands of cruel gods. Nothing – not even his gifts of prophecy and several lifespans, nor his experiences of the world as both man and woman – could spare him or seven generations of Thebans. I pored over analyses of the myths of Apollo and Daphne, Diana and Actaeon, Orpheus and Eurydice... Scholars' insights made me feel wiser only for brief intervals – days, at most. I remained baffled by the arbitrariness of fate and the elusiveness of meaning.

Yet without the urge to find out, and without the passion for worlds part-lost, part-known, I wouldn't be tutoring pupils in Latin and Greek today. I do enjoy teaching – especially A Level students. They're past the basics and can grapple with ideas which have proved worth handing on for millennia. I suppose that in them I recognise something of myself and of my father. I wonder if I'd have managed to remain tied for long to the family firm as he eventually was, the hunger for knowledge confined to scant spare time.

I had been working at the bookshop for about four years – it was March 1991 – when in walked a slim, tall young woman with long corkscrew curls and a violin case on her back. She was striking, though her beauty was not of the classical type. She had a long, angular face, with a high forehead, deep-set eyes and a thin mouth with a well-mannered and self-sufficient expression. After closing the door, she stood still, taking in the walls and the books. Edward was out. With a small nod, she acknowledged my presence behind the desk.

I walked up to her. 'Let me know if I can help you. Not all the books about music are where you'd expect.'

Her tone wasn't unfriendly but her manner confounded me. 'I wasn't looking for a book about music.' She smiled like a *kore*, an archaic Greek sculpture: unruffled, outside time. Her quiet, calm voice confirmed the feeling.

I cleared my throat. 'I shouldn't have presumed.'

Her lips opened into a wider smile. 'It's ok. I'm not looking for anything specific. Something might turn out to have my name on it, but I don't know yet.'

I couldn't believe what I said next.

'And your name is?'

That's how Zoe and I first met, more than twenty years ago. Then, as now, she lived in Earl's Court but had been rehearsing for a concert at the church near the bookshop. I wanted to impress her. I shifted the conversation towards the so-called modes of music in ancient Greece. I knew enough to tell her that different *harmoniai* were meant to convey a specific mood and to induce it in the audience. Plato would even forbid soldiers to listen to certain music as it might 'soften' them.

'There's some truth to it,' I said.

She laughed. 'To music turning brutes into ballerinas, like Monostatos's henchmen?'

I didn't know what she was talking about. 'Ballerinas? No. I just meant to music speaking more directly than words.'

She smiled at me with amused indulgence. I crossed my arms.

'Yes,' she said. 'It's the kind of thing we've known instinctively since we lived in caves. The theory keeps resurfacing – in Mozart's time, for example. I love Mozart.'

'We've got a couple of books on him.' Mustering my best professional composure, I stopped myself dashing too fast to where I remembered seeing them. 'Here,' I said.

'Sorry.' She bit her lip. 'I read those a while ago.'

'Well, if you do need me, I'll be at the desk.'

My eyes followed her through the narrow aisles till she picked out a travel guide to Madrid.

She looked for the price in the inside jacket, counted the right change and placed it before me. 'See? There was a book with my name on it.'

It struck me as bizarre that she should be paying: it felt as if she weren't a customer but a long lost friend, the kind who might appear and reappear in dreams but dissolve when I awoke.

'Serendipity,' she was saying. 'We're playing in Madrid in a couple of months. I've never been.'

'We?'

'The quartet.'

She took the violin case off her shoulder, dug inside the compartment for the music scores and handed me a leaflet. 'We've been together since music college.' The information printed in black on plain paper spelled out a programme of lunchtime concerts at the nearby church.

'We're doing the first three. Come and hear us.'

I cleared my throat. 'I'd like that. Very much.'

CHAPTER 17

When the day came, I sat in the half-empty pews, spellbound by Zoe and her three colleagues – all young women in their mid-twenties – and by Beethoven's music. How did such harmonies fill a church when they sprang from four thin wooden boxes, the rasping of horse hair on gut, the toing and froing of human arms and hands bent at strange angles like those of jointed puppets?

Zoe underwent a metamorphosis. She was first violin. After the opening phrases of the *adagio*, the collected young woman who had walked into the bookshop bent and swayed with the music, as the composition entered more expressive territory. Her bow alternately tickled, caressed and lashed the strings. On a poignant note, the corners of her mouth twitched. When finally the music eased off, she stood on tiptoes as if she and her instrument would take flight. In the *adagio molto cantabile* she regained her composure and I thought again of a *kore*, only for the *più mosso* to follow and transform her once more. A sense of relief spread through me when the quartet took a bow and I saw that Zoe's smile was unscathed by the journey.

I went to congratulate her. 'That was extraordinary.'

I was happy she recognised me.

'You're very kind. Thanks for coming.' Then she whispered, 'You must have been the only member of the audience under eighty.'

'Well, it *is* the middle of the day.'

'Come to the pub with us? We're starving.'

'I can't. I've already taken time off to be here.'

'Ah, well. But don't forget our next performance, will you?'

That afternoon Edward told me to stop being 'hyperactive' with the filing of invoices and in the evening at the restaurant I earned more tips than ever. I hadn't fallen in love. I knew that for certain because it didn't feel anything like with Anna, nor could I desecrate her memory – but I still looked forward to seeing Zoe again.

In the event I didn't have to wait till the next concert. She visited the bookshop twice, after rehearsals. We talked of the Haydn string quartet on the programme, the book I was reading, the unreliability of public transport, Putney and Earl's Court... Edward seemed absorbed in paperwork but I caught sight of him watching us.

When she had gone, he looked warmly at me. 'She's nice.'

'I thought you told me to avoid the word nice,' I teased. 'Too general, isn't it?'

'Sometimes we have to make an exception. Next time, take her to the café down the road.'

There's no point giving you all the details. Zoe and I got on effortlessly. We met over coffees. We went for walks. When friends gave her free passes to concerts at which they were playing, she asked me to go with her. We watched operas on the cheap, standing up in the slips or sitting in 'the gods'. I started taking evenings off from Signor Luciano's.

Zoe even talked me into going to a few parties. Though the smoky flats, the tipsy company and fondling couples repulsed me, I enjoyed the complicity which the atmosphere conjured between us. We'd spend most of the evening talking only with each other – on steps, in a corner, or on a balcony. Shutting out the noise around us intensified our closeness, confirming my early impressions: I felt at ease with her as with a childhood friend or even a sister.

We weren't spared the initial awkward moments, though. One occurred at a party given by a friend of hers at his Dept-ford flat. It wasn't his taste in pop and rock that drove us out onto the pavement, but the volume.

Zoe shook her head.

'Percussionists.'

I motioned towards the kebab shop across the street. 'Some water? For the throat?' A bunch of teenage boys in sleeveless t-shirts were coming out. They eyed us. 'Smoochy, smoochy,' one of them mocked. They sniggered as they walked into the night.

'No, I'm all right.' Her back against the wall, she gazed down at her feet. They looked over-long in the thick Mary Janes at the end of her boot-cut jeans. 'Can I ask you some-thing?'

'Sure.'

She lifted her eyes and fixed me. 'Why haven't you ever –'

'What?'

'Kissed me.' She paused, then blurted, 'I've made it quite plain – umpteen times – that you could, but you act like you don't notice.'

'Plain?'

'What's the matter with you? Is there someone else?'

'Someone else? No.' Or not in the way she meant.

She let out a big puff of breath. 'It's me, then.'

'No, God, no. I just...'

Till that moment I had thought of Zoe as robust and self-reliant. Now, leaning against the red brick, she looked vulnerable. Her skin was lunar under the harsh street light. I wanted to put my arms around her but a vision of my innocent embrace slipping into a kiss held me back – how would I undo that without hurting her? Yet the sight of her deflated, no, diminished, by my silence was unbearable. The temptation to tell her everything was never as strong as in that instant.

I stroked her arms and held onto them lightly. 'Zoe.' She fixed me with an inquiring gaze.

'In the months I've known you,' I said, 'You've become the person I care most about in the whole world. Believe me.'

'So why...?'

'Something years ago. Maybe one day it won't feel like it does now. Edward says time heals, but even if he turns out to be right, it might still take a very long time. You're too good to have to wait. If seeing me only as a friend hurts you and you'd rather walk away, I'll understand.'

I said it without hesitation, though I wanted to cry, 'Don't leave me.'

I saw the pity in her eyes. 'I don't want you to feel sorry for me.' I let go of her arms and turned around. 'I don't deserve it.'

What a picture we must have made, the two of us with hands and backs flattened against a wall, eyes on the potholed pavement, faces tense. My ears became alert to Zoe's irregular breathing, the music in the apartment behind us, the clacking heels of a woman, the buzzing of a moped.

Zoe pressed her lips together, straightened her shoulders and took my hand in hers. 'Ok. If friends is all we can be, let's be friends. At least it's clear – and *that* is a relief.'

She has had boyfriends in the years since. They don't last. From one she was not getting the 'emotional sharing' she calls 'vital'; with another it didn't work in the bedroom; and the next was too controlling. One or two slammed the door of her apartment in my face. They resented her confiding in me. An accountant who lasted nearly four years came knocking at my door and told me to stay clear. I was to blame for the cracks in their relationship, he said, but I wasn't. I never spoke ill of him or of any of the others. In his case I thought that an instinctive facility for arithmetic and a fixation for hoisin duck was all he and Zoe shared, though I never said it to her.

I'm not sure how helpful I've ever been to Zoe, whereas for me she has been the proverbial 'rock'. It was to her that I turned when Edward became too nosy. Over the years he had made attempts at prying into my past with innocent-seeming questions which I had managed to evade. Nevertheless, fragments of the picture must have emerged as we skirted around subjects. He sensed the existence of a secret.

One morning in April 1997 he uncorked a bottle of champagne. 'Ten years,' he said, inviting me to stand. In response to my puzzled face, he added, 'Since you started working here.'

'And you're celebrating? You're not asking yourself: how have I stood him for so long?'

He chuckled. 'I thought self-deprecation was one of *our* national talents?'

I raised my glass. 'To your health, Edward.'

'To yours – and your future.'

Call it instinct, but I wondered if this charming ceremony wasn't a preamble.

'I'm so grateful. You're as close as I've ever come to having a son. In my old age, too. I only wish – '

'Yes?'

'You won't like me bringing this up, but I do wish you'd

make more of yourself.'

'Give up, Edward, don't spoil a good thing.'

'Is it? You should be out there building something of your own – a career, a family, at least an attachment, a circle of friends, but instead... And such diffidence, even with me, even after all this time.'

I sighed.

'It's like you're punishing yourself. What for?'

'None of your business.'

'But I want you to be happy.'

'I am.'

'Rubbish. A happy man feels free to focus his energies on something or someone outside himself, to make a mark, whatever his gift.'

'Maybe I don't have one.'

'Everyone has a gift, and you, more than your fair share. It hurts to see it. Problem is, you're not free, are you? There's some kind of lead ball at the end of a chain holding you back. What is it? I'll help in any way I can.'

I gritted my teeth. 'I don't want to be nasty. If I stay here another minute, I'll say things I'll regret. I know you care, but now you're trespassing.' I picked up my jacket from the back of my chair and slipped it on.

He opened his arms. 'Tom, I mean well.'

I tugged at my shirt collar and pulled down the cuffs without meeting his eyes. 'Yes. That's why you don't know when to stop.' Before he could reply, I made for the door and was out in the fresh April air.

I walked at a furious pace to Putney Bridge Underground. By then I had come to a conclusion: I must find another way to earn my living. If I lingered around Edward, at some point he'd be tempted to make enquiries with the Italian authorities. I had never divulged my real surname to him or anyone else since arriving in the UK, but if a snapshot found its way to the consulate I might be tracked down. Unlike Edward, Signor Luciano had an instinct for steering clear of awkward questions, but now that my English was no longer a hurdle I'd welcome a job more challenging than waiting at tables.

I decided to venture to the streets neighbouring the Italian church in Clerkenwell. Over the years I had known people who received assistance of all kinds from fellow Italians in that area. When one of my flatmates was arrested for stealing from the garage where he worked, a group of Italian volunteers operating from there visited him in prison. I wouldn't stoop to asking one of the church-linked groups to help me find work, but who knew what might come from a stroll around the streets of this Little Italy? It was worth exploring, if only to collect my thoughts before discussing things with Pasquale or Zoe.

From the window of the deli next to the church, trays of *cannoli siciliani* filled with ricotta and candied fruit offered the promise of a once familiar taste. Only a few doors down was a café that could easily have been transplanted from Ostuni or Milan: chairs of wood and straw, TV in a corner, assorted Italian beers, liquors and *Serie A* football club banners behind the counter, a huge La Cimbali machine waiting to spew vapour and the aroma of freshly ground coffee. Small notices were pinned to a notice board like an untidy collection of butterflies.

'*Buongiorno*,' I said to the barman, a short grey-haired fellow in a white apron, and to the elderly couple reading the

Corriere della Sera and *La Repubblica*. The *Corriere dello Sport* and *Avvenire* hung, crinkled and tousled, from the newspaper rack behind their table.

I asked for an espresso. Cup and saucer in hand, I browsed through the notices. 'To rent: room in two-bed flat.' 'To sell: Vespa, 1990.' 'Painter and decorator available.' 'Commercial translators wanted: Italian - English - Italian.' That might be an idea. I finished my coffee and scribbled down the name and phone number of the agency.

A tap on the shoulder made me jump.

The old man who had been reading the *Corriere* spoke in Italian. 'Excuse me.' He observed me from behind thick glasses.

'Yes?'

He turned towards his wife. 'It *is* him.'

The woman huffed and got up. 'Gets worse every day,' she said under her breath as she approached me. 'I'm so sorry. When he gets something into his head...' Red faced, she twirled a finger in the air.

'That's ok.'

'But it *is* him,' her husband repeated. 'Pietro, have you still got the *Corriere* of a couple of days back?'

'Not here. Maybe in the store room.'

The old man pointed at me. 'There were notices in the *Corriere* this week, and last week too. With a photo of you – only, younger. And with a reward. Millions of lire. Millions.'

'It can't be me, sir.' I made the effort to look unruffled, and even managed to smile meaningfully at his wife. She shook her head apologetically.

'Great coffee,' I said to the barman as I left.

When I turned the corner, I leaned against a wall and

pressed my palms to my eyes. I rushed to Farringdon Station only once I stopped sweating and my heartbeat quietened down.

Zoe stared at me. We were sitting side by side on her sofa. 'Disappear so Edward can't find you? No, I'm not going to help. You can't do that to him. He loves you like... like...' Instead of dipping the celery stick in the hoummos on the coffee table, she brandished it like a pocket-knife.

I lowered my eyes. '...A son?'

'Yes. No, even better: without the tug between parent and child. What has he done to make you want to hurt him so badly? Good God, Tom. People die of heartache for less. There was this friend of my parents who –'

I interrupted. 'So what do I do? He harps on about me not putting my talents to 'better use'. He hints there's something wrong with me if I don't.'

She gaped. 'And that's why you'd disappear into thin air?'

'But he goes on and on, Zoe. I can only take so much.'

I could hardly tell her about the incident in Clerkenwell. All I needed was for Edward to contact the authorities when it seemed my mother was still hunting me down – she didn't give up, did she? She hadn't changed – and they'd put two and two together, as you English say. I had to get away from him. As if it weren't enough that he was pressing me to dig into my past. Why? Pain which couldn't be relieved was best left buried.

I didn't want Zoe, who respected my silence, to start getting ideas from Edward. She loved the person I had become, the one I had earned myself the right to be over fourteen years in London. Why couldn't Edward do as she did?

'What if he's right?' Zoe chewed on the celery and looked around the sitting room as if her stacks of cassettes, her books, the orchid on the window sill and the kilim stools could whisper back an answer. 'At least partly,' she added.

'Not you, too.'

She motioned to me. 'How can someone be one moment wise and another so childish? It beggars belief. What's so hard about keeping your mind open when people who love you give you an opinion? You can always disagree, but first hear them out.'

I picked up a carrot stick. 'Ok. I'm listening.'

'Without that raised eyebrow and the rolling eyes.'

'I didn't – '

She placed her hand on mine. 'Tom, please. An open mind, ok?'

I nodded.

'You're passionate about the ancient world. As a matter of fact, you're the only person I've ever come across who enjoys reading Latin and Greek. Rather you than me.'

'...Says the only person *I*'ve ever come across who'll drool over a Mozart manuscript.'

'You mean who has to stop herself from drooling over it. I'd never desecrate a Mozart manuscript.' She laughed. 'Ok, maybe we're similar in that respect. But here's what I was getting at: why don't you teach? Pass your enthusiasm on to kids.'

'Me, teach?'

'Why not?'

'I don't have a degree.'

'So go to uni and get one, then teach in schools.' She scratched the back of her head. 'Or you could tutor kids one-to-one, privately, for GCSE and A Level. What really matters is to know your stuff, and you certainly do.'

'Assuming you're right... I might be dreadful at it.'

She smiled. 'I doubt it. You get more fired up by the ascension of – Romulus, was it? – than by who wins elections, or the World Cup, or... You'd be infectious. I could ask around. One of my violin students might need help. Word spreads quickly among parents. And then Edward will be happy and get off your back.'

That was how my tutoring career began. Zoe was right: I could teach – and it paid well. Occasionally I also did commercial translations from, or into, Italian. Within six months I had enough work to be able to quit both the bookshop and the restaurant.

Edward said a generous goodbye. 'It'll be so sad not to see you every day, but I'm glad for you that you're moving on. Good things will come of it. And you'll pop in now and then for a chat with your old friend, won't you?'

Signor Luciano's reaction was equally open-handed. 'I've been expecting this moment for years. Good luck – and you have an invitation for lunch here any day.'

I moved out of the Harrow Road and rented a studio flat in North End Road, much closer to where most of my pupils lived. There was barely room for a hob, a fridge and a sofa bed but it was all my own. And I did visit Edward, Signor Luciano, Pasquale and Alfredo. I still do. They – and Zoe – are my friends.

Today Pasquale and Alfredo run the restaurant they have always wanted: a place in Notting Hill, constantly packed, serving Italian fare so genuine you could be in their home town in Campania. Signor Luciano lingers around his place in

Putney though it is now managed by his son Vincenzo, who sticks with his father's formula, too insecure about his roots to change anything.

Edward has closed down the bookshop and retired to a compound of assisted homes in Richmond, with a health centre and the company of other well-heeled elderly folks. Once a week we stroll together in Richmond Park or by the river and finish up at the same café where the waitresses mistake us for father and son. We talk all the time, but never of my past in Italy. Edward stopped prying once I left the bookshop, as if my 'moving on' finally sanctioned not looking back.

Zoe built as solid a career as a musician can, short of becoming a star soloist. For the last ten years, she has been first violin in a well-known quartet, performing in venues like the Wigmore Hall all over the world. She plays for famous orchestras, tutors and writes articles for magazines. As I said earlier, even a musician of her calibre can never rest, nor wholly avoid bending to audience demands; she is always on the lookout for the next source of income.

Occasionally I've checked on how things evolved in Puglia. When I first arrived here, few people had heard of it, but now it's a tourist destination. Who'd have guessed? More *trulli* and *masserie*, the typical Apulian farmhouses, have been bought up by the British than by any others, though Puglia seems to be the 'great discovery' also of the French, Germans, Americans... Do an online search and you soon lose count of the foreign celebrities who own properties there. I looked at the website of our family company. It specialises in restoring *masserie*. Trust my mother: that's where the money is.

You see, everyone moved on. It's the natural course of things. We forget our mother's breast when we progress to solid foods. We leave our train set behind when we progress to our first motorbike... I've never forgotten Anna, but she's different. There's nothing I can do to put things right with her – I was too slow, so I lost my chance. That makes it wrong – even obscene – to forget her. In order to endure, I move forward, but only as far as my guilt allows.

You, however, are young and the man you hurt is alive. If there's anything you can do to make amends, don't waste time. Even with a drink-drive conviction, a decent and bright person like you can give life a purpose. You said you felt compelled to change my fortunes for the better – channel that energy into transforming your own.

What have you received on your smart phone to make you jump like that? And why are you taking your laptop out of your rucksack? The notary was expecting you to report back, so you told him you weren't sure whether you had found the right person? And he had a letter ready for me from my mother. Well, well... You have the measure of her. He calls it 'information of which Mr. Tommaso Spagnulo would most certainly wish to be aware,' and you believe him. Do you realise that it might be her last ruse? All right, I hope I'm grown up enough to handle it.

No, I don't mind if we read it together, though it's nearly eleven. Not too tired? We can always go through it tomorrow morning. You could sleep here on the sofa. No? Too impatient? Well then, get ready for my darling *mater*'s final throw.

CHAPTER 18

My son,

I've spent longer than you might ever imagine thinking how to begin. If it really is you reading this, a 'My dearest' might provoke your revulsion, even though you are dearest to me. A 'Dear Tommaso' might disgust you by its impersonal tone and a 'Tommaso dear' by its sentimentality. 'My son' is hard fact, so it should suit us both.

How disconcerting, to write not knowing if you live or not, and aware that if this letter reaches you it'll be because I'm no longer here. I grieve at the thought that you won't be able to reply. Yet I must attempt the impossible. I want you to know the truth. I've never stopped looking for you, though everyone has long presumed you dead. Be certain of your mother's love, though I completely understand if these words arouse scorn. I deserve it.

If you are alive, I wonder where you are. I have imagined you everywhere: in the ragged Calabrian mountains, the bustle of Istanbul, the cacophony of New York, the wilderness of the Pampas – all places I've seen on TV. I have searched for glimpses of you among the crowds captured by the cameras. If you are abroad, I wonder if you remember Italian. They say memory of the mother tongue lingers even for those who haven't heard it since infancy, but I wouldn't blame you if you had expunged it from your mind.

Can you remember me putting you to bed with fairy tales when you were little? Do you recall the one about the mother kidnapped by pirates and eventually reunited with her husband and children? Oh, the bitter ironies of life – it was your favourite. After your father died, I asked Concetta not to forget to tell you that one. How could I comfort you when I couldn't suppress my grief? I thought I had to shield you from it.

How I loved your father! I fell for him when I was a girl, and years later he could still charm me. 'Charming' is how everyone described him: bubbling with curiosity and able to pepper any conversation with intriguing titbits – a real juggler of thoughts.

Sometimes his enthusiasms made him tough to live with, for someone as tense and earnest as I was. And yet those very differences were among the many reasons we loved each other. When in '72 the soprintendenza *put a temporary stop to our building project, it couldn't have put pressure on a more tender point. It took some persuading, but after some weeks, I understood – at a superficial level, at least – that your father was right: we had no choice but to go along with the archaeologists' demands. Still, they had nothing at stake. We had the banks threatening foreclosure. Had Alvaro not been so excited about the finds and about the value of the experience for you, I wouldn't have suspected him of consenting too readily to requests for delays. I was being unfair to him. But my failure of trust didn't mean I didn't love him. A rising anxiety pulled my reins, not vice versa. So, after his death, my grief was compounded by guilt: had my outbursts intensified the strain to a level his heart couldn't cope with? It's taken me a lifetime to accept that I knew myself too little to behave any differently.*

Just before he set off to Brindisi with you for the final time, your father and I had one of those quarrels which had become frequent in that anxious climate. I'd give anything for our last conversation to have been tender – for a last chance to have told him how much I loved him. Afterwards, I regretted what I said as much as what I didn't. His parting gift, the ancient loom weights, sat on my bedside table like a reproach. You'd think these thoughts would have made me doubly gentle with you, but grief isolates those it engulfs. The notion that it should awaken us to others' needs is supposed to thwart grief's power – but it doesn't always work.

During the first few weeks after Alvaro's death, stroking the clothes in his wardrobes and holding them to my nose in the attempt to hang on to his smell took me to the edge of the bearable. His scent in the fabrics soothed me but awareness that it would gradually fade to nothing brought home the finality. If only a magic box could preserve that scent. If only I had recorded his voice at the dinner table, when he and I worked next to each other at the studio, when we watched you swimming at the beach…

And then one afternoon from the doorway I caught sight of you doing the same with one of Alvaro's sweaters. How morbid for a ten-year-old, I thought. I would have to empty your father's wardrobes. That coming Sunday, I sent you away with Giorgio's parents. Concetta helped me clear the shelves, take the shirts and the suits off the hangers and place them in shopping bags. Each garment brought memories and tears.

I sobbed while holding up a blue and red checked shirt Alvaro and I had bought just two years earlier in Via Frattina on a weekend together in Rome. We had come from Piazza di Spagna. It was June. The water in the Barcaccia fountain shimmered in the sunshine. He splashed me and I called him 'childish', but his laughter was infectious. I didn't keep a straight face for long, before splashing him back. Afterwards, to make up for trying to curb his mirth, I persuaded him to buy it.

Concetta tried to pull the shirt gently out of my hands, but I kept it, and a few more of his favourites: the blue and white tie I gave him for Christmas when we were newly engaged; the jacket of Irish tweed with which he came back from a trip to Milan and which I loathed at first for making him look older than his age… I told myself that if he stepped into the room he'd be pleased. I knew he wasn't coming back, yet a part of me still hoped.

I was grateful to Concetta for dealing with the rest; she carried the bags to her Fiat Centoventisette and delivered them to Caritas. The calming pills prescribed by our family doctor didn't seem to have much effect, either that day or any other: I still felt as hollowed out as the instant I burst into the hospital and was told he had died. I could move, speak, hear and see, but my thoughts were disconnected from my actions. For months a sense of foreboding permeated my dreams and awoke me again to his absence, every dawn.

It was just you and me, now: a ten-year-old and his thirty-eight-year-old mother. I was unprepared for losing a husband. I had no parents, no degree and only limited work experience, but plenty of pressing creditors.

When you returned that evening and saw your father's empty wardrobes, you wailed and tugged at my hands, imploring me to reclaim his clothes. The torpor from the pills made me feel as if I were seeing and hearing you from behind a net curtain. Even so, your desperation connected with mine. I wanted to hug you and tell you I understood – that you were right and we'd get your daddy's clothes back, first thing in the morning. But I didn't act. I must appear strong for your sake, I thought. Seeing me crumble wouldn't be good for you. I must hold firm though you'd think me cruel: I wanted to stop you from standing at the edge of what you couldn't know was an abyss, and ensure that everyday life absorbed you.

Today I'd hug you there and then. I wouldn't get rid of your father's things until both of us felt ready. But today I'm not the young and lonely woman I was.

Nowadays there'd be no stigma in seeking a psychologist's help. Back then it didn't even occur to me: I did what I could to cope, and Concetta offered me steady support. I let the building project consume me like a widow on her husband's funeral pyre. The delays had caused urgent problems and I had to work hard to earn the respect of workmen, suppliers and bankers. Building construction was a man's industry. But the firm was our livelihood.

I have picked up some valuable know-how during four decades in the business: for example, how heavy rain stagnates on soil with poor drainage; and how toxic bacteria and moulds will follow, attacking plants' roots and smothering seedlings. So today it is obvious to me that by putting on a tough front at work and at home and avoiding grappling with our pain, I was prolonging and deepening it.

Surprisingly – no, 'appallingly', you could say – for the first few years after you disappeared I failed others as I had failed you: I couldn't respond any better to the loss of you than to your father's. I must have seemed just as distant. When I stopped to think, I found my mind spiralling down the coils of gloom and regret. Incessant activity was an anaesthetic. It worked for a while, without changing anything.

Had Alvaro lived, would you still have constantly measured yourself against him? Would you have rebelled? In your teens you charged me with comparing you to him but it was you who did it, not I. The greediness with which you drank in the classics on his library shelves or studied his travel sketchbooks alarmed me. The past – whether ancient or more recent – seemed to be your refuge from the present. It takes one avoider to recognise another.

For Alvaro, on the other hand, those books and journeys were integral to engaging with life: he was always channelling his knowledge and energy for some purpose. He had so many interests and would have acquired additional ones with the years. However, his enthusiasm for the Classical world was the one you had shared with him at a time you'd always remember. No wonder that, for you, he was forever frozen in that dimension.

Your closeness to Concetta both aroused my resentment and comforted me. I envied you your mutual confidences, yet I was incapable of narrowing the rift which had opened up between us. Your grudging *obedience and veiled resistance were exasperating. But didn't all teens rebel? We were lucky, I told myself, that you confided in Concetta.*

She is still here, you know. A kind nurse. I try not to make unnecessary demands on her — the ill can be so unreasonable, as if the healthy were an affront. Old, tired women — that's what we are. She doesn't trust herself to drive anymore: our reflexes are slow, young drivers always in a hurry. The horns honk behind her as she manoeuvres the car into a parking space, and make her break into sweats; being tailgated, then overtaken at the slenderest widening in the road, sets off her palpitations; braking too late when the car in front slows down for an indicator-less turn has cost us three visits in two years to the garage. So, earlier this afternoon she took a taxi into town and returned home a few moments ago with a present for me: a fleecy white dressing gown dotted with pink roses, the collar trimmed with two satin pink bows.

'You can't manage with just the one anymore.' She pointed to the woollen beige robe I'm wearing as I sit up in bed to write this letter. A bed tray has been doubling as my desk and dining table for the last couple of weeks. I am luckier than many: the palliatives are working; occasionally they make me retch, but it's a small price to pay.

'You shouldn't have,' I said. I'll wear it for what — a few weeks? A few months at best? Then she'll have to fold it and place it in a plastic bag headed for Caritas, I thought. But she is already feeling bereft — the three of us were her family — so I only added, 'You're always so good to me.'

I've made provision for her — she'll never have a financial worry — but money is not what's on her mind. Almost all my life Concetta felt older — wiser, for sure — to me than the three years between us. And yet now she looks so lost. As I finish making things easy for everyone after my death — all investments converted to cash, all powers of attorney given... I have to be careful with my words, not to distress her: I am only 'putting my affairs in order' for my 'departure'. I suppose all of us are a surprise to each other until the end.

The way I see it, I'm fortunate to know that I'll soon die: for years I thought of writing you this letter but was overwhelmed by the prospect; my only wish now is to be granted enough time to complete it; the doctor assures me I'll remain lucid. Does death frighten me? A little. But I have found life so hard.

Many years ago Concetta told me of her role in your story with Anna and asked for my forgiveness.

'What is there to forgive?' I said. Had each of us known the consequences of what we said or did at the time, we might have acted differently. Yet our actions could have triggered a sequence of events so unlike the one which unfolded. A happier future was a real possibility at so many junctures. That fact does not assuage my mind, though.

Shortly after you first left for Milan, Anna's father came to see me. When we heard the knock at the door, Concetta and I looked at each other. It was evening and we weren't expecting anybody. He introduced himself brusquely.

'Pietro Saponaro, Anna's father. Let me in.'

While I struggled to recall who Anna was, he strutted past Concetta and me. After trampling with muddy boots on the Persian rugs, he halted in the centre of the sitting room, looked around appreciatively and nodded to himself, arms crossed. I was shocked less by his rudeness than by what he told me. I had no idea you had been seeing so much of his daughter, let alone that she was pregnant by you.

'My son is meant for better things,' I kept thinking as I took in his unkempt hair, language spiked with dialect and uncouth gestures. He clomped about my sitting room as if he owned it.

'I want him to do 'the honourable thing'.'

I retorted that I would never consent to you marrying his daughter. Legally you were both adults, but who would want to start wedded life at nineteen without parental support? I offered instead to help keep things quiet. But no, he was adamant that the baby would be born, that you should recognise it as yours and marry Anna.

He smirked. 'That boy won't get away with it so cheaply.'

How had you allowed yourself to become entangled with unsavoury characters like these? My fault, no doubt, for having kept you so sheltered that as soon as you stepped into the real world they ensnared you. Oh, my child.

It dawned on me that you and Anna would almost certainly approach me together to persuade me to let you marry. But with a father like Pietro Saponaro, what could the daughter be like? I had no doubt how things would end if I listened to your pleas: divorce or resigned hostility between you. I couldn't let that happen. I loved you. I wanted you to be happy.

It was more than likely that you wouldn't listen to me: you were in love; you could also be so contrary and stubborn. I had to talk to Anna alone. When I called her the next morning, she agreed to meet me at Villa Emma that afternoon. I arranged for Concetta to be out.

At first Anna sat opposite me on our sofa, fiddling with her shirt sleeves or clasping her knees like a felon awaiting verdict. I didn't give her the chance to tell me her side of the story, but called her a gold-digger and swore that her father wouldn't manage to make me agree to such a foolish marriage.

She protested that until my phone call she had not known of her father's visit but that it did not surprise her.

'I don't want money. We simply love each other,' she said.

The concepts of 'simple' and 'love' in the same sentence? How naïve. I nearly laughed. But in the years since, I have learnt to recognise loves which flow effortlessly. They are the few truly blessed ones, and I realise that's what yours was. Some forbearance helps most of the others chug along. The difficulty is in telling the real thing from the unwitting impostor in the early, idyllic phase.

Anna straightened up in her seat, distaste and hurt written on her face, looking almost regal. She offered to tell you she wouldn't marry you. She had thought about it for days: in future you might regret a 'reparatory wedding' and resent her. She loved you too much to want to run that risk and said she had already told you.

Her hauteur and affronted tone at my suspicions earned her a smidgen of my respect. But it was unrealistic to imagine that her family would let her raise a baby without paternity acknowledged. I had my impression of Pietro Saponaro.

It wasn't until years later that I learnt how her family were told about the pregnancy. It wasn't Anna. Her sister saw her vomiting on a couple of occasions and guessed. Only then did Anna admit the truth. Her parents called her a whore.

'But we'll get your rights respected. He'll marry you alright,' her father repeated. When Anna said no, because you, my son, might regret it later, her parents blamed all 'her damned books'. However, they made a contingency plan: they would settle for recognition of the baby. They wouldn't allow you to get away with less.

I knew nothing of this when Anna came to Villa Emma, and I gave her no chance to tell me. Before she arrived I primed myself to act coolly: I wouldn't be derailed by her pleas. A coward, as ever, I stuck to that script. Whether I believed her or not was irrelevant, I told her. She might be sincere, but could she guarantee that her child wouldn't grow up to be greedy? Give birth to it, and the proverbial sword of Damocles would dangle over my son's head. In any event Tommaso would feel duty-bound to marry her if there was a child involved. And then, as she herself feared, what would that lead to but misery all round? Was that what she wished?

'No, of course not,' she flashed back. But a second later she looked so disconsolate that I almost took pity on her. 'What shall I do?' she asked.

'The right thing: an abortion,' I said. Afterwards she could see whether your love for each other was meant to last. Her decision, of course. I could help by making the call to the best obstetrician in Ostuni and by paying for everything – no one would ever hear about it. But if that was what she decided, you must not learn I was involved.

She shook her head and buried her face in her hands. 'No, no,' she muttered.

I told her to think it over, that one thing must be clear: this was my best offer, not a negotiating position.

After seeing her out, I watched her cross the garden and make for the gate. The unsteady step, the sinking head and stooped shoulders reminded me of enfeebled stray dogs which wander alone through the olive groves after being forced out by the pack. How long can they survive on their own? How long before she'd have to accept my offer?

She rang me the next day. I didn't know whether to despise her for surrendering so soon or to admire her resoluteness. Her thin voice at the other end of the line was like a pointed finger grating against my chest. I paid Dr. Ruggero handsomely to ensure the abortion would take place within days, in case she had second thoughts. He called me afterwards: the procedure was successful; a healthy young female; no impact on the patient's ability to bear children in future.

I found out much later what happened next. I shall explain, I promise, how I came by the information, but first things first. Anna told her parents about the abortion. She considered herself an obedient daughter – except for her relationship with you. She longed to be truthful. I imagine that won't surprise you.

Her mother charged from one room to the next, alternately wailing and covering her mouth so as not to summon the neighbourhood. Her father called Anna a 'lost' daughter – no, indeed, no daughter of his, but a whore and a murderess, as well as stupid for letting you get away scot-free. She should forget about university: this was where too much reading had led; and she couldn't be trusted not to commit further idiocies. She'd better start looking for a job in Ostuni: focus on practicalities. Her sister urged her to forget about you and the abortion – how crass.

Can you imagine how Anna must have felt? Whether a few-weeks-old foetus was or wasn't an embryonic human being was a specious legal distinction to her. In her eyes she had committed a heinous crime. The child of your love, the child she'd have cherished with or without you by her side, was lost – forever. The sin would earn her eternal damnation, and the horror she now felt at herself and in her parents' harsh words was a foretaste of Hell. On the one hand, she thought she wholly deserved the distress she was in; on the other, she longed for your understanding and comfort. But how was she to tell you what she had done? She confided in Lidia.

Her friend was stunned: of the two of them, Anna always was the one who effortlessly did 'the right thing'. So devout, too. She could not have reached her decision lightly. No surprise that her voice was so agitated and her account of events so fevered. Lidia tried to keep her own alarm in check. Anna should speak with Giorgio, she reasoned, as no one would know how to approach you better than him.

Anna followed the advice – and you arrived in front of her house just as your best friend was comforting her. I understand that Giorgio left you together. But his blind trust in the power of love – rather touching and a great deal more romantic than I'd have credited him with being – was misplaced. It was barely a few days after the abortion and Anna had not had the chance to disentangle her emotions, let alone to work out how to explain her actions to you. So she blurted out a fib about a miscarriage. And then, almost immediately, she told you the truth. Am I right? I don't think I need to remind you of your reaction.

Maybe lies are better, if a woman can't stop loving a man who doesn't truly understand her. Or maybe not, as after some weeks of reflection you clearly did understand, and loved her, proving that no love is stronger than the one which survives knowledge of the other person's worst traits and mistakes.

I won't deny the gravity of my role in pushing you to leave for Milan. The word 'regret' cannot express the anguish which grips me to this day when I dwell on the moment when in my office you told me a story to which you presumed me a stranger. I can hardly ask for your sympathy. I just want you to know.

With you gone, Anna turned again to Lidia, who suggested that she write you a letter. Anna did. Not knowing your address, she sent it to your faculty office at Bocconi. Why didn't she call Giorgio first to ask for your whereabouts? How could she trust in an impersonal system?

The letter lay unclaimed in that office for weeks until an anonymous hand scribbled on it 'return to sender'. It was delivered back long after she and you had disappeared. Her mother brought it to me, unopened. I didn't invite her in and she didn't ask. On our doorstep, the hatred and pity in our stares vied with each other.

How was Anna to know that you never received her message? What was she to make of your silence? She thought that her explanations and pleas had failed to appease you: you had deserted her for good. Abandoned by you, despised by her father, a disappointment to her mother, and spurned by me, she decided to leave.

First she entrusted Giorgio with a second letter to you. Of that, you know — and that I intercepted it, read it, burned it. For her parents she left a note — that, too, you saw, penned on the only writing paper in the house: a gift from you which still felt precious to her.

The moment when I learnt from you that Anna had disappeared is frozen in time, like the victim of a glacier: you, standing by my bedroom door, demanding to see the letter Giorgio had brought; I, trying to collect myself, with the excuse of concentrating on my cardigan buttons embossed with the Luisa Spagnoli logo; you, telling me Anna's parents hadn't seen her for days; my sudden fear of the worst after her return home from the clinic; my attempt to tell myself she must be playing a childish game and would soon be home.

When, later that day, you confronted me – after Concetta had told you all she knew – the same fear travelled through my bones like a tremor before an earthquake. And yet I dismissed it again: her disappearance would be short-lived; it was emotional blackmail of you and her parents. These seemed much more probable explanations than the possibility of suicide.

Until then I had seen myself as the one who had taken on the sin of the abortion, for love of you. Today I'm aghast at that rationalisation. The capacity for self-righteousness is the human flaw against which I most urge you to beware: not for love of me, but to avoid the anguish when you discover too late how it has blinded you. Hate me if you like, but learn from my errors. Imagine: after Dr. Ruggero told me that the operation had been successful, I went to confession. But can a sin be absolved by a priest's incantations? I wonder, especially if with each consequence the cancer grows. And I soon learnt of the consequences: Anna's disappearance, followed by yours. The moment you told me she was missing, I sensed it would crystallise your love for her.

Three days after your arrival in Milan I found out that you had fled: when I rang, one of your flatmates said he hadn't seen you for days. A mother's instinct – or bad conscience – had spurred me to pick up the phone even though I had heard you only three days earlier and normally we talked only once a week. Your composure on leaving Ostuni for Milan troubled me and aroused my suspicion. You were always capable of great self-possession – especially after your father died; it gradually turned into inscrutability – but also real passion. Your outbursts at me, when you discovered Anna had disappeared, seemed more natural than the tranquillity with which you returned to university.

The note you left with your flatmates – 'as a citizen guilty of no crime under the law', you were setting off of your own free will and should not be pursued – did not stop the police from looking for you. A friend high up in the force listened as I explained how shaken you were. I suggested you might be seeking Anna and therefore the chances of finding you might be increased by searching for her too. That double search was launched, nationwide. It was discontinued after months of dead ends.

The questore *defended himself with the tone of a surgeon who has just failed to save a life. 'We've done everything we could.'*

Although I was expecting that speech, it felt as if a black hole had opened in my belly. I held onto the handles of my chair, opposite the questore's *huge desk, and stared at a portrait of President Pertini and a plastic crucifix.*

I took on private investigators to look for you: first one firm, then another, then a third... I placed notices in local newspapers and in the national press. The P.I.s thought they had come across a few hopeful leads but these too came to nothing.

Not knowing if you were alive was like being on a raft battered by waves in the open sea. Should I give up hope? No, mourning you would be a betrayal. And yet for as long as the uncertainty continued I couldn't inhabit the present: everyday tasks felt irrelevant; I couldn't care about whether our firm continued trading or went bust; thankfully Ingegner *Forgalli stepped discreetly into my role. And what if you were alive? Had I not lost you anyway? Perhaps I should mourn you because you despised me to the point of avoiding all contact. But how could I give up hope of a reconciliation? I'm aware that I need not go into what each day was like: I swiftly realised that you must be experiencing grief too, for Anna. No wonder you had handed me down the same sentence. I deserved it.*

I lived in this limbo for nearly two and a half years. As your twenty-second birthday approached, my anguish mounted. I couldn't con-

centrate on anything at work, be it a simple negotiation with a supplier or the more complex organisation of a contract bid. At home, images of past incidents involving you hijacked my thoughts and drove me head-long into regret. When you were five and my father dismissed you from the Sunday lunch table for refusing to eat a dish, should I have stood up for you? When you were ten and I found you asleep with your teddy bear, should I have pretended not to see, rather than mortify you until you put it at the back of your toy cupboard? When you asked, at fifteen, if Horace was right to call fools those who hid their festering wounds, should I have seized the opportunity offered by that essay question for us to open up to each other? Might it have changed anything?

I don't know for sure what drove Giorgio to pay me a visit at Villa Emma on the eve of your birthday. Had he heard people whispering about what they might have called my 'fragile state' and taken pity? My secretary Elena, Ingegner Forgalli and Concetta could shield me as best they could from the dangers of my distraction, but they could hardly prevent every single person I came across noticing it. Some acquaintances alerted me by coming up to me, but I must have passed plenty more without noticing. I was past caring. The dimensions we inhabited were no longer connected.

When Giorgio told me he had spoken with you, a fleeting numbness – as if he had hit me on the head and I hadn't registered the fracture – gave way to a joy so unprecedented that I forgot to breathe. We sat down on a sofa, where I bombarded him with questions: where were you? How were you supporting yourself? Were you coming home? Had you found Anna? To none but the last did Giorgio have an answer: like us, you knew nothing of her fate. I was tempted to ask how long he had known you were alive, but I wasn't sure I could bear the reply, so held back. He told me that you would be ringing him the next day.

He said he had to tell me. He intended to persuade you to come back but expected that you wouldn't listen. He wondered whether it might make a difference if I appealed to you.

You know what followed. The next day I was at his parents' home – and so tense that I could barely hold a conversation – when you rang. You reacted angrily, as we feared. Then I spoke. You didn't even let me hear your voice.

When we plummet to the darkest point, we can either reach for a glimmer of light or take a fatal step; no one can predict which of the two it will be. Somehow, the practical side of me re-awakened and, with it, a new sense of purpose: if it was your wish to withhold contact, then I should try to make amends with Anna. Provided that she was still alive, I would seek her forgiveness, once again risking rejection, and do everything in my power to make her happy – whatever her idea of happiness might be. If by finding her I managed to tempt you back, I'd never ask for more; if you stayed away, I could still help the young woman you loved.

The private investigators' search for Anna proved even more dispiriting than for you: the time since her disappearance made success near-impossible. But six months later, in September 1985, almost three years since she had last been seen, Lidia rang me to say she had just received a call: Anna wanted to reassure her that she was ok. Prompted by the P.I.s, Lidia remembered a detail: in the background, a man with a Roman accent had shouted an order for copper wire. The search focused on electrical and building contractors and hardware stores in the Rome area.

In mid-November I received the news I had hoped for: a young woman closely resembling Anna was working in the capital in a hardware store. She lived in the studio flat above. Photos, taken without her knowledge, were faxed to me for confirmation. It was her.

I hope I've done the right thing by telling you how this came about, rather than startling you by giving you the news upfront. I imagine your relief – and hope it will prevail over other emotions.

My first thought was that I should inform Anna's parents, but I hesitated. *The catastrophe through which all of us were living had come about through my belief that I knew better than you and her. If she had no intention of being found, her reasons might be well-grounded. Should I even attempt to make contact? Was my desire to make amends for my benefit, not hers?*

Until the train pulled into Rome Termini, my inner debate about talking to Anna continued. A taxi drove me to the address: a street flanked by dull nineteenth-century apartment blocks and boxy constructions from the nineteen-sixties and seventies. Graffiti and adverts caked with grime covered the walls.

I sat on a stool in a small bar – of the type you'll find up and down the country, with an *Aperitivo Aperol* poster and a *Caffè Lavazza* clock for decoration – by a window facing the hardware store. I could peer right through its entrance door, the glare of neon tubes flooding the space. The murkiness of late afternoon descended. I couldn't see the counter or Anna, and tried to picture her serving clients, who walked in at regular intervals, though not in great numbers. Did she smile at them or had my actions transformed her into an embittered creature with a scowl?

At closing time the store lights were switched off. A young woman in a sports jacket and jeans stepped out and locked the door. I got up from my stool and walked towards her while she pulled down the metal blind, my heart beating loudly. Unaware of my presence, she sorted through a bunch of keys and inserted one in the side door.

I cleared my throat – that was all I could do, though I had visualised this moment for days. The woman turned. It was Anna. Like a film in slow motion, her initial expression of surprise became one of horror. Her eyes were wide open, her mouth gaped.

'You!' She spat the word like a viper lunging to defend itself, and yet I was relieved: her voice transformed her from stone into a living creature. 'You!' she repeated, narrowing her eyes. 'Not enough dam-

age done? Must you ruin my life a second time?'

'Please. I'll never tell a soul I've found you, and you'll never see me again, if that's what you want. But listen for a minute. One minute is all I ask.'

'That's more than you gave me.'

I shrivelled inside.

'You are right. I don't deserve better treatment than I gave you — but you do. That's why I'm here.'

She smirked, though only for a second, as if the corner of her mouth couldn't hold the expression. Did her parents know, she asked. No, I assured her. If she did not want them to, I would respect that. She raised an eyebrow as if to say, 'That'll be a first.' I said nothing.

She was fine, she told me. She had been lucky. When three years earlier she stepped into the store in search of work, the middle-aged couple who owned it had steered clear of painful questions, as if they sensed that prying would do harm. When she thought she had been wrong to trust others, two decent people trusted her.

On first impression, the man was gruff. He was not the outgoing kind, unlike his wife. They lived only a ten-minute drive from the shop but also owned the studio flat above. In exchange for being allowed to move in, she took deliveries outside opening hours. The pay was modest but she lacked nothing. Now she would have to up sticks again because of me, she said angrily. I swore it would not be necessary: she was safe. But please could she hear me out first? It was for her own good.

She laughed. 'Isn't that what you said last time?' Stepping closer, she looked me in the eye. 'What do you really want?'

'Please,' I said. 'I have learnt.'

'Then leave.'

'I thought we might find Tommaso together. And if not —' I looked at the ground. Then, mustering courage, I raised my eyes and said what I ached to convey: 'And if not, I thought I could make it up to

you somehow. I'd do anything to –'

'Leave,' she said. 'Now.'

'I beg you. Just think about it?' *I rummaged through my handbag for a visiting card.* 'Call me if you reconsider.'

I won't dwell on the journey back or the subsequent weeks. I'm not the important one in this story and I'm not trying to elicit your sympathy. Suffice it to say that one feeling pervaded me: fifty years old, two devastating losses and a colossal blunder behind me, and no purpose in my life ahead.

Did I ever see Anna again? Yes. She rang me about a month later, in early December, when I had lost all hope. I travelled up to Rome at dawn the next day.

I invited her to lunch at Mario's in Via della Vite, a real treat, I thought, but she said she'd feel uncomfortable. She suggested a trattoria in a cul-de-sac near the central station.

We arrived at the same time: she, in a pair of jeans, hands in the pockets of her sports jacket, I in a coat over a dress too light for a crisp winter's day. We stepped inside and smiled nervously at each other, saving real talk for later. The place was busy with tourists and locals, languages melding into a babble. The aromas of tomato sauce and wood-fired oven overcame that of stale frying oil. A waiter showed us to a corner table next to an artificial Christmas tree festooned with fake snow, silver tinsel and blue baubles, in which the reflections of the ceiling lights, white tablecloths, chattering diners and rushing waiters floated like sailing boats in tiny blue worlds. How puny we would be to anyone watching Earth from a rocket ship, yet how vast the space between Anna and me, I thought, as we attempted small talk. We studied our menus for too long, before ordering two pizze Margherita. *This drew smiles from both of us.*

As the waiter left, Anna spoke. 'I was so certain I'd never call you.' She straightened the cutlery either side of her plate. 'But a couple of days ago someone changed my mind. A stranger, who doesn't even know.' She sounded wistful.

It had happened on her way home from the supermarket. She was walking through a public square — umbrella pines and unkempt flowerbeds scattered around a fountain — when she spotted a young woman on one of the granite benches. Feet on the bench, hands crossed over the ankles, head hidden in her knees, torn jeans… People dashed past, carrier bags printed with Father Christmases, holly wreaths and comets.

The sight made Anna stop. It was as if a photograph was being dangled in front of her and someone were saying, 'See? That's where you're headed.'

She often wondered about the point of staying alive, she told me — oh yes, despite her protest about being 'fine' when I surprised her by the hardware store. On the day she disappeared, three years earlier, she had first gone to the beach, where she sat for hours asking herself what there was to lose by dying, now that she was damned by God and everyone she loved. And yet… Even after her guilt was compounded by your going missing, the flame of hope would not go out: hope that you might return; that you might finally understand; that she could redeem herself in the eyes of God and other people.

These thoughts engulfed her as she stared at the stranger. For a moment she was back on the beach, ears filled with the crashing of the waves. Then the young woman on the bench raised her head and got to her feet. Her jeans were only fashion-torn. She looked up at Anna's astonished face, gave her a smile and sauntered off.

Anna laughed inwardly: was that how thin the line was? Can you ever tell what's around the corner any better than she could have told the stranger's circumstances? No, so a few more years on earth might change everything. As long as she lived she could seize new chances to make a positive mark. 'What if the reappearance of Tommaso's mother is one?' she wondered. 'What if she really has learnt, like me? Maybe *in order to get my break I have to give her hers.'*

'That's why I called you,' Anna finished, studying me across the table.

My eyes stung. My prayers were answered, my remorse acknowledged. I assured her, with a choked voice, that I would not disappoint her.

So, Tommaso, you'll be asking: did I let her down? I hope not: I have tried to live up to that promise for the past thirty years.

I started by making it possible for her to go to university in Rome: I rented a flat for her near La Sapienza and gave her an allowance as if she were my child. That she still wanted to study Lettere *struck me as another victory for hope – not the Hope hammered into me since childhood, a better world beyond our earthly existence, but the one made possible by human vitality. Alvaro's reserves of that life force had been rich, too. In the years alongside him I had drunk from them. After he was gone, I had to dig a long way down to discover mine.*

Language and literature continued to fascinate Anna, though her parents had pointed to them as the origin of her 'waywardness'. Lettere, letters: the ones entrusted with crucial messages but never seen, first by you, then by her; the ones left behind, first by her and then by you, for her parents and for me; a final one she had tried to write to you but found she couldn't, crossed out and buried in sand. And yet she still put faith in letters: of the alphabet, arranged into the words with which the two of us now attempted to communicate; and of poetry and prose, to cast light on randomness.

I travelled to Rome for a day or two every month to see her. Fearful of interfering, I stayed in a hotel and spent as much or as little time with her as she wished. We walked, stiffly, through the gardens of Villa Borghese, one moment absorbed in conversation, the next drained and chewing on scraps of new information.

We sat side by side at a guitar recital in Santa Maria sopra

Minerva, for a symphony in the Auditorium in Via della Conciliazi-
one, for a play at the Teatro Sistina... I tried to guess at her reactions.
In vain: her way of feeling and thinking was alien to me, much as yours
had been. She unsettled me by pointing out details I hadn't noticed: a
shift in the music's mood, a paradox in the action on stage. She phrased
her observations as questions, professing ignorance and confident of my
superior knowledge. But my notions were scanty and her insights added
meaning. I was as deaf to the music as I had been to you.

My next thought was always the same: you, not I, should be sitting here. With the sensitivity you and Anna shared, your insights
would have built on one another's. You would both have felt richer inside, and cherished. Instead I had come between you.

Anna knew nothing that might help find you. I suggested putting more advertisements in the press, this time stating that she and I
were searching for you together. You might respond to that. However, it
meant telling her parents that she was alive and in Rome, so for months
she wouldn't agree. She'd say: 'I will, but not yet. One step at a time.'

Familiarity with each other came little by little – until the date
of your twenty-third birthday. I was in Rome. I arrived the previous
evening and spent it on my own, too weighed down by regret to be able
to face anyone, least of all Anna. I roamed through streets and squares,
so absorbed in thought that I was surprised to discover I was standing
in Campo de' Fiori when the last spot I had registered – presumably to
make it across the junction – was Piazza Barberini.

No trace of the street market which filled the square by day: no
stalls with their bright canopies; no left-over vegetables on the ground;
no stench of fish; no vendors bellowing. All dismantled and removed,
and the pavements water-sprayed. But the restaurants' windows revealed people busy living: tourists tackling spaghetti with forks and
spoons; executives and politicians negotiating; couples of varying ages,
some, no doubt, on honeymoon. Also the spring air was full of activ-

ity: the scruffy young man drawing caricatures at his easel for a few thousand lire; groups of strolling teenagers; elderly couples on their after-dinner walk.

I felt as inert as the bronze effigy of Giordano Bruno presiding over the square from the spot where he was executed. His crime? Proclaiming the sun a mere star in an infinite universe. Now the lamps obstructed the view of the firmament, leaving only the quaint buildings of varying colours and heights, and the people within the perimeter.

There was no reason to feel more cheerful the next morning. I sensed what day it was even before I woke fully in unfamiliar sheets. Dread had invaded my sleep, and the Valium I had taken had made it all the more inescapable – I felt it was a merited punishment. The impulse to bury myself under the covers was powerful, not to mention a wish never to wake up.

'Too easy. Face up to the reality you have shaped,' I told myself. 'Stay focused on making it better for Anna.' So I washed and dressed, concealing the signs of the hours of darkness with make-up, and downed a couple of espressos at the hotel bar.

When I rang the bell of Anna's flat, she opened it without speaking into the intercom. Once upstairs, I was equally surprised to find her door ajar. I stepped inside and called her name.

'Come into the kitchen,' she shouted. 'With you in a few minutes. Overslept.'

I realised that I wasn't the only one for whom the approach of your birthday had become a forced march into an emotional quicksand. For every 'what if' Anna and I shared, others flooded the mind, confounding it until we were numb. We sat at the kitchen table for hours, eyes swollen, cinder trails of mascara running down our faces, amid a litter of scrunched tissues.

I eventually realised it had gone one o'clock.

'You'd better eat something,' I said. 'You're already so thin. We could go to Lorenzo's, the trattoria down the road.'

She smiled and asked if I was hungry.

'Not at all,' I retorted.

She didn't seem to register my annoyance at the hint that my concern wasn't for her.

'I'm not hungry either,' she said, 'So we could take our time to cook – maybe some orecchiette?'

We had never cooked together: always eaten at restaurants, between and after our outings.

It wasn't as easy as nowadays to find that type of pasta outside Puglia, so I asked if she had any. She got up, opened one of the wall cabinets and pulled out a pack of flour.

'It was one of the first things I bought when you got me this flat,' she said. 'I thought the place would be a chance to start afresh.'

'It is,' I said, and got to my feet. I fought the urge to put an arm around her.

Anna pursed her lips and nodded. She handed me the flour, filled a jug with tap water and took it to the table with a glass bowl and two table knives.

'The wood is a bit too smooth but it'll do,' she said.

I pictured Concetta making orecchiette on our pastry board, rough from years of use: she insisted one mustn't wash it but scrub it – anything left added texture to the dough.

I admitted that I had never learnt how to make orecchiette, but Anna assured me it wasn't difficult. She tipped half the pack of flour into the bowl, made a hollow at the centre and poured in some water. She worked with her fingers until she had a sticky mix which she dusted with more flour and divided in two for us to knead. We pounded, rolled and stretched our lumps of dough on the table as if they were punching bags.

'I feel better now,' Anna said with a terse laugh. I agreed and let out a long breath. To my surprise it relieved the pressure I had felt mounting inside my chest.

She tore off a fistful of dough and rolled it into a finger-thick rope which she cut into small bits with a blunt table knife. Then she flattened the pieces with the blade, flicked them inside out and shaped them on the tip of her thumb. They came out with delicate hollows and thick edges, reminding me that orecchiette means 'little ears'.

I tried to copy her actions but my offering was ugly: the circles uneven, the thickness haphazard – even the odd hole. Babies' ears came to mind. Oh, Tommi... When the obstetrician handed you to me immediately after your birth, I stared at your little ears and nose, at your rosebud lips, at the fingers curled around my thumb. How perfect my baby was. How had it all come to this? And where in the world were you? Were you even in it? Why should the young woman standing next to me have lost her baby – your baby? How could I have been responsible for that?

Seeing my tears, Anna placed a hand softly on my arm. 'Basta, Emma. We've done so much crying.' She watched me while I composed myself. When I looked up, she was biting her lip.

'Please tell my parents you've found me,' she said, 'but that I don't want to see them.' Despite everything, they didn't deserve to fear she might be dead, did they? She and I, of all people, couldn't wish that on anyone. And if you were alive – if together we could find you – maybe we could all be happy again.

I stood still, eyes wide, unprepared for this unhoped-for grace. Then I hugged her.

We put notices in the national press, with a photograph, stating: 'His mother and his fiancée will reward any useful lead'. Once again the response from well-meaning strangers, pranksters and fraudsters did not stand up to the private investigators' scrutiny. But this time I wasn't alone: with each tip-off, Anna and I shared the fresh hope, *the restlessness during the enquiries, the eventual dejection. Did I say 'shared'? No: there was none of the comfort of sharing. The distress was multiplied by two. It was compounded in mid-September by the gloom which came over Anna as the anniversary of the abortion approached.*

We mourned together. We abandoned hope of finding you, Tommi — although, deep inside, I have never entirely resigned myself. This letter proves it. But we called off what seemed a futile search — everyone else, P.I.s included, must have thought it the quest of two pitiable women. We vowed henceforth to live in the present.

Anna concentrated on her studies. I reacquired the focus to manage the firm, with a detachment I wish I'd had in all the years you were with me: I could delegate tasks without anxiety, and spend regular time with Anna in the capital. Not a year went by when she and I weren't together on those days of March and September when grief rose up.

Anna obtained her degree, cum laude, *in early 1991 and began a doctorate. In 1995, towards the end of her PhD, she met Davide. He had just joined the faculty as an Assistant Professor and it was 'love at first sight' — on his part. At the age of thirty-two, for the first time since disappearing from Ostuni, Anna did not reject a man's attentions. Progress, I thought. They dated: dinner at the ivy-covered restaurant by the Temple of the Sybil in Tivoli; movies, plays, concerts; excursions to Villa Farnese in Caprarola and the Giardino dei Mostri in Bomarzo...*

'I enjoy his company, but...' she said.

'There are different levels of happiness,' I answered.

What good did it do her to compare Davide with you? Nor was she any longer the nineteen-year-old who had fallen for you. Give Davide a chance, I said, and you might find a new and different happiness. By her own admission, the two of them 'connected' in conversation; he was gentle; his daily kindnesses and constant gifts and treats showed how much he treasured her. He was handsome enough: dark-haired, dark-eyed, taller than her by a few inches, and neither thin nor fat, but sturdy.

I don't know how Davide didn't weary of proposing marriage to her for two years. She had finished her PhD by the time, in March '97, she said yes — subject to a condition which left me speechless: a final effort to find you through notices in the press. She asked me to make it; if it failed, she would resign herself to your disappearance. Even more surprising was the fact that Davide agreed, a proof of love which you might think would prompt her to re-think her proviso. But no, she did not revoke it. For my part, how could I not consent to Anna's request, if that's what it took for her to commit to Davide?

I placed notices in regional and national newspapers. Again I received tip-offs — unsurprisingly fewer than before, now that more than fourteen years had passed. Again they led nowhere. There was an unforgettable telephone call from London, of all places. It came from an elderly man so convinced that he had spotted you in a café, that for five electrifying minutes I deluded myself it was possible; then his wife seized the receiver and urged me not to believe him; she was mortified.

'Forgive him. It's not really his fault. Age is an awful beast.' I reassured her I had braced myself for disappointment.

Davide is such an attentive husband and father. They have two children — a girl of twelve and a boy of ten. Anna seems content. She would be happier, I'm sure, if she felt understood by her parents and sister, but says she accepts it won't happen. From time to time she calls on them in Ostuni. She reports back on these dutiful visits as if she had dropped in on distant relatives forgiven out of weariness for an ancient feud neither side can forget. I suppose some rifts are unbridgeable. I should know. Yet I'm obviously an optimist, after all: first, longing to make it up to Anna, and being granted that opportunity; now, hoping you're alive and that you'll be reconciled, at least with the memory of me.

Five years ago Anna was promoted to Professor at Rome's La Sapienza. She is an expert on Ancient Greek and Roman philosophy. I've read her books and articles: scholarly and insightful, as you'd expect. Some are so erudite that they seem written for fellow members of a sect who share a secret language. Many of her female colleagues work and publish under the customary double-barrelled name, maiden and married surnames combined. Not Anna: her only surname is Gabrieli.

Until illness confined me to bed, I have lived in Rome for about half the year, in a flat near Anna and Davide's. I love their children as if they were my grandchildren: the pain at a friend's stinging words; the joy of an afternoon with their best mates; the sadness at the death of a pet; the excitement of a birthday party. I have been fortunate to be allowed to be part of their day-to-day lives: the babysitting, the pick-up from school, the homework... It has brought the five of us close. When I first asked Anna to let me make it up to her, I'd never have imagined such a future. It's more than I deserve, as your continued silence reminds me.

I'm wary of telling you more about the little family. You can imagine, I'm sure, all the ordinary thresholds over the years – the children's first day of school; their learning to swim without water wings; their parents' gradual progress up the academic ranks – as well as the daily routines, though these are far more frenetic, in a city of two and a half million people and an age of space-age gadgets, than they'd have been when you grew up. My reticence is not due to any pleasure in withholding facts or my love from you. On the contrary. Behind it are my fear of hurting you by describing Anna's new life too vividly, and my respect for the sanctity of every family's own rites: the nickname which cheers one up; the favourite dish prepared to celebrate or to console; the outing guaranteed to refresh the adults and the children after a stressful period. It is for Anna to let you into her world or not, should you decide to ask her.

The other six months of the year, I have spent in Ostuni. Ever since Ingegner *Forgalli retired, Luigi Levante has looked after the firm: at first whenever I was absent, and then permanently, once age defeated me. He is willing to continue running the company for as long as my heirs – you, I hope – should wish. Until recently, though, I reserved for myself final approval of the projects we took on and of the partner firms on whom our reputation also depends. We are known for our uncompromising standards in the restoration of* masserie *– the only realm in which I haven't let go of the obduracy which once distinguished me; the only realm where it was an asset.*

There is something cathartic about renovating a masseria, *irrespective of whether its new owners wish to turn it into a stupendous villa or into a hotel. On the top floors which once housed the landowners or their stewards, layers of plaster are stripped off and replaced with fresh rendering made to a centuries-old formula. Cracks in the fortified perimeter which for hundreds of years saw off pirates and invaders are filled in. At ground level, where labourers' living quarters, storage rooms for produce, spaces for livestock and processing foods opened onto the large central courtyard, the ancient stone floors are sanded, polished and made even. They resound with the steps and voices of families on holiday, couples on honeymoon, awestruck art lovers, bustling staff. The groin-vaulted stalls, oil mills and wineries become atmospheric dining rooms. Guests sip Salice Salentino, Primitivo or Negramaro on the rooftop terrace overlooking the olive groves. In the estate's orchards and gardens they pick fruit and vegetables and inhale their fragrance with a sensuality that would make farmers blush; in its domed kitchens they take lessons in traditional cuisine. Climbing to the top of the wide staircases across the exterior fills them with a lord's contentment.*

There is something cathartic about orchestrating the work of all the craftsmen. Those best at patching up or building dry walls are farmers who used to do it to rid their arable land of rocks, and never expected this skill would become a source of wealth. The carvers of tufo *and* pietra leccese, *who struggled to make a living, now hire apprentices to help them cope with demand for tasks ranging from replacing missing balusters to repairing ornamental lintels. The children of cabinet makers, who twenty years ago might have aimed to escape to university, today choose to stay in the family's lucrative business and train in their fathers' craft.*

Why have I chosen to come to Ostuni to die, when Anna, Davide and the children are in Rome? Partly because I don't want to be a burden; Anna travels south regularly to visit me, but that's not the same as caring daily for the dying, and it won't be for long. And although hers has become my second family, my roots are here, in the house I shared with you, Alvaro and Concetta. The presence of your tata − *my old friend − anchors me to past and present. It feels right.*

I have entrusted Giorgio with ensuring that you'll come by your inheritance, if you can be found and will accept it. Our laws require that such matters are dealt with by a notary, which is Giorgio's profession. He was always your best friend − he will do anything within his powers to carry out his duty to you and me. The terms of my will couldn't be simpler: half of my wealth goes to you, half to Anna, after deducting amounts set aside for Concetta and Luigi Levante. Should the final search for you be fruitless, everything goes to Anna.

How I hope that Villa Emma will once again ring with your steps! Like you and Anna, I may be placing too much faith in a letter, but it's all that's left to me. It's not even a beautiful letter − I never could write poetically like your father, or movingly as lovers do and as I imagine you and Anna did. Nor do I expect ever to be beautiful in your eyes. I just want you to know that I loved you and love you still, however warped my expression of it was by grief and fear, mother of all cowardice.

Your loving mamma

CHAPTER 19

Me, stunned? Need you ask, Will? Exhausted, too. I never was one for staying up until the early hours of the morning. And that's the least of the reasons for feeling as if the ground beneath me were heaving. I suppose that lead-grey light, out there, is the dawn. A new dawn alright. I don't know what to think.

Do stay in your armchair. But don't mind if I pace up and down this poky sitting room.

So the notary who answered all your questions about me was Giorgio. Why am I laughing? Because I should have guessed. Who else could have provided you with the accurate answers that led you to me? He would have known anything you cared to ask about me: that I became tongue-tied in a group; that few things irritated me as much as others' lateness; that I wouldn't hand in a Latin translation until I had thought through all conceivable grammatical constructions; that I disapproved of his thirst for adventure even when we were six years old and he pestered me to wade with him through the shallow waters of the Canalone in search of tadpoles and frogs... He remained my faithful friend, and I didn't understand it.

How flawed was my love for Anna if I proved incapable of trusting her? What should I do now? If I accept the inheritance, she'll know I'm alive. From my mother's account it's all too evident that for years Anna hoped this day would come. What wouldn't I give to embrace her again, to hear her voice, to...

Thirty-three years have changed us enough for us not to be the same, and yet, I'm sure, not enough: bring us together, and our uncanny connection may well be re-established.

But what impossible choice would that create for Anna, now that she is living a serene existence? A family of her own... a successful career... She resigned herself to the thought I'd never resurface – as no doubt did Giorgio and Concetta. They all moved on. How selfish it would be for me to bring chaos to Anna's world. She'd probably be wretched if she chose me and equally wretched if she chose her husband, as I expect she'd love us both.

It is possible that she's not as content with her life as my mother believed. But how could I ever find out, when she may be hiding the truth even from herself? I wouldn't blame her – she has suffered enough.

So, no: now more than ever I cannot accept my inheritance. If I love her, I can't do otherwise.

Why did my mother want me to know? Did she think it was preferable to believing Anna was dead?

Forgive the tears. I can't remember when I last cried. But to discover that the love of your life is alive – that in this very instant she may be waking to the ring of an alarm clock in an apartment in Rome, beneath the same sky as you and me – and to have to give up the prospect of being reunited with her, all within the space of one night, is... And to realise how different our futures would have been if I hadn't broken off all dialogue...

Thank you for understanding.

Let me make the strongest espresso of which this old moka pot is capable. There: enough ground coffee in this filter to keep us awake all day.

What will you say, back at the office? 'Another fruitless venture'? I'm so sorry – and so grateful to you.

I suppose you also have a home – people who'd have expected you for supper last night. Ah, yes: your father. And his bitterness. Promise me you won't let your 'mistake' gnaw at you – that you'll make amends while you still can? And move on?

Zoe? Yes, I will tell her everything – tear down my wall of secrecy. Long overdue. But to open myself up to the possibility of us becoming more than friends? That's asking too much. Or maybe too soon.

What am I doing? See for yourself: I'm taking one of my coin casts out of the display case. I'll just fetch some cotton wool and a little box to wrap it up safely. Here we are. I want you to have it.

But our coffee is ready. See? Thick and dark, with a twirl of toffee-brown *crema*: velvet-covered steel. Let's sip it slowly, while the sky grows lighter.

Acknowledgements

I would like to express my gratitude to all those who have sustained me throughout the process of writing *That Summer In Puglia*.

To Rachel Seiffert and Maura Dooley – thank you for your unstinting support. You made a difference from start to finish.

To Richard Gray, Lynn Foote, Nicki Heinen, Bernadette Reed and Julia Rotte – my gratitude for your insightful feedback.

To Francis Spufford – thank you for your encouragement of my research into A.S. Byatt's use of art and artefacts in fiction. Its lessons have been invaluable.

To Todd Swift – I'm grateful to you for believing in this book and making it all happen.

The list of those who have helped on the journey is long: Simonetta Agnello Hornby, Josie Barnard, Elena Battista, Sue Cornish, Benito Fiore, Sarah Hudspith, Nikita Lalwani, the late Natalie Luethi, Angela Matheson, Laetitia Rutherford, Nicholas Shakespeare, Richard Skinner, Ardu Vakil and Edoardo Winspeare.

To my friends – your warmth, wisdom, understanding and encouragement have been and are ever-nourishing.

Last but certainly not least, my thanks to my husband and kids, who have 'lived' with Tommaso, Anna and their families and friends while I was writing the novel. You managed to keep me rooted in London while my mind was travelling back and forth to my native region, the quiet protagonist of *That Summer In Puglia*.